KEVIN BERRY

TO KILL A CONMAN

A contemporary crime noir novel

Cover design by Dawné Dominique, DusktilDawn Designs.

Quake City map by Ava Fairhall.

The story is written in UK English.

First edition

ISBN: 978-0-47-357579-3

This book was professionally typeset on Reedsy.
Find out more at reedsy.com

Acknowledgement

I wish to express my thanks to Charlotte Kieft (who writes as Charlotte Jardin), Eileen Mueller, and A J Ponder. These friends are talented writers who encouraged and helped me immensely with this story. I hope some of my readers will take the time to look them up and read some of their work.

Many thanks to my friend Lee Murray for the editorial review, to my wife Nadene Rogers for her endless support and encouragement, and to my teenage son James Berry for drafting the murder scene.

My cover designer, Dawné Dominique, DusktilDawn Designs, creates breath-taking covers for my stories.

Ava Fairhall designed a beautiful, detailed map of Quake City, which is reproduced on the following two pages.

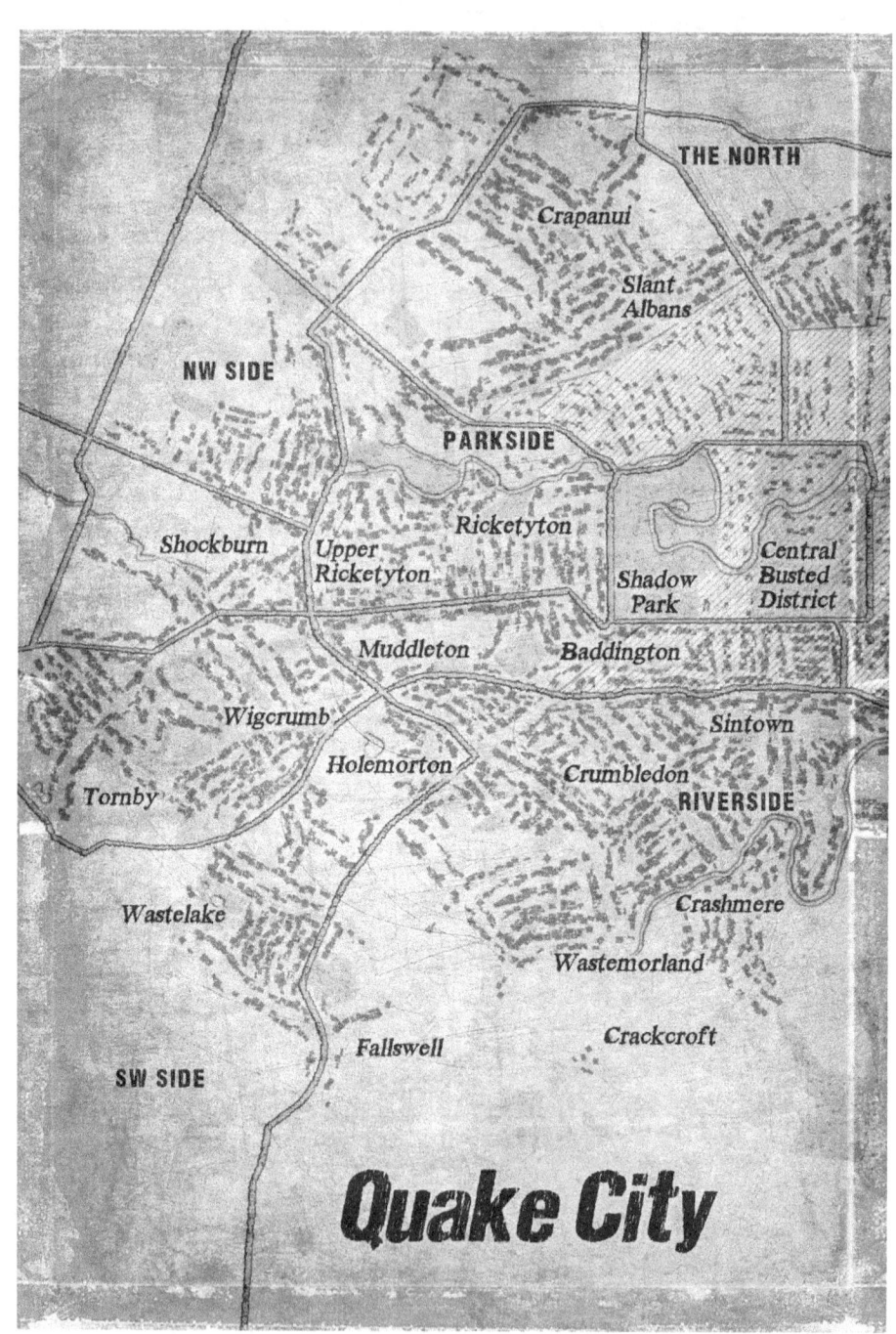

THE NORTH

Crapanui

Slant
Albans

NW SIDE

PARKSIDE

Shockburn

Upper
Ricketyton

Ricketyton

Shadow
Park

Central
Busted
District

Muddleton

Baddington

Wigcrumb

Sintown

Holemorton

Crumbledon

RIVERSIDE

Tornby

Wastelake

Crashmere

Wastemorland

Crackcroft

Fallswell

SW SIDE

Quake City

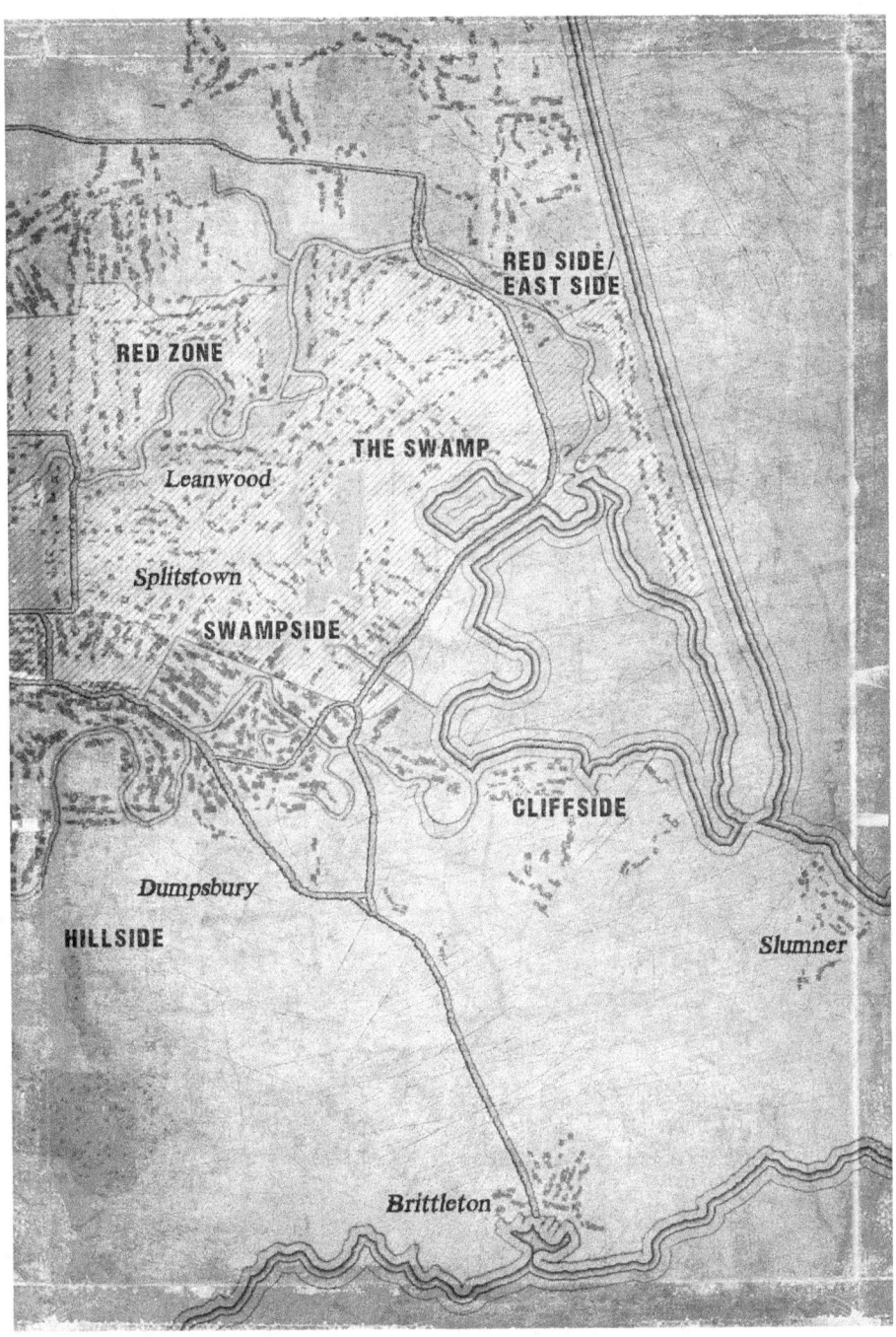

RED SIDE/
EAST SIDE

RED ZONE

THE SWAMP

Leanwood

Splitstown

SWAMPSIDE

CLIFFSIDE

Dumpsbury

HILLSIDE

Slumner

Brittleton

The Conman

STUART BAKER WORKED HARD for other people's money. He knew every scheme and scam going and ceaselessly toiled to develop new ones. There was no low to which he would not stoop, no crime that he would not consider committing, and no victim for whom he might show a little pity. He was both the most opportunistic and the most cunning of fraudsters, both the best and the worst of liars, and the living exception to the rule that crime does not pay. It paid Stuart well. Far too well for him to contemplate ever giving it up to do an honest day's work. Stuart Baker's activities had enabled him to make a lot of dough. His moral compass was that of a low life, but it enabled him to live a damn fine high life.

Chapter 1

STUART BAKER GLANCED at his Seiko watch, an old present from his ex. Five o'clock. Almost time to close the grubby antique shop he used as a front for laundering his ill-gotten cash gains. Though he had few real customers because the varied inventory was such poor quality, his fabricated accounts showed the antique shop brought in a handsome sum every year. After he'd offset that with fictitious salaries for his imaginary staff, the shop barely broke even, he'd cleaned his dirty money, and pocketed the cash tax-free.

Stuart pinched his trousers at the knees to keep the crease, leaned back in his carved wooden chair, and rested his polished black shoes on the glass-topped counter. He opened his vinyl accounts book. Handwritten figures in pencil listed several fake purchases and sales for the day. No fancy accounting software for him with its digital records in the cloud that couldn't be erased or rewritten whenever convenient.

His phone rang. He grabbed it without checking the number and jammed it against his ear. "Yes?"

"Hey, Stu, it's Gabe. I'm finished work for the day. How're you doing?"

Gabe the babe. The bank teller he'd hooked up with a few days ago. She was Gabrielle, but she preferred Gabe to Gabby as a shorter name. She was a bit of all right, but he hated how she called him Stu. He'd never liked the abbreviation.

He brushed a spot of lint off the arm of his suit jacket. "I'm good, babe.

About to close up the shop. I've got places to go, things to do."

"But we're still on for dinner, aren't we?" Her tone turned from wheedling to sultry. "I want to see you, Stu."

"I can't wait to see you, too, babe. Give me an hour. I'll call you back, all right?"

Stuart disconnected without waiting for an answer, then drummed his fingers on the counter. What did Gabe want from him? A few shags? Anything more? He hadn't figured her out yet.

The way she'd bluntly asked him out when she was serving him in the bank had seemed a little… ungenuine. He had a natural talent for detecting bullshit. It seldom let him down, and his instinct had been nagging at him ever since he'd met her.

He dragged his feet off the counter and stood, shrugging. He checked his tie and pencil-thin black moustache in an ornate but garish faux-gold mirror that would never find a buyer, and nodded. Looking sharp, as always.

Mismatched lamps of all ages were scattered around the shop. Stuart switched them off one by one, stopping occasionally to wipe surfaces and check for dust. Damned cleaners never did a proper job. He'd withhold their pay again.

Stuart exited the shop and locked the door. His premises were part of a row of dated buildings that had somehow survived the earthquakes of years before, though cracks now covered the cladding.

He sauntered down the main street in Sintown, past a busy pawnbroker's and the busier brothel next door. Beyond that, a middle-aged beggar sat propped against a shop window, a faded baseball cap pulled low to conceal her face. A fast-food box in front of her contained greasy banknotes and a smattering of coins.

Stuart paused, took a dollar coin from his pocket and bent to place it in the beggar's box. It clinked, and even as she nodded thanks, eyes staring at the ground, he discreetly palmed her only twenty-dollar note before walking on.

He turned into a side street where weeds grew from holes in the asphalt footpath. After a minute he reached a set of lock-up garages. As always,

Stuart glanced both ways along the street and ensured no one was in sight before he pressed the garage door opener in his pocket. The door rolled up with a rumble of corrugated steel.

His car, a bright red Lamborghini, gleamed, even in the dim light. He stroked the bonnet as he ambled to the door, warmth rising inside him. This was his pride and joy, a symbol of his status, the fruits of his frauds.

Stuart drove out, the garage door closing automatically behind him, and turned into the side street. The lion-hearted vehicle purred like a kitten, responding to his slightest touch with ferocious power. He dreamed about women like that, but a car was better. You never had to wait for a car to get ready in the morning.

First stop, a supermarket to get chocolates. The nearest ones, in the CBD, had been closed since the quakes had made the buildings unsafe and the entire area had been red-zoned. He drove in the other direction, to Crumbledon, cutting through the traffic without a care for the angry toots of other drivers, and pulled into the car park a few minutes later. He wouldn't be long, but there was always an opportunity to make money, so he grabbed a small briefcase from the back of the car before going inside.

The briefcase contained a sophisticated card reader like those merchants used to take payments. Stuart's model was a custom variation that copied and stored the card details, then used them for fraudulent transactions.

Now to find a victim. There, by the cat food, stood a man wearing a navy-blue raincoat. Odd. It was chilly outside, but not raining. The colour-clashing maroon fedora on his head made him stand out. What a strange guy. Likely a weirdo who lived by himself—apart from his cat.

All that aside, Stuart focused on the wallet-sized bulge in one coat pocket. He wandered over, shopping basket in one hand and briefcase in the other, and bumped into his victim with the briefcase. A faint beep sounded as the card reader detected a bank card in the victim's wallet and read the details. Stuart coughed to cover the sound.

The man turned instantly, eyes flashing, hand dropping to his pocket to ensure the wallet was still there. He touched it and visibly relaxed.

"Excuse me. My fault." Stuart moved on. Inside his briefcase, his modified card reader would charge small amounts to his victim's card until it got blocked or emptied the account. The stolen payments would ping around the world in different currencies, including Bitcoin, before the total was paid into Stuart's antique shop account. Untraceable, and easily explained as an antique purchase from a foreign buyer.

After repeating his trick with another two unwary shoppers, Stuart paid for his chocolates and left the store.

He drove to Leanwood, thinking about Gabe and how she had come on to him as if she were a filly in heat. It was odd. She'd worked in the bank for years, never any more pleasant to him than to other customers, until a couple of weeks ago, when she set out to snag him like a siren reeling in a sailor. But Stuart wasn't complaining. If she was up to something, he'd work it out. In the meantime, he'd shag her as much as possible.

It wasn't Gabe he was going to see now, though. His ex, Sarah, lived in Leanwood with their five-year-old twin sons. He'd missed their birthday the previous week, and she'd phoned angrily nearly every day since. It was time to put things right. The chocolates would help. They always did.

He parked outside the worn weatherboard property. A picket fence with peeling paint bordered a small lawn in front of the house. Stuart strode up the cracked driveway. Before he reached the door, Sarah stormed out, sleeves of her holey cardigan rolled up, her tangled black hair flying, her boots stamping on the driveway so hard they might worsen the cracks. The two boys tumbled from the house after her, half-eaten sandwiches in hand and jam on their faces. They ran towards him.

"Where the bloody hell have you been? Couldn't you spare a couple of hours to see your kids on their birthday?"

Stuart shook his head, smiling against her fury. "Work. Always busy. Trying to keep the shop afloat. It doesn't make much money, you know."

Sarah folded her arms and jutted out her chin. "That again. It's just an excuse for you to pay no child support."

"You know I don't earn enough from the shop for that. One day profits will pick up, and I'll be able to give you something."

Sarah snorted in reply.

The twins tugged at Stuart's pressed trousers. Even now, he couldn't tell them apart. Did they have sticky hands? They'd better not. They let go and dashed off down the driveway.

"Keep off the road, boys." Sarah raced past Stuart in pursuit.

One brat called out before Stuart could turn around. "Cool car, Dad. Is it yours?"

Damn. All the way here, he'd been thinking about Gabrielle, Gabe the babe, pondering her intentions, planning dinner and a lusty shag that evening. Like an idiot, he'd forgotten to park around the corner.

He turned and faced Sarah's fiery glare. She stood on the footpath, red-faced, boys cuddled under one arm.

"That's your car? The Lambo?" She jabbed a finger towards it, spittle flying from her mouth as she snapped the words out.

"Yeah, I won it."

"Ahah. Just like you won that Mercedes a couple of years ago?"

Stuart stroked one end of his moustache. "I'm a lucky guy. Look, sorry I couldn't come over last week, but I've got something for the boys now."

"You have?" Some of the fire faded from Sarah's voice.

Stuart strode over. He stuck a hand into a pocket and withdrew the twenty-dollar note he'd lifted from the beggar's cash box. "Take them to the movies." He pressed the note into Sarah's hand.

"That's not enough. You know it's not."

Stuart shrugged. "That's the best I can do right now. And these chocolates." He took them from his jacket and passed them over to her.

Sarah stared at them as if they were rat poison.

His phone rang, and he dug into a pocket for it. Gabe again.

"Yes, babe?"

"You said you'd call me, Stu, and I'm getting lonely. Let's go to that new Italian place tonight. The one near my apartment."

"Angelo's. I know it. Sounds good, babe. I'm on my way to pick you up." He disconnected.

Sarah's eyes were daggers. With a motion, she shooed the boys away. They raced inside, munching their sandwiches as they ran.

Stuart stiffened. "What? You're going to complain about me starting a new relationship now?"

Sarah shook her head, her long hair whirling. "No. You were always one for other women, even when we were together. But you're going to a fancy restaurant for dinner with her? The boys and I can't afford to eat more than baked beans and toast most nights."

He shrugged. "She's paying."

"Oh yeah. Lucky guy, you are. Piss off." She marched past, barging into Stuart's arm on the way.

Stuart grinned. This was his kind of night. He strode to his car, chuckling, then stopped short. The passenger-side window bore a brat-sized jammy handprint.

Frowning, he withdrew a monogrammed silk handkerchief from his suit breast pocket and wiped the window clean. The handkerchief was ruined now. He posted it into Sarah's letterbox before driving away.

Chapter 2

AT THE SUPERMARKET checkout, I scratched my head under my maroon fedora and tried my bank card again. The damned machine beeped at me once more. Insufficient funds.

The checkout operator glanced at the name on my card. "Do you have another bank card... Danny?" She tilted her head, chewing gum. It stretched between her teeth when she yawned.

"No. I don't understand this. I have the money in my account." I know I did. At least, I know when it's zero. I'd saved about three thousand, enough for a cheap car after paying my rent.

"Whatever. You have cash?"

I only had fifty bucks and handed it over. "Cancel everything except the coffee and the cat food."

She did so and gave me twenty dollars and shrapnel in change. I jammed it into my raincoat pocket. She stared at me with large, glazed eyes, moving the gum from side to side in her mouth. "You bring your own bag, or do you wanna buy one?"

"I'll carry them." I didn't need a bag for two items, even if I had to walk home. It wasn't far.

A light drizzle started. I didn't care about getting wet. I wanted to know how my money had disappeared.

The rain became steadily heavier. By the time I reached my apartment, it was coming off my raincoat in sheets. My shoes and my trouser legs below the knee were soaked, and my vision was blurry from the wind gusting water into my face.

I climbed the stairs to my apartment, leaving miniature puddles behind me, found my keys, opened the door and went inside. The main room was my office; the rest was my living accommodation. I liked to work from home, and sleep at work, so this arrangement suited me.

Torquemada, my cat, bounded from the top of the bookcase onto my desk, then onto the floor to greet me when I hung up my coat and hat. I stroked him and topped up his food before plopping onto the sofa.

My money. Where was it?

I phoned the bank. Their hold music had clearly been designed as a form of mental torture, but I endured it until someone finally took my call, demanded I prove my identity, and listened to my problem. A guy with a nasally voice said he'd check it out for me. I waited, the hold music on again.

He came back after a couple of minutes. "I see the issue. There have been some purchases on your card from a lingerie company in the Cayman Islands. Were you buying for someone else, or yourself?"

"It wasn't me. I didn't make those transactions."

"They were made half an hour ago from Quake City."

Heat spread through my neck into my face. I ground my teeth. "Those aren't my purchases."

"I'll see if I can reverse the transactions, if you're sure you didn't make them yourself."

"Of course, I'm sure. I'd know if I bought lingerie online half an hour ago, wouldn't I?"

The bank helpline assistant sighed. "Don't be rude. I don't have to reverse the charges, you know."

"Please do it. I'm the victim of fraud."

"What was that? The line's going bad." The unmistakable sound of a finger tap echoed through the phone.

"Just fix it, will you? How long will it take for you to get my money back?"

"*If* we decide it's fraud, and *if* we reverse the charges, it'll take six weeks."

"You're in on it, aren't you? Taking a little slice of any bank fraud to inflate your oversized profits. I'll burst your bubble if you don't help me out."

"Sorry, your support call time is up. I'm hanging up now."

The call disconnected. I threw the phone onto the sofa. It bounced onto the floor, startling Torquemada. Typical Quake City bank. They wouldn't do anything.

I'd have to track down the missing money myself. In my line of work, that was easy enough if money had been physically taken—any private investigator in town could do that. But these modern-day digital thefts were a different matter. The thief was as likely to be on the other side of the world as on the other side of the street.

My fuming thoughts were cut short by the creak of a stair. I tiptoed to the side of the door, watching through the frosted glass bearing the words 'Quake City Investigations'. A familiar shape, the silhouette of an Eastern European weightlifter, stopped outside the door and rapped on it.

Nadia Hart, my landlady. Trouble was never far away, and she had turned up at the worst possible time.

I opened the door.

Nadia's dark brown eyes pinned me to the spot. Heavy mascara clogged her lashes, dark red lipstick was smeared over her mouth, and the scent of cheap perfume blew through the doorway like a gale. Her large cleavage strained against her tight maroon dress.

Nadia bowled inside and bent to pat Torquemada, who scuttled away from her and hid behind the sofa.

She straightened up and nodded to me with a grim expression. "The rent is due, Danny. You didn't drop it off, so I thought I'd pop round and collect it. Save you a trip." She smiled and extended a chubby hand. The boil on the side of her face had sprouted more black hairs.

I met her gaze. "Nadia, there's been a problem. I can't pay it today."

"Why's that, dear?" Her gaze hardened. "You're not trying to diddle a poor landlady out of her due, are you?"

"No, of course not. It's just that… I've been the victim of bank fraud. My account was cleaned out. I phoned the bank, but—"

"They were arseholes, weren't they?"

"Yeah. They were."

"Just as well you're a private investigator, isn't it, dear? You can track down the fraudster yourself and beat the shit out of them to get your money back."

"That's my plan." If the perp was local, that is. If they were in Russia, or North Korea, or anywhere overseas, I was screwed. "So… if you don't mind waiting a week or two, I'll pay the rent I owe then."

"Look, Danny, I'm reasonable. You're a good tenant, you don't cause much damage, just the occasional smashed door and a few bullet holes from time to time. Nothing major. But I'm not running a bloody charity. I have expenses. And most of the apartments in this building have been empty for ages."

I took a deep breath. "I realise that."

"If the money's not possible, then…" She sashayed up to me, both chins wobbling, then winked. "The rent must be paid one way or another."

I gulped. "I promise I'll get you the cash. Just give me a few days."

She chuckled and turned to go. "All right, dearie. Oh, by the way, you're going to have a new neighbour. She's moving in today."

With a speed belying her build, Nadia swooped out through the door.

Hell's teeth. I had to find the money. Or find *some* money. But how could I track down a bank card fraudster who could be literally anywhere?

I couldn't track him down with my limited tech knowledge. I needed my own hacker.

My sometime partner in investigation Deepa Banwait knew of someone: Petra, a schoolgirl with a prodigious ability to access systems and information through various back-door hacks, viruses and code injections. We don't understand how she does it, and we ignore the fact that what she does is completely illegal because it's so damned useful.

I texted Deepa, and a few minutes later my phone rang. I expected it to be Deepa, but it wasn't.

"I hear you're looking for me, Danny."

"Petra?" If only the bank's service was as good.

"Yup. How can I help?"

I explained the problem as clearly as I could and with as few swear words as I could manage.

"That's too bad. It happens more and more. I can't guarantee that I'll be able to track it down, but I'll do my best."

"Thanks. It's not a lot of money, but I need it to pay my rent and buy a car. Besides, these bloody cyber thieves make my blood boil. I'd like to make this one pay."

"Look, you can pay me an hourly rate or a percentage of the funds I recover for you. Up to you."

It didn't take long to decide. "A percentage. Though that won't pay you much." It was only fair to let her know that. "Or how about I owe you a favour instead?"

"Yup, all right. You can owe me a favour. One day I might need a private investigator for something."

We discussed the details of my missing money. After disconnecting, I breathed a sigh of relief that someone would do something about the card fraudster, even if I couldn't.

There was a knock on the door. Surely not the landlady again. Should I hide? Had she come to—

The door opened. It wasn't Nadia.

A slim, bronzed woman, mid-twenties, stepped into my office. Her wavy blonde hair brushed her shoulders. Her wide hazel-green eyes met mine. My jaw fell open. I forced it shut again.

"Hey. I'm Chelsea Whitlam. I'm moving into the apartment next door."

"I'm Danny." I discreetly assessed her. Was she a party girl? She looked like one. I hoped not; I didn't like noisy neighbours. Maybe Nadia was trying to get rid of me by renting out the apartment next door to someone who would keep me awake at night.

"Just wanted to say hello. I'll be going now—ooh! You have a cat." She scurried over to the sofa—quite a feat in high heels—and bent to stroke Torquemada, who lifted his head in appreciation.

"That's Torquemada. Guard cat." I swallowed.

"Awesome name. Right. I must go, get moved in. Nice to meet you."

She turned and left, the scent of her fine perfume tingling my nose.

Chapter 3

STUART SAT SHIRTLESS in a poolside deckchair at home, his laptop balanced on his knees, a beer in one hand. In his sheltered position, the mid-morning sun warmed his shoulders, even though it was still a cool late winter day. There was no way he'd be taking a swim at this time of year. Leave jumping in icy-cold pools to the Scandinavians.

One drawback to being master of a fraud empire was the amount of paperwork—at least double that of a legitimate business. He had to maintain a set of accounts for the Inland Revenue, showing his antique shop barely scraped a profit after expenses, yet had a high turnover of stock. Much of the stock he sold was fictitious; that was necessary to launder some of the money he earned from his nefarious activities. But he also had to be sure to invent enough expenses and tweak sales numbers to avoid paying tax on his beautifully laundered money. And after fabricating a set of accounts more fictitious than Middle Earth, he had to keep his accurate, secret, actual accounts so he could see which of his illegal schemes were the most effective. It was tiresome.

He was analysing the returns from one of his businesses now: an online pirate book store. He'd paid a hacker for an app to break the copyright protection on thousands of eBooks, uploaded them to a pirate website, and sold them off to unscrupulous buyers at discount prices. When authors complained that he'd stolen years of their work, he removed their books

13

temporarily, only to upload them again a week later. This caper was a steady little earner, one of his favourites, but the accounting was a bit of a drag.

His phone rang. Stuart reached out to get it.

"Is that Fat Prophets Investments?" The voice on the other end was female, quiet, timid.

"Julie Nicholls, isn't it? I recognise your voice. This is Jonathan Goodfellow here." The spark of avarice kindled in his mind like an ember being stirred back to life. He'd almost given up on this one.

"I read the cryptocurrency investment strategy document you gave me at our first meeting. Your track record is almost unbelievable."

Stuart smirked. Yes, it was.

"I don't know how you do it, but I don't think it's for me. It sounds too risky investing in these digital coins. I'm going to have to pass on this one." She sounded almost apologetic.

Stuart dragged his feet off the deckchair and sat forward, his knuckles white on the phone, fighting to keep his words measured and assuring. "This is a once-in-a-lifetime chance, Ms Nicholls. I'm not taking on any more clients after tomorrow. My research points to an incredibly profitable opportunity that's currently overlooked by the general market. You don't want to miss out, do you?"

"Um..."

"Think carefully. There aren't any better investments around than what I can offer you today. You can make a lot of money with one wise investment in my cryptocurrency plan."

"Do you really think so?"

"Absolutely. I know you'll regret it if you miss out."

There was a pause. Stuart held his breath, letting greed do its nasty work.

"Hmm. All right, you convinced me. I'll sign up. It must be better than keeping money in the bank."

"Of course it is, Julie. Listen, I'm just walking out the door now. I've got an errand to run near your work. I'll pop by in half an hour so you can sign up and transfer your investment money."

"Oh—okay."

"See you soon."

Stuart disconnected. He had to put on a suit and get over there before she changed her mind. He plonked his beer down on a table next to his deckchair and grinned. His silver tongue had done its job again.

§

Forty-five minutes later, Stuart hustled out of a glassy office building in Baddington. Most of the lawyer firms had moved there after the earthquakes had made their CBD offices inaccessible or unsafe. Julie Nicholls, a criminal lawyer, had happily signed an investment contract and transferred forty thousand dollars to a cryptocurrency 'investment' account.

The contract was worthless, of course. Stuart chucked it and his phone into the nearest litter bin. He didn't want Julie Nicholls to phone him again. He'd simply disappear into the sunset, like her money.

He pulled out another phone, one of a dozen he had ready to go, and tapped a few keys. The fake investment account opened up. He transferred Julie's money to a cryptocurrency account in another country, then strutted to his car. An easy forty grand from another gullible mark.

Stuart got into his Lambo, gleefully aware of the envious glances from bustling pedestrians. He loved knowing he owned what most people would never have despite working their entire lives. And he'd bought it with other people's money. Did that make him a bad person? Yeah. But so what? He didn't fucking care.

He straightened his tie and combed his hair, then started the engine and brought the powerful motor to life. The thrill reverberated through him as he swung the car around and roared off.

Gabe was working today. She was a professional, never questioning where his money came from. Or maybe that was bank policy. Few banks accepted deposits in cryptocurrency, even in Quake City, but her bank did.

He drove there, parked right in front, and shoved his designer sunglasses up onto his head. He strode inside. Gabe was serving a customer. He leaned against a pillar until she'd finished.

She waved him over. "Hey, Stu. How's your day going?"

"Great, babe. Really great. You know what? We should celebrate. Come over to my place. We'll have dinner, go out to a club, whatever."

"Cool. What are we celebrating?"

"Another successful business venture. I have a deposit to make, a big one."

Gabe raised a manicured eyebrow. "Cryptocurrency again?"

"Yeah." Stuart passed his phone over the counter, a coin exchange app open on the screen. Gabe scanned it, and it pinged. She checked her bank terminal screen.

"Deposit registered. Forty thousand dollars, less fees."

Stuart pocketed his phone. "See ya later, babe."

"Hey, Stu…"

He paused, half-turned, and studied Gabe without saying a word.

"What's your secret? You know what I mean… how do you make such a lot of money? Do you want a partner?"

Stuart pulled his sunglasses down over his eyes and grinned. As if he'd share with her—or anyone. "Catch you later, babe."

He ambled out.

§

Gabrielle watched him go, her smile fading, her expression hardening. Stu strutted through the door like an over-zealous peacock. He was involved in something dodgy, but what?

There was no pattern to his deposits. This time it was forty grand in cryptocurrency. Other times, it could be a few hundred in cash or bundles of hundreds that he claimed were the proceeds from an auction.

She was sure of one thing. It had to be dirty money.

She'd tried tracing it, but her investigations had led nowhere. The source of the cryptocurrencies Stu used couldn't be traced beyond an account in Australia. And cash could come from anywhere.

Gabrielle worked hard for her money in a steady job. A J.O.B.—Just Over Broke. After she paid her rent and bills each month, there wasn't a lot left. And at least once a week, that arrogant fuck parked his Lamborghini in the disabled park outside and strutted in with another giant deposit.

It was galling. It was unfair. It was surely criminal.

But, most of all, it was tempting.

Chapter 4

Day 2 (Tuesday, 15 August), evening

STUART SELDOM STOPPED WORKING. Swindling and scamming people took a lot of time. The doorbell rang. He checked his watch: seven o'clock. Time had flown.

It was Gabe, wearing a low-cut dress and carrying a bottle of red wine.

"Hi, Stu." She bustled past him and put the wine on the kitchen bench. "We going out for dinner, or what?"

"Nah. I've spotted a new opportunity I'm working on. Research, you know."

"But you're still in your suit, and I dressed up specially. Come on, my treat."

Again. Why was she so willing to pay every time? "All right, you talked me into it. Let's go. The fancy Italian place in Parkside?"

Gabe's breezy demeanour slipped for a moment. "The expensive one?"

"Yeah, that's it. The one with the bouncers."

"I think the management call them doormen. They take customers' coats and hats and show them to their seats."

"Whatever, babe. Let's go. I'll just grab my laptop. I can work on this at the restaurant." Stuart swivelled and picked it up from the coffee table. No sense wasting time while waiting for the food. He could carry on researching his new mark. There was a lot of money in this one, potentially. Gabe could play with her phone or ogle the waiters or something while he was busy.

Gabe ambushed him with a huge kiss when he turned back. "We'll have the wine later."

Was that a slight frown?

When Stuart pulled up in his fast Italian car, the doormen scurried like busy ants. Somehow, although the restaurant was fully booked, a table at the window was swiftly found after the doormen whispered in the maître d's ear.

Stuart moved the lit candle to one side and opened his laptop, ignoring a glare from the maître d and Gabe's efforts to get his attention by playing footsie under the table. Once he had a target in his sights, he needed to find out everything he could about them without delay, before the opportunity slipped away.

SuperGames Apps. An unimaginative name. Were their games any better? According to a press release, serious gamers thought their current work-in-progress would be a major score for the small company, blowing them into the big time. That meant their intellectual property was valuable.

If Stuart could get hold of it, he'd have plenty of options to cash in on it.

"Are you going to talk to me while we're here?" Gabe batted her eyelids at him.

"Yeah. Sorry, babe." He put his laptop away and gave her a quick smile.

"Maybe you can tell me about that new investment opportunity that's taking up all your attention."

"Nah. It wouldn't interest you." Nice try, though, babe.

The food arrived, steaming with garlic and tomato aromas. Excellent food, and it tasted even better knowing he wasn't paying.

At nine o'clock, they left and got into Stuart's Lamborghini. He turned to her. "Clubbing, babe? You up for it?"

"Where, Stu?" Gabe applied lipstick, checking herself in the sunblind's mirror.

"The 88 Club is where I normally go." He'd bet she'd never been there.

Gabe twisted her head, her lipstick forgotten, with a teeth-clenched expression part-way between a grimace and an insincere smile. "A strip joint? That's not really my scene, Stu." She shoved the lipstick into a bag and reached over to stroke Stuart's upper thigh. "Let's go back to your place. We've got wine, remember?"

He grinned and gunned the car's ignition. With Gabe's squeal of delight accompanying the engine's roar, they sped off.

Stuart swept around the arc in his driveway to the front of his house and parked by the fountain. Gabe beamed at him as they climbed the marble steps. Once inside, she dashed down the hall, glancing over her shoulder at him on her way to the kitchen. "I'll get the wine and glasses."

He put his laptop on the coffee table, took off his jacket and laid it carefully across the top of one sofa, and loosened his tie. Should he do some more work? Nah, Gabe the babe was here. Work could wait.

Gabe breezed into the living room, smiling, crystal glasses clinking in one hand, the opened bottle of wine in the other.

"Hey, babe." Stuart jerked his chin up and towards the wooden staircase in the hall. "Take it to the bedroom. Let's fuck."

§

Gabrielle rolled over. In the super-king bed, there was little chance of disturbing Stu. She checked the neon clock: 2.10 a.m. He snored like a rusty combine harvester.

Gently, she eased out of bed. Best to take no chances. Wearing nothing but her Victoria's Secret knickers, she padded across the bedroom's polished wood floor and slipped into the hall. The stairs were cold and hard on her feet, but it wasn't cold in the house. She'd turned up the central heating a few notches before going to sleep.

She fetched a glass of water from the kitchen and a book from her handbag, then sat in the living room. If Stu came downstairs, she'd claim that she couldn't sleep.

But reading was not on Gabrielle's mind. Stu's phone lay on the coffee table. She picked it up. No passcode. Lucky.

Gabrielle checked the phone's messages. Nothing. Puzzled, she checked the call history. Nothing there either. Weird. Maybe he wiped his phone every day. Or maybe it was a new phone.

She put it down and moved to the laptop. This, she knew, was password protected, because she'd seen Stu tap a few keys to get into it when he'd opened it earlier. She couldn't tell what he'd typed with his podgy fingers, apart from determining the first and last characters were shifted number keys on the left-hand side of the keyboard, either '#', '$', or '%'.

Gabrielle didn't know Stu well. He liked slow dinners and fast sex. And money. With that in mind, it was a racing certainty that those keystrokes were '$'. But what of the characters in between? He'd been too quick punching those in.

Then it hit her. His car number plate. Stu loved his car, and the number plate was '$TRIP$'. That must be it.

She tried it. The MS Windows screen appeared. Gabrielle clenched her fists in silent celebration. Now to find out how he got his dirty money. To get in on the action herself and out of salary slavery, she had to either have something to offer Stu in his ventures, or find enough information to demand a slice of the profits to keep quiet.

Gabrielle browsed the recent document list. At the top was 'Clients'. She opened the spreadsheet and started reading.

It was all laid out in multi-colour, confirming her suspicions. There didn't seem to be a pattern to the colours, but the meaning of the contents was clear.

Stu was a high-frequency, high-value, fraudster.

Curiosity shot through her. At any moment, Stu might wake and come downstairs. She had to copy the file before examining it further. Gabrielle grabbed a memory stick from her handbag, inserted it, paused for a moment to listen, then copied the 'Clients' file and many others for good measure, before putting the memory stick in her handbag.

She sipped her water and listened again. Nothing. She bent over the laptop and read.

The last entry was dated the previous day and read: 'Julie Nicholls – investment deal - $40,000'. That was the amount Stu had transferred into his own account in cryptocurrency. It was obviously an investment that Julie wouldn't see any return from.

Gabrielle flipped the page. Her own name jumped out at her, in red.

'Gabrielle Hocking – free meals and shags' was the entry. Heat flushed her face. Bastard.

More entries: 'Book piracy – July - $6800', 'stock market flyers - $1700', 'worry website premiums - $3400', 'house removal - $48,000', '88 Club – July profit - $77,500' and so on. A veritable cornucopia of illicit earnings, misdeeds, lies, schemes and scams. A staggering amount of money, month after month.

How audacious. Gabrielle shook her head. She set her jaw and closed the laptop. There'd be plenty of time for her to examine the copied file tomorrow. Right now, she'd better sneak back to bed before she was missed.

Footsteps sounded on the floor above. Stu was up. Gabrielle grabbed her book, opened it, and lay on the sofa, her head on a cushion.

Stu appeared. "Why are you down here, babe? Couldn't sleep?"

"Nah. Restless. I thought I'd read, and I didn't want to wake you." Gabrielle feigned a yawn.

"You seem tired now. Come back to bed."

"Sure." Gabrielle swallowed. It had been a close call. Heart pounding, she followed Stu back upstairs.

Chapter 5

I SAUNTERED NORTH from Crumbledon along the cracked pavement of Crumblo Street, turning up the collar of my raincoat and pulling my fedora down against the pelting rain. Water streamed along cracks on the buildings with flaky facades—a constant reminder of the terrible earthquakes we'd survived.

My destination was Sintown. It was walking distance if you had little to do and you didn't mind wearing out shoe leather. Anyway, I had little choice.

After twenty minutes, to avoid the rain, I ducked under the awning of an illegal betting shop masquerading as a newsagent's, pulled out my phone and dialled.

Someone answered. "Yeah?"

"Jimmy? It's Danny Ashford here. I've gotta talk to you about something. Can I pop round?"

"Yeah, all right, Danny. See you soon." He disconnected.

I stuffed my phone into my pocket and trudged on. Quake City Auto Getaways was in the next block, in the heart of Sintown, between a fish and chip shop and a hairdresser's, both grubby establishments that should be closed down by the authorities if anyone cared to examine them—not that anyone would.

The auto shop didn't have a sign. I entered through a door next to a large corrugated aluminium roller. It would be easy enough for criminals to smash it down and raid the auto shop, but it never happened. Jimmy had connections, and no one wanted to get on his nasty side.

Tools and random parts lay scattered on a workbench that stretched the length of the shop, apart from a small office. Sometimes the fried fish smell overpowered the smell of body paint and motor oil, but rarely.

"Danny! What can I do for you?" Jimmy finished screwing a number plate on an Audi, slipped the screwdriver into his overalls pocket, and got to his feet.

"I need a car. My last one got shot up and busted to hell." Rivulets of rain ran off my hat, cascaded off my coat, and onto the concrete floor.

Jimmy eyed the growing puddles of water. "What type of car you after?"

"Something like this?" I jerked my head towards the Audi.

He laughed. "You can't afford it, Danny, if I know you."

"Okay. Have you got anything cheap and comfy, but reliable and fast. And it must be automatic so I've got one hand free. A good safety rating, not a body that bullets will pass through as if it's tin foil."

Jimmy chuckled. "That all?"

"Yeah. The best you can find." A voice at the back of my mind protested vociferously, and I ignored it. I was desperate for a car. What kind of private investigator would I be without wheels? A damn slow one.

"Colour?"

"Midnight blue or racing green, whichever."

"You need it by?"

"As soon as."

Jimmy traipsed to a small kitchen area at one side of the workplace and started making himself a coffee. He raised a mug with oil-stained fingers and eyed me. "Want one?"

"Yeah, thanks." I shivered. The winter rain hadn't been cold, but the wind had been blowing it into my face.

Jimmy busied himself with the drinks. "It might take me one, two or three days. I've got to source a vehicle for you, then make it uniquely yours. Understand?"

"Yeah. Thanks, Jimmy."

I understood only too well. Jimmy was in the business of recycling stolen cars. The problem was, I had little choice but to go to Jimmy. I'd barely had enough money for my last crappy one. My financial situation had gone downhill since.

He took our drinks to an old Formica table. We sat on rusty steel-legged chairs, sipping the strong coffee.

My conscience prickled at me. "Jimmy? When you, uh, source the vehicle, you'll do it ethically, won't you?"

He stared at me for a long moment, then laughed again. Clearly, I'd caught Jimmy in a jovial mood. All the better for when the topic of payment came up.

"Don't worry, Danny. I'll get you a car that won't be missed. Or, rather, won't be reported as stolen."

I inclined my head and said nothing.

Jimmy's eyes narrowed. "You're thinking I'm going to put together a car from wrecks. No, I won't do that to you, Danny. I have a more sophisticated sourcing pipeline than that."

"That's a relief." I took another mouthful. Whatever brand of coffee Jimmy used packed a punch like a UFC champion. I was buzzing already.

"Okay, let's talk payment. Cash on delivery. And I mean actual cash. Nothing through the banking system."

I nodded. "How about I pay you a little later? Like in maybe a week or two?"

Jimmy drew in a deep breath and leaned back. "No credit. What if you skip town?"

"Hell's teeth, Jimmy, if I was going to leave town for any reason, I would've done it by now."

"Yeah, I suppose."

"Give me a break. Some bastard hacked my bank account and emptied it. I've gotta earn some dough before I can pay you, and I need the car for that."

Jimmy sighed. "Fine. I'll get you something, and you can pay me when you're ready." Sharp eyes glinting and his gaze never leaving mine, Jimmy took the screwdriver from his overalls pocket and stabbed it in the air as he spoke, punctuating his words. "But you'd better not make me wait too long."

I flinched at each stab and tried not to read anything into that.

§

I trudged towards home through the easing rain. Across the street, a fight had started outside a bottle store. I watched for a few moments until the store's security guard raced out with a baseball bat and sent the troublemakers off in different directions.

My phone rang. I glanced at the number. Petra. Maybe it would be good news. Maybe she'd tracked the hacker who raided my bank account.

I answered. "Danny here."

"Hey, Danny, I did what I could. Here's what I've got. Your money paid for items from a fictitious online store. The funds went into an account in the Caymans, but I can't track them from there. Their banks are too hard to hack."

Dismay swept through me. "So, there's no way to recover my money?"

"Nope. But I have some good news for you."

That was something. "What is it?"

"I found the exact time when the first transaction happened."

I found cover from the drizzle under the awning for a bakery. "How does that help? The hacker could have been anywhere."

"True, but I wondered if the hacker might have copied your card details when you last used it, so I checked where you were at the time using the location of your phone."

She was spying on me? "I didn't ask you to do that, Petra."

"No... but I did it anyway. You were in a supermarket when the fraudulent transactions took place."

I took a deep breath, waiting for her to continue.

"So, I hacked into the supermarket security system and reviewed the camera footage at around that time. I located you—I wouldn't buy that brand of cat food, by the way. It's had some critical reviews."

"Wait a minute. We've never met. How do you know what I look like?"

"From a photo in the *Richter Mail* a while back, after that serial killer case."

"Oh, right. Go on."

"Just seconds before the first of the fraudulent transactions, a well-dressed dude bumped into you. Remember him?"

Yeah. I did. "You're saying he's the hacker? Someone who might live locally?"

"It's too much of a coincidence otherwise. He could've read your card details with a customised card reader hidden in his briefcase. Then it made several purchases over the next few minutes until your account was empty."

I remembered that guy. Something about him stood out, apart from his snappy suit and fine moustache. A certain glint in his hazel-green eyes. Avarice. Ruthlessness.

"Can you send me a copy of the surveillance video?"

"Yup, no problem."

"Thanks, Petra. I owe you one."

"Too right. I'm bound to get into trouble one day. I'll call you when I do." She disconnected.

I strode on. A passing car hit a pothole and splashed water over my shoes. Just my rotten luck.

Another call. Deepa, investigative journalist. My sometime partner in solving crime.

I picked up. "Hi, Deepa."

"Hey, Danny. How are you and Petra getting on?"

"She's been a great help, thanks." I explained everything, and how Petra had given me a brief video clip of the man who'd stolen my bank card details.

"Is she sure about that?"

I frowned. "Not a hundred per cent. More like ninety per cent. But it's my only lead so far."

"All right. Good luck. Call me if you need anything." She disconnected.

I shoved the phone into my pocket and clenched my teeth. What I needed most was to find that black-moustached, smart-suited guy.

Chapter 6

STUART BAKER USED A VARIETY of contacts to carry out his legwork. No point being the mastermind conman of a fraud empire without having a few henchmen to do some dirty work. Especially on riskier jobs.

He parked along the shore at Slumner. The sandy beach stretched into the distance. Across the road, a row of weather-beaten houses faced the greyish sea. It wasn't raining now, but the wind off the sea was chilly, as always.

Stuart strode to the Slug and Lettuce pub. Why it was called that, no one could remember. It didn't even serve food; though, if it did, he wouldn't order the salad. Stuart liked the place because of its discreet booths where he could conduct business deals without being overheard.

Brock Patterson rose from his seat to meet him with a misshapen smile and a callused handshake. Stuart knew him as a man used to hard work, interspersed with periods of leisure at Her Majesty's pleasure that never permanently dissuaded him from his chosen career.

"Hi, Stu. Good to see ya."

Stuart cringed inside. He hated people calling him Stu, but almost everyone did, even when he told them not to. He tugged lightly at the knees of his trousers as he sat and snapped his fingers.

The barmaid trotted over. "What can I get you, gentlemen?"

Brock ordered a beer. Stuart ordered a red wine. They sat in silence until the drinks were delivered.

"Let's get down to it, Brock. I've an important job for you. One night's work. I'll pay you ten grand if it works out."

Brock whistled softly. "I'm interested. What's the job?"

Stuart withdrew an envelope from an inside pocket of his suit jacket. "The details of the place are in here. Do it yourself, and don't tell anyone about it. Got that, Brock? This must be kept absolutely quiet."

Brock took the envelope but didn't open it. "What risks am I taking on?"

Stuart sipped his wine. "There'll be alarms. No security guards as far as I can tell." He poked a finger at Brock. "You'll have to disable the alarms so you have time to search for the information I want."

"You don't know where I should look when I get inside?"

"No. That's why I'm offering you a lot of money."

"That's fine, Stu. I'm up for it." Brock took a big swig from his beer, then wiped his mouth with the back of his hand. "I need the money."

Stuart chuckled. "You always need the money, Brock. That's why I can rely on you." He leaned forward, his mouth hardening. "Don't let me down."

§

Mary Sanchez stood at the one-way mirror in her office, a glass of wine in one hand. Below, the floor of the 420 Club, a drink, drugs and dating venue she owned and operated, was quiet. A year ago, it had bustled with activity from early afternoon until the wee hours.

Now it was a shadow of its former self. Only a handful of die-hard patrons were on the premises, and half of them were presently unconscious, so they weren't spending. The latest band's attitude and music was lacklustre. One of the barmen had nodded off behind the counter. Two of the hostesses played cards, ignoring everyone. Mary's accounts—her real ones—revealed she was losing several thousand dollars a week, on a good week, after salaries and expenses. Sometimes it was five figures.

The 420 Club had lost its mojo. She'd tried every marketing trick she knew. Dreaded karaoke and quiz nights. Two-for-one drinks. Paid dancers. Even two-for-one hostesses. Nothing had worked.

The path to its current state of desolation had begun months before when the 88 Club opened a block away. She'd just found out via a forensic

28

accountant that the proprietor, a slick dresser called Stuart Baker, owned it through a hierarchy of look-through companies, some overseas.

Apparently, Stuart's suit had deep pockets. He'd hired cooler bands and prettier hostesses, played louder music with fancy flashing lighting, and sold cheaper drinks. His venue outshone hers in every aspect. At first, he must have run it at a considerable loss.

Her clientele had hastened down the street to the newer, cheaper, more exciting club. It had become busier than hers had ever been. And when Stuart had gradually put up his prices, her disloyal clients hadn't returned.

Mary seethed. If she wanted to survive in this business, she had to take drastic action. Fast.

She clutched her wineglass so tightly, the stem broke.

§

Gabrielle sat in bed in her small flat, poring over her laptop late into the night, cradling a coffee. Two empty mugs sat on the side table nearby. She'd put her phone on silent in case Stu called her to drop around for a late-night quickie. The last thing she needed was an interruption, especially from him.

She'd been studying the copy of Stu's clients and scams files for hours. Whatever the man lacked in morals—and he appeared to have none—he made up for in energy. Stu had carried out a breath-taking number of schemes over the years, breaking too many laws to mention. If the police found out the extent of his activities, the charge list would be as long as *War and Peace*.

He illegally duplicated the hard work of struggling indie artists and sold their work on pirate sites, making money from display ads. Simultaneously, his websites infected the computers of unwary and unprotected users with viruses, which then stole their bank card information.

Gabrielle shook her head. Dreadful.

Another website, supposedly legit, offered a 'worry' service. Despairing people would fill out a form describing their problems—including a 'click here' section for extra room—and then pay an hourly rate for someone to fret over their difficulties for them. Not that anyone ever did. Instead, their money channelled straight into one of Stu's overseas accounts. Gabrielle had probably handled some transfers to his local account herself.

It made her nauseous. Making money from other people's misery, preying on their gullibility and desperation for someone to share their pain, even virtually.

She gaped at his 'house removal' scam. Daring in the extreme.

And there was worse. Much worse. Anyone, everyone, was a potential victim to Stu.

Gabrielle put aside her laptop and swapped the lukewarm coffee for a glass of red wine. As she'd suspected, Stu's money was all dirty. It couldn't get any dirtier. He'd taken advantage of so many naïve and unfortunate people. Some of his schemes were truly despicable.

They were also highly profitable.

She'd wanted a cut. But Gabrielle wasn't as hard-hearted and callous as Stu. Or did making a lot of money make it easier to live with the repercussions of the crimes?

She didn't think so.

Gabrielle shoved the duvet aside and got out of bed. It was after two a.m. There was no way she could sleep with this conundrum whirling in her head. She'd have to call in sick for work tomorrow.

She poured another glass of wine, to help her sleep. Fortunately, she'd had the foresight to bring the bottle with her from the kitchen. It was remarkable how often doing that was necessary. Especially when there was a lot to think about.

The second glass tasted sour. Or perhaps it was simply a sour taste in her mouth from thinking about Stu's nefarious activities. The first glass had been fine.

She drained the second and poured a third, opened the curtains, then the window itself, and stared out at the dark street beyond. A cat turned to stare at her, a rat dangling from its mouth, before trotting across the street and disappearing into bushes in a neighbour's property.

She'd imagined getting in on a get-rich-quick scheme with Stu, but now she'd learned his total disregard for others, she questioned her plans. Did she want to get involved with someone so heartless, so scheming, so untrustworthy?

She'd tried to get close to him so she could earn his trust before asking for a slice of the action. Spent her money to wine and dine him. Let him fuck her and treat her with disdain so she could edge closer to her goal.

Now she didn't know if she wanted any part of it.

Stuart Baker was a horrible man.

Gabrielle took a deep breath of the cold, fresh night air. Then she hurled the glass of wine into the night. It smashed on the path outside. In the distance, a dog barked. "You fucking bastard, Stu. I hate you! I hate you! I hate you!"

She slammed the window so hard the glass shook. Took a few deep breaths, feeling a little better.

She sat on the bed and swigged wine from the bottle. What to do, what to do? She could turn everything she had over to the police. Stu would get what he deserved, and Quake City would be less of a shithole without him around. But she wouldn't make any money that way. And that, the wine reminded her as she took yet another swig, was why she'd gotten involved with him in the first place.

Plan B had always been blackmail. Perhaps that would be a better course of action.

Chapter 7

MY OFFICE DOOR didn't have an Open / Closed sign on it because I figured that anyone needing a private investigator doesn't want to wait for normal office hours. When I was home, my business was open.

I hadn't even finished breakfast when someone knocked softly on the door.

"Come in." I pushed my toast and coffee to the edge of the desk.

An elegant woman in a business suit carrying a leather document holder entered. Her black hair was tied in a bun. She closed the door behind her. "This is Quake City Investigations?" Her voice was quiet, timid.

"That's right. I'm Danny Ashcroft, proprietor and chief investigator. How can I help you?" I gestured at the chair in front of the desk.

She sat. "I'm Julie Nicholls. I'm a lawyer."

Hell's teeth. This could be bad news. Maybe I'd broken some law I didn't know about, the police were on their way and she was here to say she would represent me. Or it could be about the laws I did know I've broken occasionally. Or perhaps she was delivering a warning.

"Danny, I believe I'm the victim of a sophisticated confidence trickster."

Relief flooded me. I wasn't in trouble. Instead, she'd brought me trouble of her own. I had a potential client right when I needed one.

I leaned forward, resting my arms on the desk. "Tell me everything, Julie."

She opened her document holder and took out a colourful prospectus and a business card. "This man, Jonathan Goodfellow, convinced me to buy into an investment fund. The details are all here. He said he'd call me back and email me a receipt and my account information, but he hasn't." Her words were softly spoken.

"How long ago was this?"

"Two days." Julie pushed the documents across the desk towards me.

"His office might be slow at responding."

She shook her head. "I phoned the number on the business card yesterday afternoon. It's been disconnected. Then I googled him. The only mention of a Jonathan Goodfellow, investment manager, is on his website, Fat Prophets Investments. When I examined it in more depth, I discovered the website was set up only last month. The prospectus here shows several years of outsized investment returns. It doesn't add up." She jabbed a delicate finger at the document.

I picked up the business card. It had fancy fonts and no photo. "It sounds like you're right. In that case, Jonathan Goodfellow won't be his actual name. Shame you didn't carry out that due diligence before you invested."

Julie sighed. "I blame myself. I mean, I should know better. I'm a lawyer. I tell my clients to be wary of things that sound too good to be true, and I didn't follow my own advice. I was only thinking of the big profits he promised." She looked down and shuffled her feet under the chair.

"Why did you trust him so readily?"

Julie didn't lift her head. "He seemed like a really nice, genuine guy." Her voice was so soft I could barely hear it.

I was sure there was more to it. "And?"

"I slept with him twice."

"We all make mistakes. How much money did you give to him?"

She raised her head and looked me directly in the eye. "Forty thousand."

I whistled softly. "That's a lot."

Julie sniffed. "It's the principal of the matter, as well as the money. I want you to find him and gather evidence. And find the money."

The money might be gone or well hidden. I thought about my own stolen funds. "Why don't you go straight to the police?"

"I can't. It'd ruin my reputation if it got out. Who would hire a lawyer so naïve she'd gotten hoodwinked by a confidence trickster?"

"I see your point. So, when you say you want me to gather evidence..."

"I want you to keep me out of it if you can, at least until I've formed a trust and made it appear like the money came from there instead of directly from me."

"I don't understand any of that accounting legalese stuff."

"Don't worry about it. I want you to find him, get him arrested, and get my money back if you can."

I stroked my jaw. "Can you give me a description of the perp?"

"He's about my age, has black hair, always tidily combed, and a thin black moustache. Oh, and each time I saw him, he wore an expensive suit."

My eyes widened. Could it be...?

"What? Do you know him?"

"Check out this video and tell me if that's your man." I grabbed my phone. Petra had sent me the snippet of the supermarket's security system recording. In it, the guy who had bumped into me and scanned my bank card details could be seen clearly strolling away after the event. I put the phone on the desk and let the video run from that point. It lasted only a few seconds before he was out of sight.

Julie leaned forward. "Yes, that's him. Jonathan Goodfellow or whatever he's actually called. Where did you get this video?"

"From a source. This guy scammed someone's bank card in the supermarket." I wasn't going to say I was the victim.

Over on the sofa, Torquemada glared at me accusingly.

"So, you're already after him?"

"Yes." Damn. She might demand a discount now that she knew I was already hunting him.

Julie paused for a few moments, deep in thought. "It appears you have a head start. Will you help me, Danny? Discreetly?"

"I certainly will. I charge eighty dollars an hour plus expenses, with five hundred upfront. All right?"

"Wow. You're good value. Text me your bank details and I'll transfer the money." She handed me a silver-lettered business card, then stood and stretched out a hand. I shook it. Her handshake was firmer than her voice.

Julie picked up her document folder, turned and strode to the door. There she paused and glanced over her shoulder, smiling faintly. "Goodbye for now."

She seemed confident that I'd get her money back. It was more than I felt.

Chapter 8

Day 4 (Thursday, 17 August), evening

I'D HAD ENOUGH OF BANKS by two in the afternoon. All I wanted was a new account. The first bank had rejected me because of my occupation, and when I told them I only wanted a deposit account, not a loan, they said I didn't fit their preferred customer profile. Not that they'd tell me what that was.

The second bank was more accommodating. Once I'd filled in screeds of forms, submitted my identity documents, and promised them my first-born child if my account lurched into an unauthorised overdraft, they opened an account for me.

I texted the details to Julie Nicholls and had a burger while I waited for her advance payment to come through. It was in my account within the hour.

The rain started on my way home, a thirty-minute walk from the Crumbledon mall, where the banks clustered together like guard dogs at the entrance. I didn't mind the rain; it was refreshing, and the steady beat of it on my raincoat and hat calmed me after my ordeal.

I climbed the stairs of my apartment building. My new neighbour, Chelsea, leaned against the door jamb of her apartment, wearing a light dressing gown and smoking a cigarette. I stopped beside her, and she gave me a faint smile.

"How are you settling in?"

She blew smoke towards the ceiling. "I'm all good. You?"

"Stressed. I've been at the bank, opening an account."

"I know what you mean. You wanna have some breakfast? I'm about to make coffee and toast and scrambled eggs."

"You've having breakfast now? It's mid-afternoon."

"I work late evenings into the early hours, and I sleep until at least noon most days."

"Ah, right. Well, if you're sure… another breakfast sounds great."

She led me inside. Her bare feet were silent on the polished wooden floorboards. She was wearing purple nail polish.

I hung my hat and coat on a hook on the door. I was already familiar with the apartment from when my previous neighbour lived there, but Chelsea's décor was completely different. Modern light-hued furniture with soft curves had replaced the dark, hard-edged decades-old stuff. The place was no longer fusty and dated. Now it was cool and chic.

"I love what you've done with the place." I winced. What a cliché. Couldn't I think of an original compliment?

Chelsea didn't seem to mind. "Thanks. I'll get the breakfast started. Take a seat if you like, or maybe you can help?"

"I'll do the toast." I didn't fancy the odds of the eggs surviving if I tried scrambling them, whereas burnt toast could easily be scraped to an edible state.

Five minutes later, breakfast was ready. We ate at a faux-birch table.

Chelsea started the conversation. "I saw the sign on your door saying you're a private investigator."

"Yes. Is that why you invited me in? You need help with something?"

Chelsea crunched the overdone toast and gestured that she couldn't answer while she ate. I watched her, then glanced away. I'd been staring.

"It's my boss. He's a complete prick, not just to me, but to everyone who works for him. He's always making snide remarks, or making us run errands for him. Just yesterday he made me take his watch to be repaired because it had stopped working. Other times, it's to do his grocery shopping. That's not part of my job."

Instinct and experience told me there must be more to it than that. "What else?"

"He's also making sexual advances, but I'm not interested. The last one was a week ago. He said I 'wasn't being a team player'. I told him I will not let him fuck me, no matter what. I don't think he got the message. I'm afraid he's going to try again and fire me if I don't."

Chelsea's dressing gown had slipped and exposed her right shoulder and part of her right breast. The smell of her perfume when we first met came back to me in a heated rush. I tried not to stare. My throat had dried up like the Gobi desert.

I took a mouthful of coffee. "You want me to warn him off?"

"Yeah. Can you do that?"

"I can."

"What'll it cost?"

My usual spiel about a minimum two-hour fee passed through my mind, but my mouth betrayed me. "Don't worry about it. Call it a neighbourly favour."

"That's so sweet of you, Danny. Thank you." She leaned forward and kissed my cheek.

My skin tingled. Why was I having these reactions? I thought of Deepa. A pang of guilt swept through me.

I finished my toast. "What's your boss' name?"

"Stuart. I don't know his last name."

"And where do you work?"

"The 88 Club in Sintown."

I concealed my surprise. The 88 Club... I'd heard about it, but I'd never been there. "I'll pay a visit and speak to him as soon as I can."

Chapter 9

Day 4 (Thursday, 17 August), evening

I SPENT THE REST of the afternoon searching online for any information on Jonathan Goodfellow in the Quake City area. As I expected, there was nothing. The guy didn't exist. At least not under that name.

The best, perhaps only, approach now was for me to visit places where a scumbag like him might hang out, and ask if anyone there recognised him. Eventually, I'd turn up something. But I needed a car for that. I couldn't walk all over the city.

I phoned Jimmy Wang. "Jimmy, when will my car be ready?"

"About an hour, Danny. I found you a nice one. The spray paint is almost dry. Midnight blue."

"Perfect. I'll pick it up in an hour."

"Hang on. I want a down payment. In cash. You can come up with the rest of the money later, as agreed, but you've got to pay something up front."

"I can give you three hundred." Great. That was most of my advance payment from Julie. I'd need the remaining two hundred for food.

"That'll do. See you in an hour." He rang off.

I strolled along Crumblo street towards Sintown. It was dusk. Most shops were closed or closing up, the proprietors pulling down corrugated iron shutters to deter robbers. I had a dinner stop at McDonald's, then carried on and withdrew the cash at an ATM when no one was nearby. I arrived at Jimmy Wang's garage a little after six p.m.

Jimmy answered my call and let me in. With a grin, he swept one grimy arm towards a vehicle on the workshop floor.

I nodded in appreciation. An Audi A3, midnight blue. A better grade of car than I'd expected. But could I afford it?

That might have been Jimmy's concern too. "I'll take the three hundred now, thanks, Danny."

I gave it to him. "How much is this going to cost me, Jimmy? You know my budget doesn't stretch far."

He told me. It was more than I thought, but less than I feared. I examined the car carefully. It was an automatic, just as I wanted.

"I cleaned out the interior for you, seeing as you're a friend."

"Yeah, it's nice. What's this dent on the back right-hand side?"

"No idea. I'm not a panel beater, Danny. I can't fix it. Besides, you wanted a car urgently. This was the first one I could get for you that matched your specifications."

"Okay." I completed my slow circle of the car. Despite the dent, I was impressed. I hesitated. "You sourced this car ethically, didn't you, Jimmy?"

Jimmy hummed and hawed. "Let's just say that neither you nor I should have any moral qualms about this car's previous owner."

"Right. And did they agree to you taking possession of it?"

"It's not one that'll be reported stolen. Don't worry, Danny." Jimmy clapped me on the shoulder so hard he almost knocked me into the side of the car. "You needed a suitable vehicle, and I got you one. Be happy."

"Okay. Thanks, Jimmy. I'll get you the rest of the money as soon as I can."

"Here are the keys. I'll open the garage door for you."

I slipped into the car and turned it on. The engine purred like a wild tiger. A wild tiger that was perhaps getting on in years and had a slight throat infection, but nevertheless I sensed the Audi's coiled power.

Jimmy rolled up the garage door with a clang. I drove through the gap, braked abruptly at the edge of the road to check the way was clear, then swerved sharply left and accelerated towards Crumbledon. Putting the car through its paces, finding its limits—that was important. Besides, it was fun.

§

At home, I called Deepa and told her about my new wheels. She invited me over for dinner. I hadn't seen her for three or four weeks, not since our previous case together had ended, so I readily accepted and drove over to her apartment.

Spicy aromas welcomed me when she let me in. "It's a recipe my parents taught me. Chicken korma. Mild, not hot. I think you'll like it." She chuckled. "Maybe after dinner you can take me for a drive in your new car?"

I beamed. "I sure will."

The dinner was as tasty as it smelled. Afterwards, we took the Audi for a spin. We drove around the four avenues enclosing the red-zoned, barricaded Central Busted District before going to Crashmere and over the hills to Crater Bay. The hills were steep and the sharp turns unforgiving, but after two hours I was confident with the awesome Audi Jimmy had found me.

I stopped at a bay where there was a view of the dark sea and the night sky, and turned to Deepa. "Did you get an insurance pay-out for your Vespa?"

"Yep, but I only just received it. I've ordered another one, similar model, but more powerful."

"Great. When can you pick it up?"

"Next month." Deepa gave me a sly smile. "I'm sure you owe me a few trips."

"Yeah. Call me if you need a ride somewhere."

"Cool, thanks." She smiled again, warmer and longer this time.

We returned the same way. It was ten thirty. Probably a good time to visit the 88 Club and speak to Chelsea's boss, like I'd promised.

I stopped outside Deepa's apartment in Splitstown. The illumination from one streetlight shone through the windscreen.

She swung the door open, but turned to face me before getting out. "It's good to see you, Danny. Thanks for the ride. Like to come up for a drink?"

Work and pleasure warred within me, but obligation won. "Ah, I can't, thanks. I've got a job I promised to do."

"At this time of night?"

"It's at a club where they're open late hours. I need to tell a guy to stop harassing his staff."

Deepa frowned. "That sounds risky."

"I've got to present the argument in a way that he won't forget, that's all."

The car door was still open, but Deepa hadn't got out yet. It was getting cold in the car with the night air streaming in and the warmth gushing out. Wasn't Deepa getting cold herself, sitting in the open doorway? "Sounds like there's a story in there somewhere. I could come with you."

I shook my head. "No, my client wants this done discreetly to protect her privacy. An article in the *Richter Mail* is too much exposure."

"That's a shame."

"Why don't you write an article on con artists and hackers? There's plenty of material for that."

"You want me to write about how you got hacked?"

That would dent my reputation. "No, that's not a good idea. You'd have to find some other victims."

"In my experience, most people say nothing if they get hacked or conned. They feel embarrassed and humiliated."

"Yeah, you're right. Listen, I have a client who was conned out of a lot of money. She wants me to find the con artist. But you know what? Petra says the perp who hacked my bank card is the same guy."

"Really?"

"Yeah. I showed my client the video Petra sent me, and she confirmed it."

"There's a story for me right there. I'll help you track him down if you like. The usual financial arrangement?"

"Deal." We made an excellent investigative team, and split my fees and the earnings Deepa made from any exposé or articles she wrote for the *Richter Mail*. "You mind closing the car door? It's getting cold in here."

"Even in your coat and hat?"

I nodded.

"Sorry. Are you sure you won't come in for a hot drink to warm you up?"

"Nah, I'd better get going and do this job. Thanks anyway. Another time. Call me tomorrow about the investigation."

"Will do." Deepa got out of the car and shut the door with a wave.

I drove off into the night. Next stop, the 88 Club.

Chapter 10

WHEN I REACHED SINTOWN, I parked on Crumblo Street and strode two blocks to the 88 Club. Garish flashing neon lights and the thump-thump-thump of loud music sliced through the still night air, attracting punters like moths to a flaming torch.

It wasn't my kind of place, and I was certain it wasn't Deepa's either. Thankfully, she hadn't pressed the issue when I'd said she shouldn't come with me.

The '88' of the sign was in the shape of two wide-hipped buxom women. The club was a strip joint. The kind of place where the owner would most likely have a bodyguard or two with him most of the time, and where sexually harassing the staff might not be unexpected.

I'd initially planned to confront him and threaten him with the police if he harassed the girls again. But someone who employed heavies in their club wouldn't hesitate to have me beaten up and left unconscious in some alleyway or dumped in the river. I needed another tactic.

A flashing arrow below the neon '88' pointed to the club entrance. On either side of the darkened doorway, heavy-set men wearing suits stood, watching anyone who approached. They allowed most people to enter, but occasionally turned someone away. I wondered what they would say to me, if anything, as I strolled casually up to the entrance.

One heavy leaned forward and stopped me with a hand. "You got any weapons on you?"

I shook my head.

"Any drugs?"

"No."

The other heavy moved right up to me, his hot breath in my right ear. "Want any?"

I shied away in distaste. "No."

They resumed their earlier positions and the first guy waved me through.

Inside, the overhead lighting was low. Thirty or so male patrons sprawled around small tables set up before a small stage on which a three-piece band played upbeat music as if they were drunk. Perhaps they were.

I sidled towards the bar, scanning the crowd. Three more heavies watched over the customers from shadowy recesses, poised to leap in if there was trouble. The bar was side-on to the stage and stretched three-quarters the length of the room from the back towards the stage. Toilets were opposite, near the entrance. Beside the bar was a wooden door that I guessed led to the drinks cellar. To the right of the stage, a carpeted staircase went up. One heavy stood next to it.

The musicians, despite appearing a little lacklustre, played well enough if you weren't a music afficionado. I took a seat near the bar, facing the stage.

A hostess in her twenties approached me. She must have been cold. All she wore was a bikini bottom. Her breasts bounced as she ambled over. I tried to keep my eyes off them and my mind on the job at hand.

"Want a drink?" She barely glanced at me with dull eyes.

"Whiskey, please." I didn't intend to cloud my judgement so I wasn't planning on drinking it, but I had to fit into the scene until my business was finished.

She passed me a mobile EFTPOS machine. When I saw the price she'd entered, my eyes watered. The only money left in my new account was the two hundred remaining of the advance and a few expenses Julie Nicholls had prepaid, and this one drink was going to make a big hole in that if I paid for it.

"I can't afford that."

"Cheapskate. You want a cola or something?"

I handed over a twenty-dollar note. "Will this cover it?"

She screwed her mouth up. "I'll get you a small glass."

"Fine. Is the owner is in tonight?"

"What would you want with him?"

"That doesn't need to concern you."

She jutted her chin forward, scowling. "He's here somewhere. At least, he was half an hour ago. Maybe he's seeing to the VIP customers or the poker players upstairs. Or banging one of the girls."

Heat rose in my face. In the dim light, it wouldn't be visible.

"I'll get your drink." She stalked off.

While I waited, the band stopped playing, thanked everyone for their muted applause, and left the stage. I glanced around. Chelsea had told me she was working tonight. That was the major reason I'd called in on her boss before he hassled her again. Was she a hostess? I couldn't see her.

The woman who'd taken my order brought my drink and plonked it on the table without a word. I sipped at it, wishing it was whiskey after all.

Music started up again, but it wasn't the band returning. It was disco music. A woman sashayed onto the stage wearing a long trench coat, white gloves, black boots, a red beret and a colourful umbrella. None of the outfit matched, but the customers didn't seem to mind.

I recognised her instantly. Chelsea.

Her dance act didn't seem to fit the music, but that didn't bother the customers either. The trench coat fell to the floor. She kicked it off the stage. The hat and boots followed, going in different directions. Chelsea danced on in a bikini, the umbrella whirling in circles in a gloved hand.

A voice in my head told me not to watch. She was my neighbour, after all. It felt wrong. I watched anyway. Until an opportunity appeared, I had nothing else to do, and I needed to seem like just another punter.

One of the white gloves landed on my table. A well-aimed throw, or a challenge? I caught Chelsea's eye. She gave a meaningful glance to the staircase by the bar.

I got the hint. Still, it would draw too much attention for me to move before the show ended. And when it did, I would need a diversion to get past the security heavy. He stood at the staircase, arms folded, watching the crowd, not the show.

The song was almost over. Now only in her bikini bottoms, Chelsea removed them from behind the umbrella. They also landed on my table. The last notes sounded, and Chelsea flung the umbrella across the stage, revealing herself in her naked glory under a dazzling spotlight for a few moments before the stage was plunged into darkness.

Two nearby patrons swivelled and regarded my collection of garments with envy. This was my chance to create a distraction. I glanced at them both and held up the knickers. "First one here gets them."

I dropped the panties and got out of their way. Both guys dived for them at the same time. The table toppled over, sending my drink flying. The men scrambled under the chairs in the dim light. I backed away.

The security heavy raced over from the stairs to break up the fracas. One of his colleagues approached too. The third remained by the door, watching the melee. The bartender was busy with a customer. I slipped around the corner of the bar and dashed up the unguarded staircase two steps at a time.

The top floor had the same thick, red carpet that looked like it hadn't been changed for a decade. Several rooms came off a main hallway. Every door was closed, and no one was in sight.

I didn't know what the rooms were. Bedrooms, gambling rooms, meeting rooms, offices or others. The owner might be in one of them. Or not. I had no way of knowing, but at least there weren't any bodyguards up here.

One of these rooms had to be the owner's office. I tread along the hallway, my footsteps silent on the carpet, listening for doors opening behind me. Nothing but silence. Maybe all the rooms were sound-proofed.

How much time did I have before someone saw me?

A door marked 'Private' was halfway along the hall. No light came from underneath. I tried the handle. Locked.

Internal locks often aren't secure. I grabbed an old library card from a pocket of my coat and slipped it between the door and the frame, feeling for the catch. It slid away, and I opened the door.

Chapter 11

I CREPT INSIDE, returning the library card to my pocket, and closed the door. Starlight shone through a large window. I felt for the light switch.

The room illuminated brightly. It was a large office with a desk at a right angle to the window. The desk was half-covered with papers, mainly bills and receipts for the club. A strap of fifty-dollar notes stuck out from underneath a power bill. I stared at it for several moments. Five grand. Tempting. That would solve a lot of my problems. But that wasn't what I was here for, and I wasn't a thief. I left it untouched.

A letter lying across the computer keyboard caught my eye. I skimmed it. Someone called Mary Sanchez requesting a meeting with Stuart Baker, owner of the 88 Club. Chelsea had said the owner's first name was Stuart. Now I knew the dickhead's full name.

Back to what I was meant to be doing. Rather than confronting the owner in person, I'd decided to leave a clear message for him. His office was the perfect place for that. He'd be uncomfortable at how easily I got past the security men and into his office.

I picked up a pen and a blank sheet of paper from a printer nearby. On it, in black capital letters, I wrote:

BAKER, OWNER OF THE 88 CLUB.
STOP HARASSING YOUR GIRLS
OR YOU WILL DEAL WITH ME.

Underneath the message, I drew a stick figure of a man. In the desk's top drawer, I found a drawing pin and attached my warning note to the seat of the chair by sticking the pin through the groin area of my drawn figure. For good measure, I threw one of my business cards on top of it. That'd show I wasn't afraid of him.

My message delivered, I now had to leave before a wandering security heavy found me. I opened the door a fraction and checked the hallway. Empty. I switched the office light off and slipped out.

The security guy guarding the stairs would surely be back in position by now, so I needed another way out where I wouldn't be seen. But where?

I strode down the hall in the other direction. Maybe there was another staircase. I tried to get my bearings. Which rooms faced onto the street? Could there be a way out from one of those, like a fire escape?

The music downstairs was thumping again. Suddenly, a guy grabbed my shoulder and wrenched me around.

Another staunch heavy in the same cheap cut of dark suit. He scowled. "You're not allowed up here unescorted."

"I'm looking for the toilets."

He stared at me for what must have been several seconds, though it seemed longer. Maybe he was trying to figure out if I was lying. Something he heard in my tone, or saw in my eyes, or merely because he was a mean bastard, eventually led him to a decision. I saw it coming in slow motion. His eyes narrowed slightly, his jaw clenched, his weight shifted slightly on his feet.

He moved to slam me against the wall, but I spun out of reach. His shoulder crashed into the wall. He groaned and staggered away. I kicked the back of his knee, hard. He crashed in a heap to the floor.

Doors opened along the hallway. Two similarly attired men raced out. Other people too, but the heavies commanded my attention. I didn't like my chances of getting past both of them.

One drew a handgun from his jacket. They both dashed towards me.

The heavy on the ground rolled over and grabbed at my legs. I leaped over him and sprinted. The door he'd emerged from was ajar. I darted inside as the gun fired. It echoed loudly in the hallway. Splinters of wood flew from the door jamb. Screams and shouts came from behind me.

I entered a large room. Several people were seated at a round table, playing poker. They stared at me. I had only seconds to get out. The gun-toting heavy and his colleague were only metres away.

There were no other doors. Only a window.

I lurched at the table and swept one arm across it, sending chips and cards tumbling to the floor. The players dived to the carpet, scrambling for their cards and stakes.

That should hamper the guys pursuing me.

I pulled my raincoat over my head and leaped toward the windowpane, turning side-on in mid-air so shards of glass wouldn't lacerate my face. The window shattered. A sharp pain spread across the back of my hand. My stomach rose to my throat as I plummeted toward the ground.

A canvas awning broke my fall. I tumbled forward, my raincoat falling away from my face. I dropped off the edge of the awning. I grabbed at it with one hand and swung myself down, landing on the ground in front of a grocer's shop on the main street.

My hand stung, and my fingers dripped blood. With my other hand I grasped for my hat, but it was gone. Dammit.

No time to stop. I bolted down the street, keeping under cover as much as possible. Two shots rang out as I crossed a side street, the bullets ricocheting off the stone-chipped asphalt. Shouts came from outside the 88 Club. A car revved up. Two doors slammed shut. My Audi was almost two blocks away.

I wouldn't make it.

I slid to a stop and ducked behind a battered old Toyota. A black SUV raced past. Good. They hadn't seen me. That gave me a little more time. I edged out onto the road. The heavies' car was a block distant. I glanced back the way I'd run to see if anyone was pursuing me on foot. No one.

But a taxi was close. I stuck out my hand eagerly. It skidded to a halt. I yanked the back door open and threw myself inside, lengthways, on the back seat.

The taxi driver, a guy with white hair and moustache, peered around. "You all right, man?"

"Yeah."

"You're bleeding."

"It's only a scratch." It wasn't. My hand oozed blood onto my raincoat.

"You get blood on the upholstery and I'll charge you cleaning fees. Where are you going? The hospital?"

"Take me two blocks down the road. Don't draw attention to us."

The taxi driver nodded slowly. "I get it. You're on the run from someone. That's why you're injured. Are you a bad man?"

"No. I'm running from bad men. Will you just drive?"

The driver turned back to the front and sped up gently.

"Tell me if you see a black SUV anywhere."

"Man, in this part of Quake City, there's a lot of black SUVs. They're the favourite wheels of criminals. Two have gone past already, one in each direction."

"Okay, good." Maybe the guys hunting me had given up and returned to the club. "Drive another block or so until you see a dark blue Audi. Stop there."

A few seconds passed, during which I may have forgotten to breathe.

The taxi came to a halt. "We're here."

"Great. What do I owe you?"

"Come on, man, I won't charge you for driving you two blocks when you're on the run from gangsters. Get out of here and take care of yourself."

"Thanks. I appreciate it. You're a good guy." Fortunately, there were still some around.

I opened the road-side door and scanned both ways. Nothing in sight, so I scooted out of the taxi and crossed the road to my car. The taxi left. With a sigh of relief, I started my car, pulled a U-turn, and drove off.

POLICE INTERVIEW 1

Day 6 (Saturday, 19 August), afternoon

POLICE: *The time is two forty-five p.m. Present in the interview room are Inspector O'Toole and Sergeant Hilton. The interviewee will now state his name.*

DANNY: *Come on, Inspector. You know my name.*

POLICE: *It's for the recording.*

DANNY: *(Sigh.) Danny Ashford.*

POLICE: *What is your occupation?*

DANNY: *You know that already.*

POLICE: *Will you please cooperate for the recording?*

DANNY: *Sure. I'm a private investigator. Maybe the best in the area.*

POLICE: *You think a lot of yourself, don't you?*

DANNY: *Is that one of the interview questions?*

POLICE: *No, not really. It's just an observation.*

DANNY: *Well, for your information, it's a marketing slogan I use. I wouldn't get any business if I said I wasn't the best, would I?*

POLICE: *I suppose not.*

DANNY: *Do I need a lawyer for this interview, Inspector?*

POLICE: *I don't know. Do you?*

DANNY: *I have done nothing wrong.*

POLICE: *Then let's just have a friendly chat. That all right with you?*

DANNY: *Fine. Please get on with it. I've got things to do.*

POLICE: *What things?*

51

DANNY: *I can't tell you. I have to respect the privacy of my current client.*

POLICE: *And who is that?*

DANNY: *I'm not saying who my client is.*

POLICE: *Very well. Maybe you can tell me why your face is bruised?*

DANNY: *(Pause.) I walked into a door.*

POLICE: *This door have a name?*

DANNY: *What?*

POLICE: *I don't believe you walked into a door. You got that bruise in a fight, didn't you?*

DANNY: *(Indistinct sound, possible obscenity.)*

POLICE: *So, why don't you tell us who you were in a fight with?*

DANNY: *I couldn't say.*

POLICE: *Why not?*

DANNY: *Because I don't know who it was.*

POLICE: *You in the habit of getting into fights with people you don't know?*

DANNY: *No. He caught me by surprise. Are you going to charge me for being beaten up by a stranger?*

POLICE: *Of course not. Let's move on.*

DANNY: *Fine with me.*

POLICE: *Do you know a person by the name of Stuart Baker?*

DANNY: *(Pause.) I know the name. I haven't met the man himself.*

POLICE: *In what context do you know him? A mutual friend, a business associate, anything like that?*

DANNY: *Nothing like that. His name turned up during some investigative work I was doing.*

POLICE: *Interesting.*

DANNY: *Why is that interesting?*

POLICE: *We're asking the questions here.*

DANNY: *You said this was a friendly chat. Can we take a break? I'd love a coffee.*

POLICE: *You think this is a café, do you?*

DANNY: *Come on, I know you've got a coffee machine in the hall right outside.*

POLICE: *(Sigh.) All right. Let's have a break. Stay here. Interview paused.*

Chapter 12

THOUGH STUART BAKER delighted in the art of the con, he was enough of an astute businessman to have invested some of his ill-gotten gains in a profitable business to smooth out the variations in his illicit cash flow. When the previous owner of the 88 Club hastily sold up to leave town, Stuart was ready with a lowball cash offer.

The amount had perfectly matched the blackmail demand the unfortunate owner had received only a few days earlier, and it soon found its way back to Stuart through his labyrinth of offshore companies and bank accounts.

The 88 Club performed well, gradually attracting customers from nearby establishments, and provided a steady source of income. The only problem Stuart had was creating a fake set of accounts showing the club never turned a profit, like his antique shop, to avoid tax.

But there were always opportunities for an imaginative dishonest guy like Stuart to use to his advantage. Like now.

He'd noticed one of his exotic dancers, Chelsea Whitlam, wore a valuable sapphire ring on her right hand. The size of that sparkling blue rock had almost made Stuart's eyes water. The girl probably didn't know how much the ring was worth. But he did, and he wanted it. So, a few days ago, he'd slipped into the performers' dressing room when she was doing her act and taken several photos.

A jeweller he knew had easily fashioned a passable replica with a much cheaper gem of the same colour. He'd picked it up earlier in the day.

Stuart felt for the replica in his pocket as he made his way to the dressing room. Chelsea might never notice the switch, or, if she did, it might not be for ages. She'd probably have moved on by then. He liked to replace the dancers every few months to keep the punters happy with fresh flesh.

He slipped inside. Where would she keep her jewellery? In her bag? In the dressing table drawers? In the wardrobe? The options were limited, but her act only lasted a few minutes.

As luck would have it, he tried the dresser drawers first and quickly found what he was searching for. He pocketed the valuable ring and left the fake in its place. In a couple of days, he'd sell the sapphire ring for a handsome profit.

Grinning, he strolled out towards the bar. Time for a drink.

§

Chelsea bustled offstage and grabbed a light robe to cover up, a creepy sensation rising from her stomach as usual. Being perved at by a bunch of leering middle-aged men while she stripped wasn't the best use of her dance skills. She'd trained extensively to hone her classical and modern moves. But needs must, and the money was good. Better than that of a hostess.

Her neighbour, Danny the private detective, had turned up after all. She'd thought his offer of threatening her boss had simply been a ruse to get into her good books and then into her pants. She'd have to wait to see if he followed through. She'd made it clear that she'd seen him in the club. Like all men, he'd watched her entire show. Hopefully, he'd picked up her hint to go upstairs.

The dressing room that she shared with the other exotic dancers wasn't large, but the mirrors made it seem that way. She sat, sipped from a half-empty glass of wine, and waited until a quiet knock sounded.

"Come in, Carl."

A big, muscled man entered, bearing her trench coat, umbrella, boots, gloves and hat, and nodded a greeting. "I couldn't get your swimsuit, Chelsea. The patrons pocketed it."

Chelsea shrugged. That wasn't unusual. She seldom got the bikini top and bottoms back. She'd learned to buy in bulk during sales. "Thanks, Carl. Will you get me a sandwich and some hot chips, please? I'm starving."

"Will do." He left.

Carl was tough, but a sweetie. He was gay, so she knew he wouldn't try anything with her. That, and his size, was the reason he had the job of picking up the performers' discarded clothes.

Chelsea packed her performance costume away in a wardrobe, then dressed in her home clothes. The musicians hadn't started up again. Stuart, the boss, thought that a quiet few minutes after an exotic dance led to more alcohol sales. Give the punters constant entertainment and they don't drink as much, he'd said.

Bang!

She gasped and put her hand up to her mouth in shock. What was that? A gunshot?

Thumping. Something that sounded like a window smashing. More thumping. More gunshots.

Chelsea's eyes widened. Had Danny caused trouble? Surely not. She'd only asked him to speak to Stuart, not start a shoot-out.

Carl popped back with her food and put it on a small table for her.

"What's going on, Carl?"

He shrugged. "I don't know. I didn't see anything on the way back from the kitchen. Sounded like gunshots."

"That's what I thought. Jesus. Are we safe here?"

"Yeah. I'll wait outside the door until you're ready to leave, and I'll walk you to your car."

"Thanks, Carl. I appreciate it."

Chelsea ate quickly. The sooner she finished, the sooner she'd go home and maybe find out what really happened.

She opened the top drawer of her personal dresser and took out her watch, keys and rings.

Odd. Her sapphire ring seemed a little loose. Yet she'd put it on the right finger.

Chelsea checked her other rings. They were all costume jewellery and fitted perfectly. She wasn't going crazy. She hadn't lost several kilos while dancing. Something had happened to the sapphire ring.

Unless it wasn't the same ring. The one she could now easily spin on her finger didn't seem so tarnished. It even appeared... new.

She slipped it off her finger and examined it carefully. She'd found her ring in an op shop, a lucky bargain. It had three tiny, barely noticeable, scratches on the inside of the band. This one didn't.

Someone had swapped the rings.

Chelsea clenched the fake in her fist. That bastard boss! Had he done this? She wouldn't be surprised. Or had it been Carl? No, not Carl. He wasn't that kind of person.

Challenging Stuart would be a waste of time. He'd deny stealing the ring. Calling the police wouldn't help either. They were next to useless.

And if she did either of those things, she'd be out of a job.

Chapter 13

BROCK PATTERSON double-checked the dossier Stuart had given him the previous day. He'd memorised everything, but he liked to be sure. The company: SuperGames Apps, some small tech firm who'd announced the impending release of a highly awaited kickboxing game. The building layout, the location of the alarm control system, and the location of the server room were imprinted in his mind.

He dressed completely in black, his working clothes for breaking-and-entering jobs, grabbed his vocational tools from the bottom of the wardrobe, and proceeded outside.

Brock was looking forward to this job. It seemed easy enough, and the ten grand payment was generous. Setting off the alarms was the only risk, and he'd figured out how to deactivate those with an hour of research on the Dark Web. But if that went wrong, somehow, he'd still have time to get away in his trusty old Audi A3.

That car had been his pride and joy since the day he'd stolen it from a Quake City mall parking building. A quick change of number plates and a paint job had made it unrecognisable. Even when some asshole had dented the side of the car in a minor accident, it hadn't diminished his pleasure in driving his Audi.

The overcast sky hid the moon and stars. Dim streetlights cast islands of light in an otherwise dark street. Brock stood at the side of the road, car key in hand. His car wasn't there. A tatty old Ford was parked in its place.

Had he parked the Audi further along the street? He marched up and down the block, his blood boiling. Nothing.

"Fuck!" Some bastard had stolen his car.

He shoved the key into his pocket and took some deep breaths. He hadn't had the vehicle long, only a few weeks. That wasn't much more than the auto equivalent of a one-night stand. Well, maybe a frisky weekend. Or a frisky few weeks. But, anyway, he'd soon forget about it. Wouldn't he?

No. He loved that car.

There was nothing he could do about it at the moment. He had a job to do for Stuart. When he got paid, maybe he could spend some of the money on paying someone to steal another car for him.

Brock started walking. At least it wasn't raining.

He reached SuperGames Apps at around half-past eleven. The small, two-storey building was dark. No dogs or guards roamed the area.

Brock glanced around. No one in sight. On this side street, there'd be few vehicles or pedestrians going past at this time of the night. This job was going to be easy.

At the rear of the building, he found the concealed control box for the internal alarm and pried the cover off. Red, green and black wires ran from a chip sensor inside through a tiny hole in the wall. Brock drew a pair of garden clippers from his bag and cut all three wires. He waited. The alarms remained quiet. He smirked.

Next, he swapped the clippers with a glass cutter and cut out a windowpane large enough for him to squeeze through. With a huge suction cap, he gently removed the windowpane and laid it against the side of the building. He scrambled inside.

SuperGames Apps was on the ground floor. Brock swept low with a torch and skulked past a few desks in an open-plan area to the CEO's office. Jaxon Coles was a young business whizz-kid who'd overseen the development of a new mobile phone app, but rumours were that he was naïve regarding security. Brock had confirmed that for himself with the ease by which he'd entered the property.

Jaxon's office was plain, boring. A computer with two large wide screens. A few books on coding and marketing. No pictures or anything personal. Brock shook his head. What a loser.

His computer was password-protected. That made Brock's job even easier. There was probably a company-wide password policy enforcing complex passwords. If so, Jaxon would have written it down. Brock found it on a scrap of paper in the top drawer.

He plugged a high-capacity memory key into the computer and started browsing the contents of the hard drive, hunting for the source code and design plans for the app.

He downloaded the design specifications. Eventually, he found the source code on the main server and copied that too. Easy.

Brock glanced at his watch. He'd been inside the building for fifteen minutes and had everything Stuart had asked for. Stuart must think the information valuable to pay so much for a simple office raid.

He thought for a minute, then took another memory key from his bag and made another copy of the same information. This one he'd keep himself.

The last step was the fun part—wiping the contents of the main server and the CEO's hard drive. Another few minutes and that was done.

Brock left, chuckling. It wasn't even midnight yet. He'd walk to the 88 Club and hand over the first memory key to Stuart, as arranged. That way, Brock could collect his money straightaway. He remembered his stolen Audi and frowned. No matter. He'd splurge some of the money on a taxi to get home.

What an easy night's work.

He slipped through the dark offices, thinking about what he'd stolen. Stuart wanted this information so badly he'd pay ten grand for it. Therefore, it must be worth a lot more. Maybe many times more. If that was true, then what he was getting wasn't fair payment. After all, Brock had taken the risk of the burglary himself.

In his mind, Brock renegotiated the terms of the deal he had with Stuart. He'd demand twenty thousand. Maybe thirty thousand. Or he'd go for a percentage deal with whatever Stuart planned to use the information for.

But he knew, in reality, he was kidding himself. No matter how brilliant his renegotiation arguments were in his mind, once he opened his mouth, they'd come out all wrong.

Just as well he'd kept his own copy on another memory key. Maybe he could use it to make himself rich, somehow. Stuart need never know.

Chapter 14

Day 4 (Thursday, 17 August), evening

I UNLOCKED THE DOOR to my apartment and stumbled inside, almost tripping over Torquemada, and switched on the light. I staggered to the bathroom, the cat trailing me. My hand stung. It was still bleeding. Smears of blood stained my raincoat.

The gash might need stitches, but that could wait. I disinfected it. It was midnight, and the last thing I wanted to do was spend hours waiting at A&E with a bunch of injured drunks and drug addicts before being seen by a nurse. I'd go in the morning if I had time. The bathroom cabinet had bandages; they would have to do. Using my teeth and my other hand, I wrapped up my injured hand.

Now for the pain. Paracetamol or whiskey? After a moment's thought, I poured myself a drink and sat on the sofa to pat Torquemada and contemplate my day.

I'd got a case, though I'd made no progress on finding the mysterious conman who called himself Jonathan Goodfellow, despite extensive searching online. Also, I'd got a car, and the debt that came along with it. I'd had an evening out, seen rather more of my new neighbour than I'd expected, and done a job for her pro bono, only to get shot at as I crashed through an unopened window. So, yeah, busy day.

I knocked back the whiskey. Tomorrow, I'd go scouting for the conman. Deepa had offered to help me. We'd always made an excellent investigative team. When we weren't arguing, that was.

The stairs creaked. Someone was coming up.

My heart thumped in my chest. Was it the thugs from the 88 Club? I gritted my teeth. My carefree attitude in leaving my business card behind didn't seem so clever now.

I raced round the desk and wrenched my Glock 17 free from the tape that attached it out of sight underneath. I rushed to the edge of the room behind the door. I held my breath, keeping the handgun level. Would they kick the door open, or shoot out the lock?

A gentle tap came. "Danny? You still up? I can see light under your door."

Chelsea. I exhaled and opened the door.

She strode in without waiting for an invitation, and I shut the door behind her. She spun to face me, about to speak, then jerked back.

"Shit! What are you going to do with that?"

I put the gun on the desk. "I can't be too careful in my business."

Chelsea nodded and sat on the sofa next to Torquemada, who smooched up to her for a pat. "I guess not. I heard gunshots at the club. Was that you?"

I sat on the other side of the cat. "No, it was some bozo shooting at me."

Chelsea gasped. She examined me, her gaze finally resting on my inexpertly bandaged hand. "You're hurt. Oh no! Were you shot?"

"No. I cut myself on the glass when I jumped through a window to escape. It's nothing to be concerned about."

She shook her head, smiling now, and took my hand gently to examine the dressing. "You did all that for me?"

"Yeah, well, I didn't know I'd have to jump through a first-floor window when I agreed to do it."

She poured me a drink and leaned in closer. Between us, Torquemada purred softly. "I dropped by to thank you. Whatever you did, or said, worked. My boss actually apologised to me and to another girl he's been harassing for coming on to us, said he didn't know we had a protector. I think you shook him up real good."

My bandaged hand was still in hers. She stroked it tenderly. Somehow, it seemed to dull the pain, like she was one of those mystic healers laying on hands. Or perhaps it was the whiskey taking effect. "As long as he stops bothering you, that's all I wanted to do."

Chelsea leaned right over Torquemada, so close to me, and squeezed my injured hand, sending a jolt of pain up my arm. At the same moment, she put her other hand at the back of my head and pulled us together. Her lips met mine in a kiss that she deepened.

My head spun; whether from the adrenaline of the evening, the whiskey, the pain in my hand, Chelsea's dramatic kiss, or the heady combination of it all, I couldn't tell. The rush of powerful sensations made me giddy, entranced, bewitched. My will was no longer my own.

Ever so slowly, she stood, pulled me to my feet, and led me into the bedroom.

Chapter 15

Day 5 (Friday, 18 August), morning

A TONGUE IN MY EAR woke me. I knew it didn't belong to Torquemada because I could feel him curled up between my feet, asleep.

Then it all came back in a rush. Fleeing the 88 Club, pursued by heavies. Losing my hat. Injuring my hand. Chelsea's gratitude. A long, deep kiss. And then...

Oh. Right.

My eyes opened wide, squinting against the bright light creeping around the edges of the blinds.

The tongue in my ear stopped wiggling. Chelsea loomed over me. "Morning, handsome. Ready to go again?"

Confusion engulfed me. My mind raced. How had I got into this? Did I want to be in this situation? If not, why not? Logic failed me. My head wasn't working right. I'd slept well, but I was tired, groggy, and my head hurt worse than my gashed hand. My memory of the time after midnight was shredded.

Chelsea waited for an answer, and I sensed she would not wait much longer before she made the decision herself.

I rolled over to the edge of the bed. "I shouldn't sleep with a client. It's unprofessional."

"LOL. Too late now. Anyway, I'm not a client, because I didn't pay you."

I couldn't argue with that, but I needed time to process everything. Also, I wasn't really capable of wanting anything at the present time except a strong coffee.

I clambered to my feet and stumbled towards the en-suite bathroom. The doorway was moving about, so I aimed for the middle. I bounced off one door jamb but reached the shower on my feet somehow.

The hot water refreshed me. I emerged and headed for the kitchen.

Chelsea followed me. Naked. "You're no fun." She pouted.

"I need coffee." My recollection of the time after Chelsea turned up at my door was hazy, like a dream—or a nightmare. Had we had sex? We must have, but I couldn't remember.

The questionable ethics of sleeping with a pseudo-client niggled at me. Though she didn't regard herself as a client, so why should I? It had been a while since any living being other than Torquemada had shared my bed.

But what about my friendship with Deepa? How did this bedtime jaunt with my new neighbour affect that?

Chelsea interrupted my thoughts. "You shouldn't have had those whiskeys. Overindulgence is bad for you."

"I'm sure there are worse things." I hadn't been drunk from two whiskeys, surely? Maybe I'd had more than two. I couldn't remember.

"My mother drank herself to oblivion and then committed suicide by hanging herself. That's why I never drink much."

I stopped getting the coffee ready and turned towards Chelsea. Her face was drawn. I shook my head. "Sorry. I shouldn't have been flippant."

Chelsea's gaze dropped to the floor. "My father abandoned her before I was born. He left her with almost nothing. She couldn't bear it. She was too afraid of him to claim child support. We lived in poverty because she spent most of her money on booze. She killed herself when I was sixteen."

"Oh, I'm so sorry." It reminded me of my own trauma: my parents being gunned down by bank robbers, though that was a sudden tragedy, not a long-drawn-out one.

She raised her gaze to meet mine. "I'm okay. It made me resilient. But it's why I never have more than one drink."

I shrugged off my memory lapse. Water and coffee would help me feel better. Paracetamol, too. Or codeine. Whatever painkiller I could find, in fact. I found some paracetamol in the bathroom cupboard, and swallowed it while waiting for the kettle, then made the coffees.

"It's ready." I put the cups on the table.

"Be out in a few minutes." Chelsea returned to the bedroom.

Torquemada purred at me. I gave him some food and water. At least he seemed happy.

A creak sounded on the stairs outside, followed by a knock on the door. For a moment, a chill passed through me. Had the 88 Club owner changed his mind and sent his heavies around to give me an early morning beating? But then I realised the knock was familiar. Deepa.

Shit!

She didn't wait for me to answer. She opened the door. I'd not locked it after letting Chelsea in last night.

Deepa bustled in, wearing her purple puffer jacket and holding a paper bag and a cardboard tray of takeaway drinks in one hand. "Morning, Danny. I brought pastries and coffees. We can start on that investigation after breakfast." She paused in front of me. "Are you all right? You don't look so good."

Hell's teeth. What time was it? A glance at the clock on the wall told me it was already mid-morning. How was I going to get out of this?

Deepa put the food and drinks on the coffee table and noticed the steaming cups already there. "Were you expecting me?"

Something in my expression must have suggested otherwise, for her smile faded.

"Hey, hello there. Are you Danny's girlfriend?"

A plummeting sensation turned my stomach inside-out. I sank to the sofa. Chelsea stood by the bedroom door, wearing only panties and an unfastened dressing gown—mine—that barely covered one breast and made no attempt to cover the other.

Deepa took a step back and faced me. "I'm—I'm sorry. I didn't think you'd have company." Her voice was chilly, shaken.

Torquemada swivelled his head between them and me. I could swear he was enjoying this.

Chelsea swanned into the room. "No problem. Maybe we can have a threesome later." She giggled.

Deepa glared at me. I could see the hurt in her eyes. "No, I'm leaving. Call me later when you want to do some actual work, P.I. Ashford. Or maybe don't bother."

She turned and left, banging the door closed behind her.

I groaned. "She's not my girlfriend. Deepa's my sometime investigative partner." I remained seated. The coffee table swirled in my vision. The paracetamol hadn't had time to take effect yet.

"Then why did she seem upset?"

I didn't answer that. My head was reeling. I took a swig of coffee to see if it would help. It didn't.

Chelsea sat. Torquemada snuggled up against her, the traitor. "Thanks again for warning off my boss."

"Don't worry about it. It comes with the profession. Look, Chelsea, last night was great." What I recalled of it, anyway. "Don't get me wrong. I'm not brushing you off, but I have to get straight to work. I need to find a low life who conned a client of mine out of a lot of money. He hacked my bank account too." And I had to make things right with Deepa.

"Yeah, sure. Last night was a one-time thing, anyway. I'll get dressed." She noticed the takeaway coffees and pastries. "Did your friend bring those?"

"Yeah, she did."

Chelsea picked up a pastry and took a bite. "So, this guy you're trying to find. He got a name?"

"Not a real one."

"How about a photo or a description?"

"I've got a photo. Hang on." I'd printed out the image Petra had sent me, and I showed it to Chelsea.

She gave it one glance, then contemplated me. "That's my boss, Stuart. Didn't you recognise him?"

I shook my head. "I never met him. He wasn't around. I sneaked into his office and left him a threatening note instead of confronting him."

"Great. I hope it works."

"Are you sure this photo is of him?" What a coincidence? I could have confronted him last night.

"Totally. That's him."

POLICE INTERVIEW 2

Day 6 (Saturday, 19 August), afternoon

POLICE: *The time is four p.m. Present in the interview room are Inspector O'Toole and Sergeant Hilton. The interview with Danny Ashford will now continue.*

DANNY: *Is this still a friendly chat?*

POLICE: *Of course. Did you enjoy your coffee?*

DANNY: *It would have been better if it came with a few biscuits.*

POLICE: *Budget cuts have eliminated the biscuits, I'm afraid. Now, we were talking about a man called Stuart Baker. You said he is a subject of one of your investigations?*

DANNY: *In a manner of speaking.*

POLICE: *We'll take that as a 'yes'. We're interested in him too.*

DANNY: *You want to exchange information? No problem, but why all the formality? Why'd you bring me in to the station?*

POLICE: *So you could enjoy our hospitality. How about you tell us what you know about Stuart Baker?*

DANNY: *I know he runs an establishment in Sintown called the 88 Club. It's a strip club, and I'm damned sure they offer other vices too.*

POLICE: *Hang on. The Stuart Baker we're interested in is the registered owner of an antiques shop in Sintown. We don't know anything about any involvement he has with the 88 Club.*

DANNY: *I don't know anything about an antique shop. Have you got a photograph of him?*

POLICE: *You said you haven't met him.*

DANNY: *In the course of my investigation, I've seen a video of him, and a still image.*

POLICE: *All right, let's compare. For the recording, I'm passing a photo print of Stuart Baker's driver's licence photograph over the table to the interviewee.*

DANNY: *Yeah, that's him.*

POLICE: *Sure?*

DANNY: *Positive. Same thin, black moustache under an aquiline nose.*

POLICE: *Interesting.*

DANNY: *Then I'm sure you'll find this piece of information fascinating. Stuart Baker is a conman and a computer hacker.*

POLICE: *Is that why you were investigating him?*

DANNY: *Yes. He conned my client out of a large sum of money using a false name. I tracked him down with the plan of forcing him to repay it.*

POLICE: *'Forcing', you say?*

DANNY: *A better word might be 'persuading'. You know how it goes, Inspector.*

POLICE: *Yes, I'm well aware of your methods, Danny. Did your client report this crime to the police?*

DANNY: *No, but she said I could report it once I've gathered evidence. My client only wants her money back discreetly.*

POLICE: *By any means necessary.*

DANNY: *I didn't say that.*

POLICE: *You said 'forcing', though.*

DANNY: *What's this about, Inspector? You wanted to know what I know about him. I've helped you out. Now it sounds like you're accusing me of something. You said this was a friendly chat.*

POLICE: *Yes, it is. Perhaps you can tell us why a letter addressed to you was delivered to Stuart Baker's house?*

DANNY: *(Pause). I have no idea.*

POLICE: *The envelope contained a bank debit card in your name.*

DANNY: *That bastard. He's trying to steal my identity. I could kill him. Figuratively, I mean.*

POLICE: *If you say so.*

DANNY: *Look, as well as conning my client, he stole my debit card details and emptied my bank account. Obviously, he then ordered a replacement card in my name to his own address so he could rob me again.*

POLICE: *All right, I can understand that, but how did you know he was the one who stole your money?*

DANNY: *(Pause). (Sigh). I really can't say.*

POLICE: *Can't or won't?*

DANNY: *I have my own investigative sources, and it's unethical for me to reveal them.*

POLICE: *I see.*

DANNY: *Do you?*

POLICE: *Sure. We'll let that slide for now. What's more important is that you managed to track him down.*

DANNY: *Yeah. It wasn't easy.*

POLICE: *So, what did you do then? Confront him and demand your money back, and that of your client? Is that how you got the bruise on your face?*

DANNY: *No and no. I've already told you I don't know who hit me. He was like a ninja.*

POLICE: *Yes, there are plenty of ninjas running around in Quake City.*

DANNY: *I said 'like a ninja', not an actual ninja.*

POLICE: *Okay. So, let's summarise. Someone conned your client and emptied your bank account. Using your unspecified investigative sources, you identified the perp was Stuart Baker. And you're saying you didn't confront him, but you got attacked by an unknown ninja-like assailant.*

DANNY: *Yeah, that's pretty much it. So, why are you looking for Baker? Has someone else reported him?*

POLICE: *We're not looking for him. We found him this morning.*

DANNY: *Oh? What did he have to say for himself?*

POLICE: *He said nothing. He's dead.*

DANNY: *Dead? How?*

POLICE: *Later. It's time for another break. Someone will get you another coffee and a sandwich.*

Chapter 16

DEEPA STORMED OUT of Danny's apartment building and paused on the footpath to size up what the hell just happened. Emotions swirled through her: surprise, disappointment—and a burning anger, hotter than her nana Ji's chicken vindaloo. Bloody men—who needs them? Certainly not her. She was better off on her own. She had more freedom that way.

She ducked into a café to buy a coffee and calm down. Stupidly, she'd left the drinks and pastries in Danny's apartment. No way was she going back for them. He and that bitch were probably tucking into them right now, and laughing at her expense.

No, she mustn't think about it. It would only make her mad all over again.

Deepa made her order and stepped aside to wait for it, still fuming. She plonked her bag on a nearby table a little too heavily. Damn. Her laptop was in there.

Some of the contents spilled out. She made a grab for a metallic cylinder rolling towards the edge of the table and caught it before it toppled over the edge. She glanced about to see if anyone had noticed as she shoved it back into her bag. She'd bought the telescopic metal baton over the internet for self-defence after having been attacked during previous investigative cases. It mightn't be legal, but she felt less vulnerable having it with her at all times.

As she waited for her latte to arrive, she analysed her feelings the way she could break down a story.

Why was she so upset? It's not as if she and Danny were together, or even had some kind of casual arrangement. They worked together and caught up sometimes, but nothing more.

"Takeaway for Deepa," the barista called. She scooped up the paper cup, and headed back outside and along the road.

Her shoes clicked on the pavement in time with her rapid heartbeat. Her parents would never approve of her dating a private investigator. They'd had an arranged marriage before emigrating to New Zealand. Although Deepa had grown up here and had modern Western attitudes and goals, in some way, she still wanted their approval—and they would definitely not welcome their daughter dating a down-on-his-luck PI.

Sure, she enjoyed Danny's company. They made a good investigative team. They solved crimes together. Perhaps she'd started to think there could be something more between them, which was probably why she'd asked him to come in for a drink the other night—not that she'd had romance on her mind at the time. Would he have come up if he hadn't had a job to do? And, if he had, would they finally have got together?

Then, to find him with that half-naked hottie… that was a gut-punch. God, was she the "job"? Had he just used work as an excuse to fob her off?

Deepa took a few deep breaths and slowed down. She didn't have any claim over Danny. He was free to sleep with whoever he chose, just as she was.

But, man, it hurt that he'd chosen that fake blonde instead of her.

She resolutely turned her attention to journalism. The conman story sounded interesting. It would make a great article for the *Richter Mail* if she could interview a few victims. Even better, if she could identify the conman himself. Though she'd need Danny's help to do that.

Deepa clenched her jaw. She didn't have a choice but to work with Danny if she wanted the story. Though she'd have to wait until he could pull himself away from his girlfriend, or hook-up, or whatever she was. And that comment about a threesome! What the hell?

§

Gabrielle Hocking called her manager at the bank to report in sick. She wasn't ill, but she was sick of working there, and today she hoped to secure her way out.

She stood at the window of her small flat, staring down at the tiny front garden. The mid-morning sun glinted off a piece of broken glass she'd missed when sweeping up her smashed wine glass the previous day. The flash of light reminded her how much she despised Stuart Baker. Her study of his criminal activities revealed him to be as scheming, callous and ruthless as any warlord of the Dark Ages.

Gabrielle didn't want to be an active part of that. But blackmail was acceptable in her mind. She wouldn't be committing the crimes, after all. Stu would continue to do that. She wouldn't even have to know exactly what he was doing. But she knew enough now, and had evidence, to make him pay for her silence. She'd effectively be punishing him, so in a way she'd be doing some good. And scoring a nice little earner by doing so.

She picked up her phone and dialled Stu.

It rang several times, and Gabrielle wondered if Stu was avoiding her until he answered. "Hey, babe. What's up? You not at work today?"

"Hi, Stu. I took the day off. Hey, I need to talk to you about something important."

There was a long pause. "What's that, babe?"

"Not over the phone. Let's meet. You can take me out to lunch this time. You need to hear what I've got to say, Stu."

No reply. Gabrielle could hear him breathing, so he was listening. What was he thinking?

She continued. "It's about your unusual income sources, understand? We need to discuss some things, or..."

"Or what?" His voice hardened.

"Or I'll have to consider my options."

"Is that a threat?"

"Doesn't need to be."

"Are you at home? I'll pick you up. Where do you live?"

Gabrielle had been careful to keep her address to herself. She'd only met Stu at his house or at public places, and he'd only ever picked her up from her work, never her home. She certainly would not let her guard down now.

"No, it'll be quicker if I meet you there. That fancy Italian place you like. At one o'clock. Don't be late." She disconnected, smirking.

Chapter 17

MARY SANCHEZ PARKED on Crumblo Street, a few doors down from the antique shop. When the losses at her 420 Club kept mounting, she'd downgraded her car from a high-end Jaguar to a low-end Honda to save money. It hardly fitted her profile of an underworld boss, but it was cheaper on fuel and easier to park.

She spent a minute or two scanning the area for threats or hired heavies. A few street hooligans hassled shoppers as they exited stores. A man sat spread-legged on the footpath on the other side of the street, drinking from a bottle. No one paid any attention to her.

Mary sauntered to the antique shop. Her shoulder bag hung heavily, weighed down by an illegal handgun. She didn't go for the small, lady-sized weapons—she preferred a gun that you only had to fire once.

A chime sounded when she pushed the antique shop door open. She entered warily. The shop appeared empty, and no wonder. The interior was poorly lit, the surfaces dusty and grubby. Even to her untrained eye, the wares on sale weren't antiques—they were overpriced tat.

She turned as a door closed on the far side of the shop. A well-dressed man strode over, hand extended. His moustache was finely groomed, and his impeccable suit was undoubtedly expensive.

"I'm Stuart Baker. You must be Mary Sanchez."

She nodded and shook his hand. He seemed a charmer. "Thanks for meeting me. As I said, I want to discuss how we might work together."

He gestured to a small circular table and chairs beside the sales counter. A cafetiere and two mugs sat there. "Coffee?"

"Yes, thanks."

Mary sat and sipped a little of the hot, strong coffee. It was excellent, as much out of place in this tatty store as the owner.

"So, Mary, you wrote me two letters, one to the 88 Club and one here. You're in the antiques business too, I assume?"

"No, actually." She leaned forward to emphasise her words. "I'm in the clubbing business. I own the 420 Club, down the street from your 88 Club."

Stuart leaned back in his chair, chewing his lip. "Ah. I see. I thought so. You've done your homework if you've worked out that I own this little shop in addition to the 88 Club."

Mary narrowed her eyes. "I have. I know a lot about you, more than you'd realise. And I know your club is successful because you stole my customers."

Stuart shrugged. "I didn't *steal* them. I provided a superior clubbing experience, and they came voluntarily."

"You had your goons outside my club handing out fliers!"

"It's a public footpath. They had every right to be there." Stuart banged his mug onto the table. "What do you really want, Mary?"

"I want my customers back."

"It's not my problem if you couldn't keep them."

Mary sipped more coffee. "Look, I have a suggestion. Let's combine forces and work together. There's more than enough customers and profit for both of us, especially if we both save on costs and put up our margins."

"You're suggesting a partnership?"

"No. More like an oligopoly. The two of us working together as one, fixing prices, screwing the customers."

Stuart pursed his lips. "That's illegal. I assume you know that."

"Do you care?"

"No. But I don't see how it would work to my advantage when I already have all the punters."

Mary groaned inwardly. Didn't he understand? "We'll both make more profit because we'll control the prices in both clubs instead of competing, and we'll be strong enough to force other clubs out of the area too. We'll eventually get everyone's customers and make greater profit margins."

Stuart nodded slowly but kept silent.

Mary tapped her foot on the floor and drained the mug. Maybe he did get it, but couldn't trust anyone but himself. Or maybe he didn't want to work with a woman. Either way, she was getting nowhere.

Finally, Stuart answered. "I'm not interested."

Mary could have grabbed him by the lapels and shaken him for letting this opportunity slip. But she wouldn't give up. "In that case, how about I buy the 88 Club from you? You've made it successful. Take your profit, and you can spend your time selling antiques or whatever else you want to do."

"If you have that much money, why don't you simply invest in your own club? Why buy mine?"

She took a deep breath. It gave her temper time to cool a little. "I can't compete against your 88 Club. You think I haven't tried? I'd only be throwing good money after bad. That's why I'm trying to make a deal with you here, or buy your club outright."

"I see." Stuart twirled one end of his moustache.

The hooligans Mary had observed outside passed in front of the shop window, shouting, swearing and jostling. Had they spotted a new target, someone to mob and rob? Or was it a setup to grab her as soon as she left the antique shop? She hadn't told Stuart she owned the 420 Club when she requested a meeting with him, but perhaps he'd done his homework too, and had decided to eliminate his competition—her—in a direct, permanent way.

Discreetly, she reached for her shoulder bag and felt inside for the handgun.

Stuart inclined his head. "I'm not interested in selling or in some kind of partnership, Mary. I'm sorry, but you've wasted your time."

Two loud reports came from outside. Gunshots. Stuart's eyes widened. His hand jerked for an inside pocket. She pulled out her handgun and levelled it at Stuart at precisely the same moment as he levelled a revolver at her.

They sat frozen in their seats. Mary's heart thumped. What was happening outside? Were those thugs about to burst into the store to seize her? They wouldn't dare when they saw she had a gun levelled at their boss, would they?

Stuart spoke first. "That was nothing to do with me. Those thugs are low-level hoodlums. I've seen them around. They're independent." His voice was quiet, slow, reassuring.

Mary almost believed him. "I'm the one taking an enormous risk coming here. You might have prearranged something."

Stuart laid his gun on the table and spread his hands in a gesture of peace. "I didn't. Listen. Those guys are running away. Their footsteps are fading. They probably grabbed someone, fired a couple of shots into the air when he didn't give up his wallet, shook him up a bit, then bolted. It happens all the time in this area. It's Sintown."

"I know it's Sintown. I work here too, you know." But he was right. The footsteps were receding. She lowered her gun and put it into her bag. "Think about my offer. We'd both do a lot better working together than separately."

He sneered. "You only say that because your club is failing and you're desperate."

"Desperate women do desperate things. I will not let my life's work go to waste. I'll be seeing you again."

She stood and strode out of the shop, slamming the door behind her. The ting-a-ling of the little bell diminished the effect of her dramatic exit, but she hoped she'd made her point.

No way was Stuart Baker going to push her around and bankrupt her club and her personally.

Somehow, she'd stop him.

Chapter 18

Day 5 (Friday, 18 August), morning and afternoon

I FOUND DEEPA at the Coffee and Cheesequake café, drinking a latte and typing on her laptop. I dropped into the seat next to her. She didn't even glance at me.

"Deepa, I'm sorry about before. Last night just… seemed to happen. I don't remember much about it. I guess you're upset."

"Don't assume to tell me how I feel. I could see you had company, that's all. I didn't want to interfere. Anyway, it's none of my business who you sleep with." Her voice had an edge to it.

I didn't know how to respond to that, so I bided my time until my cappuccino arrived before speaking again. "Are you still keen on writing a story about the conman I'm after? I'm sure he's conned many people. He's crafty, computer savvy, and completely unscrupulous."

"Is he dangerous?"

I shook my head. "I don't think so, but his hired goons sure are."

Her deep, intelligent brown eyes sought mine. Was there hurt in that expression? If so, she disguised it quickly, but that didn't dampen how bad I felt about what I'd done. I had to make it up to her somehow.

Deepa appraised me for only a moment before returning to her typing. She may have been typing nonsense for all I knew, deliberately giving me as little of her attention as possible. "You lost your fedora again?"

"Yeah. I was being shot at. It fell off when I made my escape."

"Sounds like you had an exciting evening, all round."

I pursed my lips. I deserved Deepa's snarky remark, but there was a case to solve. I had to find Baker and recover Julie Nicholls' stolen money and my own. "Look, I know the dude's name, I know where to find him, and there's a story there for you if you want it. Do you?"

Deepa exhaled audibly, faced me, and this time held my gaze. "Sure, I do. But wait a minute. Let me say this. I didn't mean to put you in an awkward spot when I walked in on you and your... uh..."

"My new neighbour."

"Your new neighbour. Wow. So, she got the full *personal* welcome." Another sardonic comment.

"It wasn't like that, Deepa." My voice and my breathing quickened.

"Anyway... I got a surprise. I thought you and I were..."

I stared at her, unblinking, unmoving, silently demanding she finish her sentence. But she didn't.

At times, I'd wondered if we might develop more than a working partnership, but the work always got in the way. Now there was no chance. I'd blown it.

Deepa closed her laptop. "I must have been wrong. Tell me about this conman. What's the plan?"

Deepa and I usually argued about our investigation strategy, though she called it something fancy like 'creative brainstorming'.

"The best approach is a show of strength." I spoke louder now, emphasising my point. Other customers in the café turned to stare and, probably, to listen. That didn't stop me. I was on a roll. "I'll retrieve my gun from the office, drive to the club, and force my way inside."

"No, no, no." Deepa had her elbows on the table, head in her hands. "How have you survived this long as a private investigator? That's too dangerous. We need to find out where he lives, catch him off guard there or en route, not confront him where his goons shot at you last night."

"His house might be guarded too."

"So? We take a discreet peek and back off if we can't safely get close."

I ground my teeth. "Patience isn't one of my virtues."

Deepa rolled her eyes. "Let's not talk about your virtues—they're running low at the moment. You know, the simplest plan is to call the police."

"Then I'll never get my client's money back, or mine. It'll be hidden too well. That's why I have to force him to pay it back."

"All right. I get it. Your masculinity makes you feel you've got to confront him—"

"It's my professional opinion."

Deepa fixed me with a stare. I returned it in kind.

"Are you two finished here?" The waitress leaned across the table, wiping it pointedly. We'd finished our coffees long ago, so we took the hint and left.

Once outside, Deepa swivelled to face me. "Do me a favour, Danny. Don't go charging into the club and getting yourself killed. Let's figure out where the bastard lives or where else he hangs out. Spend the rest of the day on that, as least, before doing something reckless."

She was almost pleading. I conceded. "Yeah, okay, Deepa, we'll try it your way. But this guy's an expert at hiding himself in plain sight. He might disappear on us."

"Trust me, he won't. Conmen like him are narcissists. He's probably feeling invincible."

POLICE INTERVIEW 3

Day 6 (Saturday, 19 August), late evening

POLICE: *The time is 8.50 p.m. Present in the interview room are Inspector O'Toole and Sergeant Hilton. The interview with Danny Ashford will now continue.*

DANNY: *I've been here for hours already, Inspector. How long will this take?*

POLICE: *Not long. We just have a few more questions before you can go.*

DANNY: *Well, I have one too. How did Baker die?*

POLICE: *It appears that he fell from a balcony at his house to the bottom of the cliff below.*

DANNY: *So, it's an accident, then.*

POLICE: *I said it 'appears' that he fell, but we're investigating to see if it wasn't an accident after all. It's likely he was helped over the side.*

DANNY: *I don't see how I can help you any further. I don't know anything about that.*

POLICE: *Then let's talk about the 88 Club you mentioned. You're familiar with the establishment?*

DANNY: *I've been there in the course of my professional work.*

POLICE: *Nice place?*

DANNY: *I wouldn't say so.*

POLICE: *Were you there late the night before last, Thursday night?*

DANNY: *(Pause.) Yes, I might have been there then. Why are you asking?*

POLICE: *Mind telling us why you were there?*

DANNY: *Client confidentiality prevents me from doing that, as you know,*

Inspector.

POLICE: *Naturally. Know anything about some gunshots fired there?*

DANNY: *I heard them, but I don't know who fired them, if that's what you're after.*

POLICE: *So, you were there at that time. Were you involved in that altercation at all, Danny?*

DANNY: *Do you even need to ask me that? How long have you known me?*

POLICE: *(Chuckles.) All right, we'll move on. We understand there may have been a minor break-in at the 88 Club minutes before the shots were fired.*

DANNY: *Was one reported?*

POLICE: *Not at the time. A member of staff mentioned it to one of our officers informally earlier this evening.*

DANNY: *I see. I assume you're going somewhere with this, Inspector. What was taken?*

POLICE: *Nothing, apparently. Instead, the perp left something.*

DANNY: *How unusual.*

POLICE: *For the recording, I am now passing a note across the table to the interviewee. Danny, have you seen this note before?*

DANNY: *(No answer.)*

POLICE: *You might as well admit it. You left your business card with it. But let me be more specific. Did you write this note addressed to the owner, Stuart Baker? And draw the accompanying picture?*

DANNY: *Actually, I did, but—*

POLICE: *Let me guess. It was part of your professional work.*

DANNY: *Yes, he had been harassing his staff. My job was to politely persuade him to stop.*

POLICE: *You stuck a drawing pin through the crotch area of the stick figure you drew.*

DANNY: *Okay, I did, but I didn't mean anything by that. It was metaphorical.*

POLICE: *Metaphorical. What an interesting word. But what happened to Stuart Baker less than thirty-six hours later wasn't metaphorical, was it?*

DANNY: *I told you I had nothing to do with that.*

POLICE: *So, that was merely a coincidence, then?*

DANNY: *Absolutely.*

POLICE: *So you say. We'll take another break. Coffee? Another sandwich?*

DANNY: *Sure. Thanks. Why the hell not?*

Chapter 19

Day 5 (Friday, 18 August), afternoon

GABRIELLE SAT AT A TABLE in the window of the fancy Italian restaurant where she could see the entrance and the road outside. A suited waiter hovered nearby, ready to take her order.

This wasn't as easy as she'd expected; with each passing minute, her palms grew sweatier, her stomach spawned more butterflies. At this rate, her appetite would be gone in minutes.

But she wasn't here for the food.

Stu's Lamborghini slid into a disabled park outside the restaurant. He exited quickly, glanced up and down the street, then marched inside. He ignored the maître d' and approached Gabrielle directly.

The chair scraped on the wooden floor as he jerked it out. His customary warm smile was gone. "You've got something to talk to me about, babe?"

Gabrielle nodded. "I've ordered for us already."

"Tell me." Stu's gaze drilled into her.

Gabrielle paused, her spine chilling. It wasn't too late to back down. He need never learn that she knew all about his illegal money-spinning activities. She could simply tell him she was breaking up with him, go back to her mundane bank job with her mundane monthly salary, and live an ordinary, mundane—but safe—life.

Or she could go for the gold mine. He wouldn't miss a small slice of his ill-gotten gains, would he? The blackmail money would allow her to live in luxury.

"Babe? What's going on?"

She went for it. "Look, Stu, I've helped you in the bank, do you know that? You've deposited significant sums of cash and transferred untraceable cryptocurrency into your business accounts. I'm supposed to flag those transactions and raise them to my manager, but I didn't. You know why that is?"

Stu grinned. "Because you've always fancied me."

Gabrielle shook her head. "No. It's because I envied you. I wanted to know how you made so much money. But now"—she was silent as their meals were served, then continued with her voice lowered—"I know that you're banking the proceeds of crime, Stu."

"Nonsense." Stu made no movement to pick up his cutlery.

"Don't bother denying it." Now she'd started confronting him on the issue, her appetite had returned. Gabrielle tasted her carbonara dish. Excellent. The wine was a perfect accompaniment. It helped with her anxiety too, the warmth of the alcohol relaxing her.

"You don't know what you're saying, babe. I work hard for that money."

"I'm sure you do. It must take a lot of effort to con people out of their savings, scan their bank cards and empty their accounts, or pirate and sell the books of struggling authors. And that's just the tip of the iceberg, isn't it?"

Stu's expression darkened. He stared daggers at her. "How do you know this?"

"Never mind. I know a lot more. I know the details of all your illegal schemes."

"You fucking bitch. Keep your voice down."

Gabrielle ate slowly, savouring every mouthful of the delicious meal. On the other side of the table, Stu didn't eat; he seethed.

She tilted her head, as if what she was about to say was merely a casual observation. "I haven't told anyone. Your secrets are safe with me. But, for security, my lawyer has a copy of everything I know."

"What do you want?" Stu's knuckles were white where he clenched his fists on the tabletop.

"I want a cut. Not much. Ten thousand a month, cash. You'll hardly miss it with what you're making."

Stu stared at her with his eyebrows drawn together so tightly they formed a mono brow. Slowly, they parted. "You'll continue to let my deposits go through without flagging them to risk managers?"

"Of course." Damn. She'd have to keep her job at the bank for a while. In the meantime, she could build her nest egg.

"All right." Stu reached into an inner pocket.

A thrill of fear went through Gabrielle. Was he pulling out a gun?

Stu placed a padded envelope between them.

He gestured at it. "There's three grand. Consider it a down payment for your first month."

"I want the other seven thousand today. Payments are in advance." She concealed a grin and attacked her meal. This was too easy.

"Fine. Let's go." His words were curt.

"Go where?"

"My place. I've got the rest of the money in a safe in the bedroom."

Gabrielle considered. "All right, but let me finish my meal first. And remember, you're paying."

She ordered another wine, then ate and drank leisurely, passing the time by watching the other diners. Stu didn't touch his food or even speak. Finally, she put her knife and fork down together on the plate to show she was finished. She glanced up at Stu. "Dessert?"

"Don't push it."

Gabrielle chuckled. She loved seeing Stu on the back foot for once.

She waited while he paid the bill, the envelope containing the three thousand dollars a pleasant bulge in her handbag. They stepped outside and got into Stu's Lambo. Gabrielle fancied one last ride in it. After today, she probably wouldn't get another.

Stu's clifftop house, a mansion compared to Gabrielle's tiny flat, was half an hour's drive across town in Cliffside. Stu relaxed as he drove, becoming more like his usual self, chatty and arrogant.

They parked by the fountain outside the house and went in. Gabrielle followed him upstairs, eager for the rest of her first payoff.

In the bedroom, Stu raised an eyebrow suggestively.

Gabrielle chortled. "Don't even think about sex. The nature of our relationship going forward is purely business. Got it?"

"Right. Whatever you say. The safe's in the wardrobe. Give me a minute."

Gabrielle opened the French doors to a balcony with a view of the sea. Stu had told her that prior to the earthquakes, the cliff side was ten metres from the house. Now it was two metres, and the balcony overhung the edge. He hadn't owned the house until recently, but he said he thought it gave him good luck.

She leaned against the railing and peered over the edge. The near-vertical cliff face dropped to a rocky patch of boulders and rubble at the edge of a small park with a children's playground at one end. Kids were playing there. The sea was a hundred metres away.

Stu grabbed her arm and spun her around. She hadn't heard him approach. Gabrielle gasped as he clenched both of her arms and pushed her further. She seized the lapels of his suit jacket and clung on as she balanced precariously, the rail of the balcony digging into the small of her back, her toes barely touching the ground. Shit—he was going to kill her! Her breathing rasped.

He didn't push her any further, but held her in stasis, her centre of balance on the balcony's railing. Her heart pounded. Seconds passed. They seemed like hours.

Stu leaned closer. No, this couldn't be happening! Was she about to topple over the side? But he held on to her tightly.

"You've got some nerve, babe, I'll give you that. But I've decided to change the deal. You can have five grand a month, and you'd better be sure no one at the bank investigates my deposits. You'll be my money girl, twenty-four-seven—if I have any questions about money, I'm calling you. Got it?"

"Yes. Got it. Don't let me fall, please, Stu." Sweat dripped down Gabrielle's face. Her body trembled.

Stu nudged her. One of her toes lost contact with the ground. "The Romans used to have convicted criminals thrown off the Tarpeian cliff to their deaths. What do you think they thought about on the way down?"

"I—I don't know. I'm not your enemy, Stu."

"Don't fuck with me or my business. We're partners now. We're in this together. If I go down, you're going down too. Understand?"

"Yes. Pull me up. Please."

Stu jerked her upright. Gabrielle staggered across the balcony towards the French doors, grateful to feel solid ground beneath her feet. She was dizzy. Nausea roiled in her stomach. She made the last few steps to the bed and collapsed on it, face down, breathing heavily, adrenaline pumping, glad to be alive.

He took hold of her and pulled her back. Gabrielle didn't resist.

"Another thing, babe. In our renegotiated partnership, I'm going to fuck you whenever I want."

Gabrielle's exhausted panic gave way to simmering anger. She could kill him for this. "You bastard. You're going to regret doing this to me."

§

Brock Patterson trod the filthy footpaths of Sintown, shoulders slumped, heading south towards Crumbledon. He ignored anyone he passed, paying more attention to his feet than the path ahead. Though he was ten thousand dollars richer for a simple theft the previous night, his mouth was turned down in disappointment.

His negotiations with Stuart Baker hadn't gone as well as he'd hoped. In fact, Brock hadn't even tried asking for more money. His sometime employer had plugged the memory key into the laptop in his office, viewed the contents and shaken his head disconsolately. Not what he'd hoped for, Stuart had said. Completely worthless, he'd said. And then he'd thrown the memory key into the wastepaper basket beside his desk.

Nevertheless, Stuart had handed over two straps of fifty-dollar notes, ten grand as promised. Brock had taken the money and gone home, well after midnight.

In the clear light of day, after some sleep, food and lots of thought, he'd gone out for a walk. Maybe he'd see some decent wheels to buy, or, preferably, to steal. So far, he'd come across nothing suitable. Certainly nothing like his beloved Audi A3.

He strolled past a ruined line of shops in Crumbledon. Magpies dwelt in the visible rafters of a partially collapsed pharmacy. What trinkets and treasures had they stolen for their nests?

The spare memory key bounced lightly in his pocket. He took it out to throw to the birds and drew his arm back, ready to fling it into the rafters, but froze.

What if Stuart had lied to him? What if the information was valuable after all? He hadn't seen Stuart destroy the memory key. There was no reason he couldn't have taken it out of the rubbish bin as soon as Brock had left.

Stuart conned everyone: strangers, friends, family. Even if he didn't have a reason to con them, he'd do it for the hell of it. Brock couldn't trust a single word Stuart said or anything he did. It was that simple.

He had to check his copy of the stolen information himself, not rely on what he'd been told. Find out if Stuart had tricked him.

Carefully, Brock slipped the memory key back into his pocket. He'd examine it later. First, he needed some wheels.

Chapter 20

Day 5 (Friday, 18 August), afternoon

I RETURNED WITH DEEPA to my apartment to research Baker's address. There'd have to be some official records of him somewhere—if Stuart Baker was his actual name. Eventually, we'd discover where he lived.

At the top of the stairs, something hanging on my door caught my eye. My fedora, a nail passing through the brim into the centre of the wooden frame underneath the frosted window. I tugged the nail free. There was no note with it.

"What the hell, Danny?" Deepa glanced around as if she expected whoever had attached the hat to be watching, though there was nowhere to hide.

I shrugged. "Maybe it's a friendly way of returning lost property." The hat was still usable, though rain might drip through the hole in the brim.

Deepa shot me a glance to see if I was being serious. "It's a threat."

We went inside. I started making coffee while Deepa took off her purple puffer jacket, pulled her laptop from her bag and booted it up at the coffee table. I breathed a sigh of relief when she didn't mention her encounter this morning with my lightly dressed neighbour again.

I'd barely sat down with the drinks when there was a rap on the door. Deepa glanced at me sharply. Maybe she thought Chelsea was coming back, but I knew it wasn't her. I recognised the knock. It was Nadia, my landlady.

Sighing, I opened the door. Her mascara, lipstick and fingernails were purple today, and she wore a matching low-cut blouse. She already had her hand out, expecting the money I owed her. I pretended to misunderstand her intention and shook her hand instead.

"Danny me boy. I've come about the rent from last week. This week's rent is nearly due too."

"Three more days. That's what you promised."

"Are you sure you won't take me up on my offer to pay by other means?" Nadia waddled through the doorway, tugging her blouse over her head. Budget perfume hit me in the nose like a brick in a sock.

I stepped back. The landlady smirked. Torquemada hissed from his position atop a bookcase.

Deepa gasped. "Not another one."

Nadia turned towards her. "Excuse me, darlin'. I didn't know Danny had company. Well, I better be off." She tucked her blouse under one hairy armpit, turned, and left, glancing over her shoulder. "I'll be back."

I plonked myself onto the sofa, my face red, my legs too weak to hold me up. "She's becoming more persistent."

Deepa sniggered. "Will you find the rent money in time?"

"Hey, would you lend me a few hundred dollars to get me out of this jam?"

"Not a chance."

I gritted my teeth. I owed money to Jimmy Wang and to my landlady, and I didn't know who to pay first. But I couldn't pay either of them unless I forced Baker to return the money he'd stolen from me and from my client, Julie Nicholls.

Ah. My client. It was time to give Julie a call. I dialled her number.

"Hello?" Her voice was so soft I could barely hear her.

"Julie, it's Danny Ashford here. Look, I want to update you on the case. The name of the man who tricked you out of your money isn't Jonathan Goodfellow. It's Stuart Baker."

"Thanks, Danny, but what are you going to do about it?"

The contrast between Julie's quiet voice and her challenging words sent a chill down my neck. "I'm tracking down where he lives, and then I'll go and see him. I'll get your money back. I have a way of persuading people like him to cooperate." As long as I remembered to take my Glock 17 handgun with me, of course.

"Good. I'm counting on you. Thanks for the update." She disconnected.

§

It didn't take long to find Baker's home address. An internet search revealed a fancy home in Cliffside leased to the 88 Club. I could imagine Baker in his snappy attire living in a place like that.

I was all for rushing over there to confront him, but Deepa held up a cautioning hand. "Wait, Danny. This guy must have left plenty of other victims along the way to fund his lifestyle. How about we try to trace some of them?"

"Why do you want to do that now?"

"I thought it would make a better news story. More victims, more lines of print, maybe even a serialised article. More earnings for both of us." She inclined her head, smiling. I never could resist that cute look. And her indisputable logic.

"All right. Let's see what we can find this afternoon. I'll pay him a visit this evening before the club opens."

We set to work, scanning news articles and crime reports.

After a while, Deepa leaned back on the sofa with a satisfied smile. "He's got an ex-partner living in Quake City. She doesn't appear so well off, according to her Facebook profile. I'll go visit her later, see what information she can give us. For the article, I mean."

"Sounds good."

We hadn't eaten lunch. I didn't even think of it until I heard Deepa opening and closing cupboards and the fridge. Moments later, she returned to the living room, my office.

"Danny, there's no decent food in your apartment. Only cat food and mouldy bread."

"I know. Want to go out for a burger?"

"No. How about you get us some fresh coffees and pastries? You owe me that." Deepa glared at me. I turned away and winced inside.

Torquemada had slunk along the desk and now lay across the keyboard of my laptop. The screen showed at least a dozen tabs with fruitless search results. A notepad on the desk bore nothing but pen marks of frustration. I needed a break. "All right, I'll go."

Deepa smiled and brushed a tuft of hair across her forehead as I put on my coat and hat. The knots of tension eased. She was starting to forgive me. I returned her smile with a nod, and left.

I slipped past Chelsea's apartment and sauntered downstairs, deliberately stepping over the stair that always creaked. Outside, the wind whipped discarded fast-food containers along the footpath like tumbleweeds. I held onto my hat as I crossed the road to my parked car and got inside.

"Don't move."

I froze, the key half way to the ignition. Sharp, cold steel pressed against my neck. A knife. I swallowed, and it nicked me.

A gruff voice sounded next to my ear. "You stole my car, asshole."

"No, I didn't." Who was this guy? Did Jimmy Wang steal this car from him for me?

"Don't deny it. You repainted it and changed the plates, but I know it's mine. That dent on the right-hand side gives it away. If you still don't believe me, try this key. It's the spare." He dropped the key into my lap.

I picked it up but didn't bother testing it. A glance in the rear-view mirror revealed the man holding the knife. No one I knew.

"What do you want?" It was a pointless question, but it gave me time to think.

"I want my car back. And you to pay compensation for taking it."

"Honestly, man, I bought it in good faith." Neither parts of that statement were true. I hadn't been interested in the likely dubious ownership history, and I hadn't paid for it either.

"You're lying."

The knife drew tighter against my skin. Sweat beaded on my brow and ran down the sides of my face. I raised one arm slowly. Could I snatch the knife from him in time?

"Keep your hands in your lap."

"I don't have any money, so I can't pay you anything, and you're not taking this car either. So, what are you going to do? Cut my throat? For what?

You might get the car, but it'll ruin the upholstery and you'll be wanted for murder."

"Shut up." The knife wavered. I'd put doubt in the mind of my assailant. He didn't know what to do next. As I'd thought, he wasn't a killer. If he was, I'd already be dead.

"I'm just telling it how it is."

"All right. You said you bought the car. Who from?"

I didn't want to drop Jimmy Wang into the middle of this, so I said the first name that came into my head. "Stuart Baker."

"Stuart Baker? He sold you my car?"

"Yeah. You know him?"

"Sure, I know that conniving bastard. This is exactly the sort of thing he'd do."

The pressure from the knife eased. Inwardly, I breathed a sigh of relief. Somehow, I'd talked my way out of this.

The rear passenger-side door flew open. "Drop the fucking knife, you perp."

Deepa. She must have seen what was going on from the window.

"Don't shoot!" The knife dropped, impaling itself in the edge of the car seat a centimetre from my leg.

I turned. Deepa leaned in the doorway, my Glock 17 in her hand levelled at my attacker. "Deepa, I had this under control. This guy was just leaving."

"Your neck's bleeding."

I felt it and inspected my finger. There was a drop of blood on it. "It's only a scratch."

"This still counts as a rescue, Danny, whatever you say." She gestured with the gun slightly, keeping it aimed at her target. "What are we going to do with this perp?"

"Don't shoot. Please. I don't want anything. I'll go quietly."

I finally beheld the guy who'd held a knife to my throat. Now that his advantage was gone, he was trembling. His face had a grey pallor. Even his three-day shadow was grey.

"Let him go." I got out of the car and grabbed his arm as he exited from the seat behind. He stared at me, eyes wide. I glowered at him. "Don't come back here."

Deepa came around the car, still pointing the gun. The guy glanced at us both and fled.

Chapter 21

Day 5 (Friday, 18 August), afternoon

STUART DROPPED GABE—humiliated and pissed off—at a taxi stand near his house and drove off, grinning. She'd tried to take him for a ride, but he'd outsmarted and assaulted her. The five grand a month was an extra cost, to be sure, but he'd get his money's worth. Now he knew she'd definitely cover his tracks at the bank. If not, he'd implicate her in his money laundering crimes and she'd go to prison too.

He accelerated, relishing the raw engine noise and its echo off the boulders at the bottom of the cliffs. When the earthquakes hit, the cliff edges had crumbled like brittle rock cake to the park and road below. He always sped along this section in case there was another one and more rocks fell.

Fifteen minutes later, he eased off the speed as he came into the southern parts of the city and made his way to SuperGames Apps. Stuart drove past slowly, ignoring the impatient beeps from a driver behind him, who probably couldn't comprehend why someone in a Lamborghini would crawl along the road.

Two police cars were parked nearby. There was an officer in one, speaking on a phone. The others must have been inside the building.

Stuart drove on. He knew that Brook would have been careful. There'd be no clues for the police to find. At this very moment, they were probably telling Coles they couldn't do anything, that he should claim the costs on insurance, that they had more important matters to attend to.

This was good. It meant the CEO, Jaxon Coles, would be desperate. The insurance would pay out for a broken window, maybe. But the value of software that hadn't been released? Questionable. They wouldn't pay a cent for that loss.

Stuart drove to his antique store. There, he quietly dusted some of the items and listened to talkback radio. The talkback topics were mildly interesting, but the callers were invariably angry, anxious, despairing or all three. He loved sensing those emotions. It was good practise.

After an hour, he phoned Jaxon Coles' company.

"SuperGames Apps. Hello." The receptionist was young, male, and sounded stressed.

"I'd like to speak to Jaxon Coles, please."

"I'm sorry, but Mr Coles isn't taking any calls today."

"And why is that?" Stuart spoke in a slow, measured voice.

"I can't divulge that information, sir."

"Believe me, he'll want to take my call." Stuart twirled his moustache, his eyes glinting with delight.

Pause. "What's your name, sir? Is there a message I can pass on?"

Stuart beamed. "My name's Jonathan Goodfellow. Please tell Mr Coles that I've come into some information that I believe he desperately needs for his business today." Stuart twiddled the memory key in his pocket. "If he still wants to have a business, that is."

"Please wait, sir."

Half a minute passed. Stuart stopped fiddling with the memory key and resuming dusting the bric-à-brac and other miscellaneous junk on the shelves.

A fresh voice sounded from the other end. "Who are you? What do you know about my business and what's happened here?"

"You are Jaxon Coles, the CEO?"

"Yes. Please answer my questions, Mr Goodfellow."

"Very well. I'm a businessman. I was in a bar late last night and overheard an unsavoury character boasting that he'd broken into the offices of a software company. I paid little attention at the time—"

99

"I'm listening, but get to the point."

"Certainly." Stuart paused for effect. He quit the dusting, put the duster under the counter and reclined in an old chair he'd never sell because he found it too comfortable. "The rogue left a memory key on the table. I only noticed it once he was gone. I picked it up. I don't even know why."

"Go on."

"I examined the contents earlier this afternoon to figure out if what's on it is important or not. It seems that it is. There are hundreds of design documents and a considerable amount of source code, if I'm reading it right."

Jaxon Coles remained quiet for some time. Stuart waited patiently. Eventually, Coles would speak. He was desperate, after all.

"You found all that on the memory key?" Was that a hint of relief in Coles' voice?

"Yes. That's how I knew to call you. I thought it might be important."

"It is."

"Really? I thought you might have that backed up on a server or something."

Coles sighed. "The server was wiped during the burglary."

"Is that a fact? In that case, this memory key must be valuable to you."

"It sure is. I'd be grateful if I could pick it up from you as soon as possible."

"Of course. There's just one minor matter to discuss first." Stuart brushed an imaginary piece of fluff off the arm of his suit. "Price."

There was a sharp intake of breath. "That's extortion. I could report this conversation to the police."

"You could, but you wouldn't ever find this memory key. They're so small, aren't they? So easy to misplace—or lose forever."

"Damn you to hell."

Stuart chortled. "By the time I get to hell, I'll already own a little corner of it."

"I hope you fucking rot there."

"I'd like to help you, Mr Coles, but if this is your attitude, I don't think I will. We were about to discuss price?"

Another pause. Stuart could almost hear Coles seething on the other end of the line.

"Goodfellow isn't your actual name, is it? If it is, you're not living up to it."

"Of course it isn't. You don't need to know my actual name. What's your offer?"

"One thousand dollars. That's more than generous."

Stuart tut-tutted. "Don't insult my intelligence, Mr Coles. I'm not asking you to pay for my time and effort. I'm asking you to pay for the value of the information. Please, think of a number with a few more zeroes."

"That's ridiculous."

"Shall I sell on the information to another company? I'm sure someone will pay a pretty price for these designs and the source code."

"Don't you dare, you bastard."

"I don't have all day, Mr Coles. Let me suggest a price for you. A quarter of a million dollars."

"What? That's outrageous. No fucking way am I paying you that."

"Didn't you say to the *Richter Mail* this information was a year's work of your company, and this is the only copy?"

Stuart heard teeth grinding.

"Where am I supposed to get that kind of money?"

Stuart grinned. "Why, from your company bank account. According to your official filed financial statements, you have more than enough cash for that."

"That's for running my business!"

"Without this memory key, Mr Coles, you don't have a business, do you?"

"You're evil, you know that?"

"I prefer to think of myself as ruthless. Look, you sort out the money for me by noon tomorrow. Two hundred and fifty thousand dollars' worth of Bitcoin. If you can do that, I'll give you a Bitcoin wallet address into which you can pay it. When that's done, I'll leave the memory key somewhere safe and tell you where you will find it."

"How can I trust you? You're despicable."

Stuart laughed. Coles' hatred of him was palpable. "This information's no good to me. I'll keep my word, if you get me the money by tomorrow."

"All right. You've got me over a barrel."

"I have, indeed. Until tomorrow, then." He rang off, eyes gleaming, pleased with himself. If it all worked out as planned, he'll update both sets of accounts and his personal diary of profitable cons, schemes and extortions. This would be one of the most lucrative he'd carried out. He loved this game.

§

Jaxon had no intention of paying over a quarter of a million dollars if he didn't have to. What he did have, however, was a bunch of tech-heads worried about whether they would still have jobs next week.

He left his office and surveyed his team. They were a bedraggled lot with below-par personal hygiene habits, but brainy. Without the ability to do any work, all six of them were as lost as sheep without a shepherd.

"All right, everyone, listen up. Our project, our company, is dead unless we get that source code back. We can't rely on the police to do it for us. Let's do it ourselves. Anyone know how to trace a hidden phone number?"

Seven hands shot up. The junior techie, who'd also jumped to his feet, was always the keenest and had raised both arms.

Jaxon grinned. "Great. I knew I could count on you all. Find me the guy's real name, find me his address, and I'll go pay him a surprise visit."

POLICE INTERVIEW 4

Day 6 (Saturday 19 August), night

POLICE: *The time is 10.20 p.m. Present in the interview room are Inspector O'Toole and Sergeant Hilton. We are continuing the interview with Danny Ashford.*

DANNY: *You told me hours ago it was a friendly chat.*

POLICE: *I think we've been friendly. We're all friends here, aren't we? We've provided you with food and coffee, haven't we?*

DANNY: *You have. I really can't complain about the lukewarm coffee and dry ham sandwiches. Can I go now?*

POLICE: *Not yet. We have a few more questions now that we've had more time to investigate the crime scene and Stuart Baker's house.*

DANNY: *Not again.*

POLICE: *Let's start with you telling us where you were last night, Friday, between seven and eleven. We're especially interested in where you were around eight.*

DANNY: *I was home from about eight. Before that, I'd been out for a walk.*

POLICE: *Anyone see you on the walk?*

DANNY: *Only my assailant.*

POLICE: *Oh, right. That's how you got that bruise on your face. So, no one can verify your whereabouts before eight. What about after you got home?*

DANNY: *My neighbour and I spent some time together between eight and about nine thirty, when she left to go to work. I think I fell asleep then.*

POLICE: *All right, we'll have to speak to your neighbour. What's her name?*

DANNY: *Chelsea Whitlam.*

POLICE: *And where does she work at that time of night?*

DANNY: *(Pause.) The 88 Club.*

POLICE: *Well, if it isn't another one of those coincidences.*

DANNY: *Is that all? Can I go now?*

POLICE: *Oh no. There's something else I need to ask you about. Where exactly did you go for your walk? Did you leave on foot from your apartment, or did you drive somewhere first?*

DANNY: *What does it matter? Is this leading anywhere?*

POLICE: *Mind taking your right shoe off, Danny?*

DANNY: *What for?*

POLICE: *Because I asked nicely.*

DANNY: *(Something inaudible)*

POLICE: *For the purposes of the recording, Danny Ashford has removed his right shoe and put it on the table between us. What size shoes do you take, Danny?*

DANNY: *Size eleven.*

POLICE: *I'm now examining the shoe. It is indeed a size eleven. There are signs of wear on the heel on the right-hand side and on the toes on the left-hand side.*

DANNY: *So what? You're saying I should buy a new pair of shoes?*

POLICE: *Have a look at this photograph. For the recording, I am now showing the interviewee a photograph of a footprint found in a flowerbed at Stuart Baker's house. Our forensics department, Jenny, says it's a size eleven and bears a pattern of wear that appears to me very much like that on the sole of your shoe. What do you have to say about that?*

DANNY: *(Silence.)*

POLICE: *Well, perhaps you'd like to see this instead. For the recording, I am now showing the interviewee a broken flashlight found outside Stuart Baker's home. Danny, does this belong to you?*

DANNY: *(Silence.)*

POLICE: *If it helps your recollection, your initials have been carved into the side.*

DANNY: *All right, I was there for a short time, Inspector, but I never entered the house and I didn't see Baker at all. That's the truth.*

POLICE: *Is that so? Let's sum this up, Danny. The victim had stolen your bank card details and taken all your money. He'd also scammed a client of yours. You visited the club he owned and threatened him with a note and a graphic drawing. You admit going to his house last night, where you left a flashlight and a footprint. Your face bears the result of a fight, and the victim was killed last night at around eight o'clock. It doesn't look good for you, Danny.*

DANNY: *I told you, I was home by eight o'clock, and my neighbour can verify that.*

POLICE: *Maybe our time of death is out by twenty minutes or so. Maybe your neighbour will remember you came home at a different time. We'll have to see.*

DANNY: *I want to phone a lawyer.*

Chapter 22

Day 5 (Friday, 18 August), evening

DEEPA COULD HARDLY WAIT until her new Vespa arrived. A 300cc classic-styled machine, mint green, an upgrade on her previous model. Riding it would be cool, but more importantly, she'd get to places without the crippling expense of taxis or the unpredictability of public buses.

She stepped off one of those buses in Leanwood at about seven thirty p.m. and checked her phone for directions. Baker's ex-partner lived about four blocks away. She strode along confidently, her boots clunking on the footpath. This wasn't the kind of area to hang around in alone after dark; hell, almost everywhere in Quake City was like that, but Leanwood was one of the worst areas. It was late winter, and sunset had been an hour ago. She tugged her purple puffer jacket around her body and zipped it up to keep out the chill.

A shadow moved, separating itself from a large shrub at the edge of a property, coalescing into the form of a man as he emerged into the dim moonlight.

Deepa stopped, instinctively glancing behind. No one there. Good. At least there was only one.

The man approached. A streak of light illuminated his face before the moon was once again covered by clouds. Young. Glazed eyes, possibly a druggie on the hunt for cash to pay for his next fix.

"Hand over your money and phone, quick. Don't force me to take them from you." He sneered.

Deepa slipped a hand into her shoulder bag. "If you want them, come and get them."

"Stupid bitch. You're asking for this."

The man charged Deepa, one arm raised as if to strike her. His unfocused eyes failed to adjust when she adroitly stepped aside at the last moment, ducking under his arm, catching his foot with her outstretched leg. He tumbled to the ground.

"Piss off. I won't tell you again." She withdrew a narrow metal cylinder from her bag and pressed a button. It telescoped into a thin, flexible baton half a metre long.

The guy either didn't hear or was too enraged to care. He stood and stepped towards her. "You fucking bitch. You'll regret that. I'll have you—"

Deepa raised the baton. He kept coming. When she saw him take his gaze off her to glance at the weapon, she stepped forward and kicked him between the legs. Hard.

He dropped to the ground, screaming. She brought the baton down on his shoulder like a whip. It wouldn't cause any lasting damage, but it would hurt like hell and leave a welt. He rolled on the ground in agony, one hand on his shoulder, the other over his crotch.

Deepa collapsed the baton and thrust it into her bag. She pulled off the guy's shoes, being careful not to get kicked, but he wasn't paying her any attention now. She threw them down the street as far as she could, one in each direction. That would slow him down if he decided to follow her when he'd recovered.

Lights flicked on outside nearby houses. Faces appeared at windows to see what the commotion was. Deepa turned and ran.

When she reached the street she wanted, she stopped and peered behind, listening carefully. Nothing. Her assailant hadn't followed her.

Deepa relaxed and carried on. Sarah Bailey lived a few doors down in a weather-beaten wooden house typical of the area. The remains of the fallen chimney had been piled up against the side of the house. Few brick chimneys in Quake City had survived the quakes.

There was no gate. Thankfully, that indicated there wouldn't be a dog. The driveway and path to the front door were cracked. Deepa knocked loudly on the front door, then took her reporter's I.D. card from her purse. She glanced at her watch. It was eight p.m.

A light above the porch switched on. A woman's face appeared at a narrow window. "Who are you?"

Deep held her I.D. card to the glass. "I'm Deepa Banwait, a reporter. Are you Sarah Bailey? May I talk to you about your ex-partner Stuart Baker?"

"Wait a moment."

Two locks clicked, and the door swung open. A dark-haired woman wearing a raggedy cardigan stood in the doorway, a kitchen knife clenched in one hand. Deepa took a step back. When the woman saw Deepa was alone, she put the knife on a side table.

"I'm Sarah. Come on inside. Please excuse the knife. You can't take any chances in this neighbourhood, especially at night."

"I understand." Deepa followed her in. "Do you live here alone?"

"I have twin boys aged five. They're asleep now." Sarah led the way into the living room and gestured to Deepa to take a seat. "How can I help you?"

Deepa took in her surroundings: worn mismatched sofas, an old television, a bookcase half-full of battered books, a table and chairs. Everything appeared like it had come from op shops. Not that there was anything wrong with op shops—Deepa used them herself—but Danny had told her that Baker oozed money. His ex didn't seem to receive any of it.

"What's your relationship with your ex like? Are the children his, if you don't mind me asking?"

"Oh, I don't mind. Yes, they're his. He barely sees them, yet they adore him anyway. The boys are too young to understand that their dad's a scumbag. He pays the absolute minimum in child support even though he's rolling in cash himself. Would you believe he came round here the other day driving a Lamborghini? He said he'd won it."

"But you don't believe him, do you?"

Sarah shook her head. "Not for a moment. He's got money coming in from somewhere that the tax office doesn't know about, and it's not from his business, that's for sure."

"What business does he have?"

"He owns a crappy antique store in Sintown, but it doesn't have any antiques, just junk that no one wants."

Deepa inclined her head. "So, do you suspect he's involved in some other business on the sly? Maybe something illegal? Any idea what that might be?"

Sarah shook her head, her forehead creasing. "I don't know. He's up to something, though, I'm sure. He's a pathological liar and a charmer. He could talk his way into and out of anything."

Deepa nodded and didn't reply, hoping that Sarah would say more.

Sarah interlaced her fingers, her hands in her lap. "Why are you investigating him?"

"I believe he's scamming people out of their money. I'm working with a private investigator to get to the bottom of it."

"Oh, I can tell you he's capable of that, but he's cunning. I've never been able to find out exactly what he's doing. If I could, I might get more child support money out of him."

"It must be upsetting for you, seeing that he's living an extravagant lifestyle while you…" Deepa left her words trailing.

"While me and my kids are living below the poverty line, you mean. Of course it is. You'd think he'd want to provide for his boys financially. He's got no other family. I know he's going to leave his money to them in his will; he told me. But the boys won't get anything until he dies, and if they're under twenty-five, it'll go into a trust for their benefit."

"Who'll administer the trust fund? You?"

"Yes. I'm best placed to know the needs of the children."

"Of course. Can you tell me where to find Stuart's antique shop, please? I'd like to check it out."

"Sure. Don't waste your money, though. It's full of crap." Sarah grabbed a pen and a post-it note and scribbled an address. She handed it to Deepa. "Anything else you want to know? His home address?"

"No, thanks. We've got that."

"Good luck, then. I'll show you out." She got to her feet.

Deepa stood. "I'm going to call for a taxi, if you don't mind me waiting until it arrives."

"No problem. You can't be too careful around this neighbourhood at night."

Chapter 23

Day 5 (Friday, 18 August), evening

THE ROAD FROM THE SHORE wound sharply and steeply uphill. Brief periods of moonlight helped illuminate the way and, also, the lack of road-side barriers between the road and the near-vertical drop. I kept the Audi's headlights on high beam and drove with care. Near the top, where the road was relatively level, I checked the house numbers as I drove past and parked the Audi fifty metres from Baker's place. It was already dark at seven p.m.

I pulled my coat closer to ward off the cold easterly wind. Quake City was one of those rare places where the properties by the beach were much cheaper than those by the airport on the other side of town. This wasn't merely because the eastern suburbs had been decimated by the earthquakes, but also because of the beastly wind off the South Pacific Ocean. Although Baker's place, situated with the best view on the hilltop, wasn't one of the cheaper ones.

From across the street, I scrutinised his property. A high fence obscured all of it except for what I could see up the driveway in the moonlight. That led upwards at a slight incline to a stylish and modern two-storey dwelling. No lights were on. Maybe Baker wasn't home yet. I frowned. I needed to confront him to get my money and my client's money back.

No 'Beware of the dog' sign adorned the gate. Good. I hated guard dogs. I sauntered up the driveway, keeping to the shadows of the adjacent trees as much as possible. All was quiet. I reached the house and strode up to the front door and rapped the bronze knocker on it.

No answer, and no sound from inside. There was no sign of a car anywhere either. Perhaps he really was out.

I stepped away from the front door. Narrow flowerbeds with neatly spaced blooms edged the front of the house. The con artist, hacker or whatever he called himself was a proud gardener, or employed someone to do it for him. I stepped into a space between purple flowers and peered in a window, shining my torch inside to reveal a tidy living room with luxurious furniture. In the far upper corner, a sensor for an alarm blinked.

I continued around the side of the house, searching for a way inside that wasn't covered by the alarm sensors. The windows were all locked. I reached the back of the house. The beam from the torch vanished into a void. I froze, inhaling sharply, the hairs rising on the nape of my neck. The cliff edge was a mere two paces away. I could have stepped over it in the dark and fallen to my death.

Another severe earthquake could take more of the cliff, and the house with it, to the ground below. Baker was crazy to live here. But he seemed to be the sort of man who lived on the edge.

I grinned at my pun and retreated along the side of the house towards the front. I'd hide somewhere until he turned up. Hopefully, that wouldn't be in the early hours of the morning when the 88 Club closed. By that time, I'd be freezing.

A fleeting movement near the front entrance caught my eye in the moonlight. A man dressed all in black, including a mask, crept up the porch steps. I hadn't heard a car, and there wasn't one parked by the house, so he must have walked in like I had. Suspicious. From his outfit and the way he moved, he was up to no good.

"Hey, you." I flashed my flashlight in his direction so I could see him better—he'd be dazzled, unable to see me.

The figure snapped to a defensive pose facing me. "Who's there? Baker? That you?" His voice was gruff.

I moved closer, the soft sound of my steps covered by my voice. "No, it's not. Who are you, and what are you doing here?" I patted a pocket of my raincoat, feeling the hard, cold form of my Glock 17.

I never had a chance to draw it. The black-clad man moved like a lightning bolt. One moment he was in the glare of my flashlight. In the next, he dived out of sight. I darted the flashlight left and right for a second but couldn't find him.

His boot powered into my stomach so hard I doubled over, wheezing. All the breath left my body. I gasped for air. The flashlight went flying and smashed, its illumination dying. I staggered, no idea where my opponent was. I regained my balance and glanced up just in time to see him in mid-air, his boot arcing towards my head.

Everything turned black.

§

When I came to, the man was gone. It was seven thirty p.m. I'd been unconscious for several minutes. If I hadn't turned my head away at the last possible moment, the head kick wouldn't have given me merely a glancing blow. I brushed my head gingerly. My hair was wet and matted, and my fingers came away slick. Blood.

Was that man one of Baker's thugs? No, he wouldn't have left me here after beating me up. He would've dragged me off to his boss. Maybe he was a thief, or someone else with a grudge against Baker; there was surely no shortage of those. Whoever he was, he moved like a ninja and attacked like an expert kickboxer.

I retrieved my hat and got to my feet. My head thundered in protest. I was in no condition, or mood, to face Baker now. I'd go home, get a good night's rest, and return in the morning.

Moonlight intermittently illuminated my path as I staggered through the shadows down the driveway to my car. I slumped into the driver's seat and immediately reached for the glove box, where I kept medical supplies. The painkillers were what I needed; bandaging the cut could wait until I got home.

I took two tablets. They'd take twenty minutes to take full effect, but I wanted to leave this place in case Baker drove past and noticed me sitting there. I did a U-turn, put the car into neutral and let it coast down towards the main road, foot on and off the brake to control its descent. As long as I didn't pass out again, I'd probably get there.

I lowered the windows so the chilly night air would keep me alert, but it just made me colder.

By eight p.m., I was home. My headache had subsided to a mere throbbing rather than a thundering. I left the car opposite the apartment building and wearily made my way up the stairs, the muscles in my sternum sore as hell. The step near the top creaked, as usual, when I trod on it.

Chelsea opened the door of her apartment at the top of the stairs. She came out and smiled at me when I reached the landing, chatting away on her phone, a cigarette in her other hand. For a moment, it reminded me of my previous neighbour, a busybody who ambushed me whenever possible to demand details of my private life.

I returned Chelsea's smile, but weakly.

Her expression changed, her eyebrows knitting together in concern. She apologised to the person on the phone and told them she'd call back. She stuffed her phone in a pocket and turned her full attention to me. "Danny, what happened to you? Your head's bleeding."

"I bumped into a martial artist." I touched my hair. The blood was drying. Good. Maybe the wound wasn't too bad, but I had no medical training, so that was more optimism than evaluation.

She shook her head. "I think you're keeping the wrong company. Come on, let me help you." She took my arm and steered me towards my door. It wasn't necessary, but I didn't protest.

I unlocked it. Chelsea followed me inside and extinguished her cigarette. She took my hat and coat off and hung them up, then gently pushed me back onto the sofa. She kicked off her shoes and padded silently to the bathroom. I lay back on the sofa and closed my eyes.

Chelsea dabbed at my head with a wet cloth, then a dry cloth, and finally wrapped a bandage around it. I opened my eyes and saw her step back to admire her handiwork. I didn't know if she knew anything about infection control, but I appreciated her attention.

"Feeling better?"

"Great, thanks." I stood and immediately regretted it. The effort to get to my feet tore at my stomach muscles. I grimaced and groaned.

"You've got another injury?" Chelsea tugged at my shirt, loosening it. She pulled it up. "Jesus. That abrasion must be painful. There's going to be an enormous bruise. I'll get ice."

It wouldn't be comfortable, but it would help reduce the swelling. I sat, then lay on the sofa. When Chelsea laid an icepack wrapped in a towel on my bare stomach, I yelped.

"Be brave, Danny. Look, I have to go to work soon. At the club. Can I get you a drink before I go? Coffee?"

"Whiskey, please. Thanks, Chelsea. I appreciate it."

"No problem."

She poured me the drink, smiled, and left. The door clicked closed behind her. The scent of her fine perfume swirled in the air.

My mouth was dry. I gulped my drink and glanced at the clock. It read nine thirty p.m.

Chapter 24

Day 5 (Friday, 18 August), evening

STUART BAKER LOCKED UP his antique shop for the night. He'd opened only for the afternoon, and in that time two people had browsed inside and left without buying anything. He didn't mind. It gave him more time to research and plan his next nefarious scheme.

He sauntered down the main street in Sintown, past the nearby pawnbroker's and the brothel next door. Across the road, an argument broke out between two guys sitting in a shop doorway, drinking. He didn't recognise them. Regulars in the area knew from experience not to trouble him. Stuart paused in case they got up and scurried over to accost him, but they ignored him, so he kept strolling.

Around the corner, he unlocked the rusty lock-up garage that concealed his Lamborghini and drove it out. He gunned the engine and headed home through the darkened suburbs to Cliffside, reflecting on his day.

Gabe the babe. She'd finally shown her true colours, trying to blackmail him with what she knew, or thought she knew, about his business. Stuart frowned. She actually seemed to know a lot. But how?

He shook his head. He'd figure that out. The key thing was that he'd kept her in line.

And tomorrow he'd collect a pay-out from Jaxon Coles for the information he'd had Brock steal for him. One of his biggest pay-outs to date. Perhaps he'd celebrate it with a trip to Tahiti or somewhere else nice and warm.

The Lambo handled the steep road up to his house with consummate ease. Stuart parked in the forecourt by the fountain and strode inside. After deactivating the alarm, he went upstairs to the bedroom.

Stuart hung his suit carefully in the wardrobe, then finished undressing before heading into the double-size en-suite shower. Steaming water massaged him, and he took his time to let go of the stresses of the day.

He stepped out, wrapped a towel around his body, and strode across the bedroom to the French windows. He threw them open and stepped out onto the balcony, relishing the fresh, cold air against his face. Invigorating. Before him stretched the stunning view of the sea and the city at night.

The bedroom lights turned off. He spun. Was it a blackout, or an intruder?

A dark patch in the bedroom moved, coalescing into an approaching figure. A silhouette stepped onto the balcony, where moonlight illuminated them.

Stuart gasped. "You!"

A vase shattered on his head. Pain exploded in his skull. Stunned, Stuart hit out, but his fist merely brushed the intruder. "What the fuck? You, of all people."

The figure didn't answer. Instead, it grabbed for Stuart's throat and shoved him backwards.

A shiver ran down Stuart's spine when it pressed against the cold edge of the balcony railing. In a panic, he tried to wriggle away from his assailant's grip, but it was no use. The blow from the vase had made him dizzy. Icy fear gripped his heart like a vice. He was losing his balance. His attacker shoved him—hard. Stuart made a grab for the railing, but it was futile. He fell backwards over the side.

Time slowed down as he plummeted toward the rocks below. His towel fluttered away. The cold air rushing over his naked body made him gasp. Every good memory he had raced through his mind, and every sad one too. Every joke and laugh. Every scam and scheme he'd pulled off.

This was it. He was going to die.

Chapter 25

INSPECTOR O'TOOLE parked behind another police car and got out. The early morning mist had cleared, and he could see two scene-of-crime officers (SOCOs) across the park, searching the ground. The bulky figure of Mikey, the coroner, bent over something on the ground that O'Toole couldn't see. That'd be the dead man someone had found this morning while walking their dog.

O'Toole stroked his moustache and ginger beard as he took in the view in the other direction, across the estuary towards the open sea. Nice view, if you liked that sort of thing, which he didn't. Too bleak. Seagulls swooped and squawked. A couple jogged past.

"Inspector! Over here."

He turned back with a sigh. Mikey waved to him. O'Toole ambled across the narrow park. At one end, a children's playground sat empty. No one would be allowed near it for a few hours, at least until the body had been removed. The grass underfoot gave way to stones, then larger rocks, as he approached the cliff bottom where Mikey stood waiting.

A naked man lay across the rocks, a purple bruise covering one side of his face. The back of his skull was caved in, and an arm and leg were twisted at extraordinary angles. Blood, now dried, had run in rivulets over his body where the rocks' sharp edges had cut into him, and had splattered onto the surroundings.

O'Toole remained impassive. He'd seen so many dead bodies in Quake City that nothing much fazed him anymore. Mikey, being a medical examiner, was likewise unaffected. It was a different matter for the SOCOs, though, who were young, and both kept their eyes averted. One of them had a green tinge to his face.

Mikey came up to him. "Good morning, Inspector."

O'Toole nodded his own greeting. "What do we have here, Mikey? A dumped body? Or a jumper from the cliff top?"

"It's not suicide. Not all the injuries were inflicted by the fall."

"So, he did fall, then?"

"Yes. Can you see the pattern of blood on the rocks? That confirms it."

O'Toole squinted up. He knew there was a house up there. He'd spotted it when he arrived. A balcony protruded over the edge.

Mikey continued. "If the blood splatter pattern isn't enough to convince you, there's a towel over there." He pointed behind a nearby boulder. "I would bet you there are matching ones in the house above."

O'Toole slid on the gravel as he moved around the boulder to the towel. It wasn't blood-stained. "You think this came off him when he fell from the house above?"

"Exactly. But he didn't just fall. Someone hit him before he fell. Maybe they also pushed him over the balcony."

"What makes you say that?"

Mikey bent over close to the body and pointed at a bloodied, gouged ear. "He was hit with something ceramic, like a vase or a pot. There's a broken, curved piece of it stuck in his ear. One of the SOCOs also found a few shattered pieces nearby."

"Right. I need to get someone up to that house. If he was hit with something up there, the rest of it might be present. And it's obviously murder, not suicide." The inspector groaned.

Two more of his team arrived on the scene. Debbie, his new detective sergeant, and Peter, detective constable. They surveyed the body fleetingly.

"Perfect timing, you two. See that house above us? I need you both up there. Get inside and check around. Someone clobbered this guy, and he fell over the balcony."

"Fell? Or was pushed?" Debbie gazed up, then at the body, and winced.

"One or the other. We're assuming it's murder."

"Do we know who he is yet?"

O'Toole shook his head. "No I.D. on him. Nothing except a towel, and that came off on the way down."

"Okay. We'll drive up there. It might take a few minutes to find the exact house."

"No problem. The victim's not in a hurry."

Debbie and Peter returned to their car and sped off, lights and siren on. There was no need for that, of course, but Peter was renowned for racing police cars.

O'Toole scanned around. The two SOCOs were still combing the area. Mikey was bent over the body, making notes.

The inspector approached him. "Estimated time of death?"

Mikey prevaricated. "Well… rigor mortis hasn't completely set in yet, but the body's been lying here on the rocks overnight in the cold weather, which would delay that somewhat. And see the blue-grey lividity obvious in the lower part of the body except where it touches the rocks."

"Mikey. In English, please. How long's he been dead?"

The coroner scratched his nose. "My professional estimation is he's been lying here between ten and fourteen hours."

"That's a window of four hours. Can't you narrow it down?"

Mikey gave O'Toole a stern glare. "That is the narrowed-down window. It's the best I can do. Remember, he's been outside in the cold overnight."

"All right, all right. So, he would have died between…" The inspector paused. His lips moved as he calculated.

Mikey finished for him. "Between seven and eleven last night."

"I was just about to say that."

"Inspector. Over here."

O'Toole swivelled. One SOCO, Jenny something, a young woman with blonde hair and light freckles, new to the team, waved frantically from barely three metres distant. The inspector stepped over. "What is it?"

"Look, sir." Jenny crouched and pointed to an object nestled among the stones. "A broken watch. Maybe it flew off the victim's wrist when he landed on the rocks."

"Excellent work, Jenny. Well spotted. Bag it up as evidence. We'll see if someone can identify it as belonging to the victim."

She did as she was asked. She lifted the transparent evidence bag for O'Toole to examine. The watch was a Seiko. Some of the glass had broken away. The hour and minute hands were frozen at eight o'clock.

The inspector turned to Mikey, who had come over to see for himself, and grinned. "We've got an exact time of death now."

"If it's his watch."

Jenny held the bag up for better light. "It doesn't seem like it's been out here long. There's no grit or sand inside. And we can check the battery. If it's still got juice, we'd know the watch stopped when it was smashed, and didn't simply run out of power afterwards."

O'Toole considered this. The young SOCO was smart. A lot smarter than the usual Quake City lot. Reluctantly, he included himself with them.

"Where did you do your training, Jenny?"

"Wellington, sir. I graduated top of class. Excellence in forensics."

The inspector nodded. What was she doing working in this accursed city, then?

She seemed to read his mind. "I've got family down here, sir."

"Very well. I'm fortunate to have you. With your help, we might up our solve rate, which is currently between dire and hopeless."

"I'll do my best, Inspector."

O'Toole stroked his ginger beard. "Excellence in forensics, you said?"

"That's right, sir."

"Then you're our new forensics team. The old forensics team lost their jobs due to budget cuts. I'll sort out the paperwork for your promotion later today. Congratulations."

"Wow. Thank you, Inspector."

"Take your car up to the house above. I need you digging around there for evidence. That's if there's any left after my two detectives have been stomping around."

"On my way. My SOCO colleague—"

"Never mind him. He can get the bus back to the station."

Jenny, now Head of Forensics, raced off, taking the evidence bag containing the watch with her.

O'Toole turned to Mikey. "I can't believe we've got someone who might know what they're doing."

The coroner grunted. "Speak for yourself. I know what I'm doing."

"Yeah, but your job isn't difficult, Mikey. Cause and time of death, that's easy."

Mikey reddened. "It's a lot more complicated than that."

"If you say so." O'Toole harrumphed. His phone rang. It was his sergeant. "You found the house, Debbie?"

"We did. It wasn't locked or alarmed. There's no one here."

"I sent our new forensics team up to you. The new SOCO, Jenny something."

"I'll watch out for her. By the way, we found a smashed vase or pot on the balcony. And I found a wallet with a photo I.D. in it and letters addressed to the same guy. I'll text you a picture. See if it's our victim."

O'Toole's phone buzzed. He checked the snapshot of the photo I.D. against the dead man's face. He reconnected to his call with Debbie. "Yeah, it's him. What's his name?"

"Stuart Baker. Apparently, he's a wealthy antiques dealer."

"Is that so?" Could be a motive there.

"There's another letter here, Inspector, that's not addressed to him. It's..."

"Yes?"

"It's from a bank. Feels like there's a bank card inside. But it's addressed to..."

"Come on, Sergeant. Spit it out."

"I don't understand, but it was sent to Danny Ashford at this address."

O'Toole frowned. A bank letter addressed to the private investigator who was always interfering in their investigations. Found at the scene of a probable murder.

"Sounds like we need to talk to him urgently. Debbie, take Peter with you and bring that private investigator in for questioning. He's got some explaining to do."

Chapter 26

Day 6 (Saturday, 19 August), late at night

I'D BEEN IN AN INTERVIEW room at the police station in Crumbledon since mid-afternoon. Four windowless walls, a table, three chairs, harsh florescent lights. A digital recorder somewhere. Bleak and unfriendly. Not a suitable place for a friendly chat, as O'Toole had put it, but quite apt for an interrogation.

For over eight hours I'd answered Inspector O'Toole and Sergeant Debbie Hilton's relentless questions. I knew the inspector's technique, of course, having worked with him on interviews in the past. He varied between being methodical and random, wheedling information, and eventually confessions, out of suspects by wearing them down through pure chaotic tedium.

It was at that point that I'd asked to speak to a lawyer. I even had one in mind.

Debbie allowed me to make a call, though she stayed in the interview room while I did so. O'Toole left for a few minutes, perhaps to celebrate breaking my resolve.

A little after eleven o'clock might be too late for a business call, especially on a Saturday, but I dialled anyway.

She picked up after five rings. "Julie Nicholls."

I breathed a sigh of relief. "Julie, it's Danny Ashford here. Sorry for calling so late."

"That's fine, Danny. I'm still up. Have you got any more news for me? Did you track down the guy who stole my money? Stuart Baker, wasn't it?"

She spoke so quietly that I had to press the phone against my ear to hear her voice clearly.

"Actually, Julie, I've been working closely with the police on that matter today—"

"The police? I told you I didn't want you to go to the police on my behalf."

"I didn't. They came to me."

Julie paused before answering. "Why did they come to you?"

"That's why I'm calling you. I need help. They think I'm involved with Baker's untimely death."

"What?"

"Yeah, that's my reaction too. I need a lawyer. That's why I'm calling you. Will you help me?"

"Of course. You're still going to get my money back, though, right?"

"I will. I'm not giving up."

"All right. I'll be there as soon as I can." She disconnected.

§

Julie Nicholls was shown into the interview room at around midnight. I'd half expected her to turn up in a sweatshirt and jeans, but she was sharply dressed in a business suit. She thumped her briefcase onto the table. Debbie, who had shown her in, flinched at the sound. She may have been half asleep.

Julie fixed Debbie with a glare. "I want a few minutes in private with my client." Her quiet voice commanded obedience.

Once we were alone, she sat. "What's going on, Danny?"

I filled her in with everything that had happened, skipping the more personal stuff. She listened intently and made notes on a legal pad until I finished.

Julie laid down her pen and faced me solemnly. "You haven't done anything, Danny. The evidence they have isn't enough to arrest you with, otherwise they'd have done that. Do you want to get out of here?"

I nodded. "Yeah. Absolutely. More than ever, I need to get back to the case."

"Then we'll get you out." She turned and rapped on the door.

Debbie came in, drinking from a steaming cup. O'Toole was nowhere to be seen. As if she could read my mind, she grinned. "Can't you hear him? He's snoring like a hippo in his office."

Julie challenged her. "Do you intend to charge my client? If not, we're leaving now."

"I need to ask Inspector O'Toole—"

"No, you don't. My client has cooperated with you fully, and you have no actual proof he was involved in any crime."

I butted in. "I never even met the victim."

Julie pressed her attack. "Either you charge him immediately or he'll exercise his right to leave."

Debbie frowned, then pursed her lips. "You're free to go. But, Danny, don't leave the city. We'll want to talk to you again."

We were shown out.

Weariness swept through me, and I noticed for the first time a headache that must have been brewing for some time. The cold post-midnight air hit me in the face like a glass of iced tea.

Julie took my arm as if to steady me. Perhaps I'd stumbled or appeared faint. "Do you need a lift home?"

"That would be great, but what I need most is something to eat. Could we stop at Quake Burgers on the way?"

She laughed. "No problem."

Chapter 27

I ROLLED OUT OF BED at about ten in the morning. My headache had gone, and I felt pretty good. Then I remembered I'd spent hours at the police station the previous day and the good feeling popped.

Torquemada meowed incessantly as I dressed. He'd been hungry when I'd finally got home at about one in the morning, and I'd fed him before crashing into bed. It seemed he bore me a grudge for not being around earlier to meet his food needs.

After a shower, toast and coffee, I phoned Deepa.

"What's up, Danny? Where were you yesterday? I couldn't get hold of you."

"The police took me in for questioning. You know the guy we were tracking down? He's dead. O'Toole grilled me about it for hours. He thought I'd done it."

"Shit. They let you go, though, so that's good."

"I've done nothing wrong."

"You know, this sounds like a damn good story. Local private investigator unjustly questioned by police over the death of a conman. Can I write it up?"

"That's why I'm calling. Come over for lunch and I'll give you every detail."

§

The day was racing by when Deepa arrived a little after noon. She'd brought chicken Madras to share. I was slowly adjusting to the unfamiliar spicy tastes of these dishes. This one left me sweating and my throat burning, but I loved it.

She laughed. "I made it a little milder for you."

I almost choked. "You mean you usually have it spicier than this?"

"Sure. You get used to it."

"It's delicious."

We didn't discuss the case or my questioning by the police until we'd finished lunch. I cleared up and poured us cold drinks while Deepa set up her laptop and got ready to interview me.

That took an hour.

Three o'clock and I hadn't even started work on the case itself. Not only did I have to recover Julie's money—and mine—from a dead crook, but I had to evade the police and prove my innocence. If I couldn't find the murderer myself, I'd remain the only suspect. The thought of spending ten or more years in jail for a crime I didn't commit made me shudder.

I needed a game plan.

Deepa wasn't a lot of help with that. She took off home to write the article for the *Richter Mail*. Even though I'd agreed to it, I was already having second thoughts. It would be good publicity for my business—unless readers thought I might be guilty.

My mind returned to the two tasks I had to do: find Julie's stolen money and get it back to her, and work out who killed Baker to prove to the cops that I hadn't done it. Which would be more difficult? Where should I start? I didn't know.

I put on my coat and hat, slipped my Glock 17 into a coat pocket and left the apartment. I paused on the landing for a few moments, then knocked on Chelsea's door.

Fortunately, she was home. She answered the door wearing a green sleeveless vest and torn denim shorts.

"Danny. Nice to see you. Are you feeling better?"

"Yeah, thanks. Have you heard what happened to Stuart Baker?"

She hesitated, then took a couple of steps back. "Someone told me when I got to work last night that he'd died the night before."

I didn't wait for an invitation but stepped inside, pushing the door closed behind me with a bang. "What did they say about it?"

"Nothing much. Just that the online news reported he'd fallen from a balcony at his home, and the police are investigating. No one knew more than that. Danny..."

"Yes?"

"Why are the police investigating? Wasn't it an accident?"

"They think it's not. The police questioned me for hours last night."

Chelsea paled. "Oh god. You didn't have anything to do with it, did you? When I said to you, please have a word with my boss about harassing me, I meant just have a word with him. You didn't... did you?"

"Of course I bloody didn't."

"Then why did the cops question you?"

"Remember, I was tracking him for a client. The police learned I'd been hanging around at the 88 Club and outside his house. But that's all I did."

She exhaled heavily and sank into the sofa, where she picked up a can of Coke. "Thank god."

I sat on a chair opposite her. "Is there anything you can tell me about the other staff and the patrons at the 88 Club? Anyone have a grudge against Baker, for instance?"

"It'd be easier to tell you who *didn't* have a grudge against him. None of us girls liked him, as you know. He was too touchy-feely, and not in an appropriate way, if you know what I mean. Propositioning us and threatening to fire us if we didn't fuck him regularly. I wouldn't do it. I mean, who wants to put up with that?"

"What about the other staff? Security and bartenders?"

"I don't know much about them, but they were mostly transient. No one stayed long at the club."

"All right. So, everyone disliked him. What about the patrons?"

"No idea. I ignored them usually, just did my thing."

"Any of the staff hate Baker enough to kill him?"

"Not that I know. I can't think of anyone who would do that, no matter what he'd done to them. Do you want a drink?"

"Sure. Sparkling water, if you have it." This wasn't helping. Baker had so many enemies, and any one of them could've thrown him off that balcony.

"I do. I'll get it and a glass." She ambled to the kitchen and came back after a few moments with my drink.

I took it thankfully and sipped at it. "You probably think I'm grilling you for information—"

"You are."

"It's only so I can sort this out. I have to work fast. If my questioning makes you feel uncomfortable, then—"

"It's fine, Danny, I get it, but I can't help you. Are you sure he was murdered? He didn't just fall?"

I nodded. "The police are sure. That doesn't mean they're right, though."

"So, how will you know what really happened? What are you going to do?"

"I have an idea. But I need to ask for your help."

"I just told you, I can't help. I don't know anything."

"I don't mean with the investigation. I have a problem with Nadia, our landlady. She's going to be looking for me soon. I'm, er, a bit behind on the rent."

"Are you, now?"

"And I'd rather not bump into her until I've got this case solved, the money returned to my client, and been paid."

Chelsea giggled. "And what about the police? Do you want to avoid them too, if they come for you?"

"Now that you mention it, yes."

She sat forward, her fingertip poking her chin, expressing an exaggerated pose of puzzlement. "Hmm. Does that mean you don't want to be found at your place?"

I nodded.

"Let me guess. You want to stay here. Is that right?"

"Until all this is over. If it's not too much trouble."

"That's damned forward of you, Danny."

"I'll sleep on the sofa. I need to keep a low profile at the moment."

"And why not crash at your friend's place?"

"The police might look for me at Deepa's. They know we work together."

Chelsea smiled. "All right, then. I'll think about it. Ask me this evening. But let me know what you find out. Even though I didn't like him, he was my boss after all."

"Sure." I sipped more of the sparkling water. It was refreshing and cool. A thought struck me. "Who's running the 88 Club now? Was there a second-in-charge, or what?"

Chelsea shook her head. "Someone called Mary Sanchez has taken over. Maybe she bought it from Stuart before he died. I don't know. She turned up last night with a lawyer and ownership documents."

"That was quick." Maybe too quick. Coincidence? I'd seen a letter from her to Baker in his office. Maybe they'd done a deal.

"No one knew anything about it until she came in and said she was the new owner. We were all talking about it afterwards. Have you heard of her?"

"I know the name. She owns a night club herself, doesn't she?"

"Well, now she has two of them."

Chapter 28

Day 7 (Sunday, 20 August), afternoon

I DROVE TO THE Cracked Up Café in Crashmere. A strong cappuccino was exactly what I craved, and theirs were consistently good. I sat at an outside table with my drink and a notepad, watching the ducks on the riverbank and making a list of people with a solid motive to kill Baker.

The list didn't take long. I came up with Mary Sanchez and his ex-wife Sarah Bailey. There would be many more, but I'd have to dig into his business life to find them. With a pang of self-recrimination, I even considered the guy who confronted me about the Audi, because I'd told him that Baker had sold it to me.

I ordered a second drink. Besides talking to Mary and Sarah, I needed to get into Baker's house to search for anything that might reveal the identities of his previous victims. Any of them might have exacted revenge. I'd also check around for any evidence that the police might have overlooked. The crime scene perimeter could have been removed already. If not, I'd sneak in anyway.

My phone rang. Deepa. Good. I'd been missing her.

"Hey, Danny, I'm making good headway with this article. Do you want to see it later before I submit it to the editor?"

"No, I won't have time. Just don't make me sound guilty. Hey, I'm about to search for Baker's antique shop. It's in Sintown somewhere. After that, I'll go out to his house and have a reconnoitre, see if the police missed anything."

"I've got the antique shop address. His ex gave it to me. I'll text it to you. And let's talk later. Maybe I can help."

"Thanks. I'd appreciate it." I disconnected the call.

Deepa's text came through. I drove to the address and parked in a side street a couple of blocks from the 88 Club, in the centre of Sintown. I got out of the car. Rain splattered on my head, the chilly, heavy drops customary for late winter. I tugged my coat closer around me and started walking.

The rain remained light and steady. Puddles formed in the cracks and holes in the footpath. I splashed through a few, stumbled in one when its depth was concealed by the pooling water, and jumped over many others.

Sintown stretched a few blocks along Crumblo Street if you were only interested in shops and businesses. The side streets contained a mixture of run-down century-old wooden houses that had remarkably survived the earthquakes, set among the rubble of collapsed brick buildings. A few minor businesses were scattered about. I concentrated on the main street.

Baker's shop was closed, despite the opening hours posted on the door declaring it should be open. Presumably, he didn't have an assistant.

The door remained firmly closed when I tried opening it. I had my lock pick set in a coat pocket, but could I use it in daylight? A quick glance up and down the street revealed no pedestrians nearby. Maybe the rain had driven them inside.

It only took me a few seconds to open the door. I sidled inside, leaving the lights off, and moved towards the back of the store, in the shadows where I wouldn't easily be seen from outside. Why hadn't he put a better lock on the door? Wouldn't any shop owner, in this area? It had a high crime rate.

Maybe the local criminals knew to stay clear of Baker's shop.

I searched under the counter. A drawer, unlocked, contained an accounts book, a few unopened chocolate bars and Coke cans, and miscellaneous stationery. I pulled out the accounts book and flicked through it, pausing when I got to a recent date.

The entries were handwritten in a neat, almost pedantic style, the numbers lined up carefully on the right-hand side. On this particular day, the shop had apparently spent ten thousand dollars on a Louis XIV writing desk.

I shook my head. This was absurd on so many levels. There was no way a sizeable piece of Louis XIV furniture would cost as little as ten grand unless it was firewood. Even I knew that. But just in case it was true, I searched the shop. It wasn't there.

I flicked back a few pages. Items bought and sold were listed. Many were sold at a loss or at a minor profit only. Vendor and customer details were either absent or illegible.

A section on staff wages caught my eye. Two staff supposedly received fifty thousand a year. Each. But where were they? The shop wasn't attended.

Clearly, this accounts book was fiction, a method for Baker to disguise and launder money he'd raised from scams. A shop with imaginary staff that dealt in non-existent goods. The crap on the shelves was probably worthless and would never sell. It gave that impression, anyway.

From what I'd just observed, Baker kept careful records. The fake accounts book was a perfect example of that. So, could there be a real one, possibly with details of who he'd stolen money from and where it ended up? If so, I had to find it.

I had to search the rest of the shop to be sure, but surely, he wouldn't have been stupid enough to keep the fake and real accounts in the same place. So, they'd probably be at his home. Maybe on his computer. Probably encrypted.

I gritted my teeth. The police would have taken all that away when they searched his house. Wouldn't they?

So, that left me... where?

Chapter 29

Day 7 (Sunday, 20 August), afternoon

I LEFT THE antiques shop, locking it behind me. The rain had slowed, and a few people had returned to the streets. A beggar, a couple of local thugs, and a few wary shoppers trod the wet footpaths as I hurried back to my car. All I could think of doing was getting inside Baker's house to search for clues for my investigation. Maybe the police had missed something.

I phoned Deepa and explained. "Do you want to come with me?"

She didn't need asking twice. "Anything for a story."

Cliffside was a twenty-minute drive from her place. I hoped the muted tension between us would ease now that we were working together again.

Deepa turned to me in the car. "What are you hoping to find? Anything in particular?"

I shook my head. "Evidence of Baker's contacts and previous victims. One of them may be the killer. Also, keep an eye out for an accounts book or some way of storing information, like files or folders or a memory key."

"The police may have taken all that already."

I sighed. "I know. This is a long shot. But we have to try."

Deepa took in the sea view while I drove up the winding, steep road to Baker's house. We parked in the driveway and got out.

Crime scene tape made an 'X' across the door. I ripped it free from one side, leaving it dangling on the other, and tried the door. It was locked, but I'd expected that.

I got out my lock pick set and knelt in front of the door. The first two picks I tried didn't work.

Deepa loomed over me. "Can't you open it?" Her confidence in me was heartening... not.

"Yes. Give me time." I jiggled the tools in the lock a little more and it clicked open. "See? Got it."

"We'll be in trouble if we're caught in here. Breaking and entering. Disturbing the scene of a crime."

I glanced at her as I stood. "Then let's not get caught. Obviously, we'd say we're here to investigate on my behalf. I have to prove my innocence and find that stolen money."

"I hope that's enough of a reason for the police to let us off."

"Don't worry. The police will have done all they need to do here for now. They'll be busy analysing whatever it is they found yesterday. They'll only be back if they have to take a second look."

We entered the house through a wide, tiled entranceway, the walls framed with prints of luxury cars. We stepped into the expansive living area off to the right. Three large sofas and a huge flat-screen TV dominated the space.

Deepa stopped in her tracks and gazed around. "Wow. Crime does pay. Where shall we start?"

"How about I search down here, and you head upstairs?"

"Sure." The wooden stairs were at one end of the living room. Deepa went up.

The modern kitchen was fitted with top-of-the-line appliances. I opened every drawer and cupboard. Plenty of kitchen accessories were still in their original packaging. I had no idea what some of them were for. To me, anything beyond an electric jug and a toaster was a mystery.

One drawer contained papers, and I took my time rifling through them. They included receipts, booklets, advertising for gardening and cleaning services, but nothing helpful. What I really wanted was some evidence of Baker's criminal activities that the police had missed.

There wasn't anything like that in the kitchen. I moved on to the living room, where I checked the cabinet under the television and the bottom shelf of the coffee table. In a nook was a desk with some loose papers. There, I found something of interest at last: a post-it note with the words 'Job for Brock, $10K' and a telephone number. I pocketed it.

Everything was devoid of dust. Baker's home cleanliness appeared to be the same high standard as his clothing. A mouse mat lay on the desk. There had probably been a laptop on it that the police had taken.

I would have loved to get my hands on that laptop. It might have what I needed to prove my innocence. But in the hands of the Quake City police, I couldn't be sure they would even examine it, let alone find any leads on it.

I pondered that while I searched under the sofa cushions. That yielded nothing, not even loose change.

I took the stairs. Deepa was standing on the balcony off the main bedroom, gazing out at the sea.

"Splendid view." I joined her there. "Find anything useful?"

"No devices, no personal papers. Lots of clothes in the walk-in wardrobe. I searched all the pockets, but they were empty. This is one tidy guy."

"Was, you mean."

"Right. He had a nice place here. Paid for with other people's money, I guess."

"That's what I think." A light breeze came up, and I grabbed my hat so it didn't blow over the balcony. It'd be a pain to search for it down there amongst the rocks at the edge of the park.

"He fell from here, didn't he?"

I nodded. "Or he was pushed. Apparently, someone hit him with a vase or something like it before he fell."

"So… the attacker might not have intended to kill him. It could have been an argument that got out of hand."

"That's possible. We need to figure that out somehow. At the moment, I'm the number one suspect. Possibly the only reason I'm not yet in the cells is the police are disorganised and confused. And I had an excellent lawyer."

"Disorganised and confused? You mean Inspector O'Toole?" Deepa smirked. "Surely not."

I chuckled.

The front door opened and closed. We became dead quiet. Our eyes met. Deepa mouthed something to me like 'someone's here'.

I tiptoed through the bedroom to the stairs and descended carefully, keeping my footsteps as quiet as possible. Half way down, there was a gasp of surprise, and a blonde woman in a smart blue jacket fled from the living room and out the front door.

Deepa called from the top of the stairs. "What's going on?"

"A woman was here. She took off when she saw me. Hurry. We've got to catch up. She might know something."

I took the stairs two at a time, but Deepa didn't bother with the stairs themselves. She flung herself onto the bannister and slid down, then nimbly jumped off at the bottom and raced for the door. I followed as fast as I could, but her athleticism was too much for me.

She reached the car and spun to face me as I exited the house. "The keys. Throw them to me."

I dug into my pocket, pulled out the car key and tossed it to her as I ran. She caught it one-handed. By the time I reached the car, she was already in the driver's seat and had switched on the engine. I'd barely got inside before she backed out of the driveway, tyres screeching.

Deepa glanced over at me. "She's driving a white Mitsubishi."

I hadn't seen it. "She'll be too far ahead. We'll never catch her."

"Yes, we will. Hold on." She floored the accelerator, and the Audi jumped forward like a jaguar chasing down its prey.

I'd forgotten how Deepa drove. She wasn't familiar with my new car, either. I hung on to the handle above the passenger door as she took the first turn without slowing. She skidded around the second turn, almost a hairpin, the car's rear perilously close to the edge. Gravel from the narrow shoulder of the road kicked off into space.

"Try not to kill us." I didn't recognise my strangled voice.

"Look. There she is." Deepa pointed at a car disappearing around the next turn. "We'll catch her by the time she gets to the main road."

I gulped as Deepa took another swerving turn, now with both hands back on the wheel. She'd certainly missed her calling as a rally driver.

The road levelled out as we came to the intersection with the main road, but the white Mitsi was much closer now. Deepa had closed the gap so rapidly that the woman didn't seem to notice that we'd almost caught up. She paused, about to turn right, and Deepa swerved the Audi around her, braking sharply, and cut off her exit.

I swung my door open, only just becoming aware that in the haste I'd forgotten to put my seatbelt on for our wild chase. I raced over to the driver's door of the Mitsi and yanked it open.

Chapter 30

Day 7 (Sunday, 20 August), afternoon

THE WOMAN IN the white car stared at me, aghast. "Who are you?"

"I'm Danny Ashcroft, a private investigator looking into the death of Stuart Baker. Mind telling me who you are?"

"I've done nothing wrong, so I don't have to answer any questions of yours. Move your car, please. I want to get past."

I leaned against her frame of her car, preventing her from closing the door. "I'm sure my partner has recorded your licence plate number. How do you think the police would react if I told them you'd illegally entered a crime scene?" Of course, I wasn't going to say that Deepa and I had done the same.

Her whole demeanour changed. She sat back in her seat, deflated. "I don't want any trouble. I'm Stu's girlfriend. I came to his house to… to collect some personal items. The police tape had been pulled away, so I thought it was okay to go in. Then I heard noises and thought it was burglars, so I fled. All right?"

"Okay. I accept that. But I need to talk to you for a few minutes. Will you pull your car over so it's not blocking the road, please?"

Out of the corner of my eye, I saw Deepa reverse the Audi off the road and park. The woman in the Mitsubishi did the same, while I stood on the road to make sure she didn't make a run for it again. She'd have to run me over if she did that.

She got out. Deepa too. The three of us convened on the footpath beside the Mitsubishi.

I smiled wanly at her. "Thanks for cooperating."

The woman scowled. "You're not really giving me a choice, are you?"

I cocked my head. "No. Now, I've already introduced myself. This is my investigative partner, Deepa Banwait. And who are you?"

"Gabrielle Hocking. Friends call me Gabe."

"Gabe? Not Gabby?"

"That's right. I can't stand being called Gabby."

Deepa spoke up. "When did you last see Stuart?"

"Friday evening. He met me for dinner at a restaurant in Parkside, but he left about seven thirty."

"After dinner?"

Gabrielle looked away. "Stu didn't stay for dinner in the end. We'd had an argument earlier in the day. He tried to smooth things over with flowers and chocolates and shit like that. I wasn't having it. He got pissed off and left me to pay the bill."

"And that was the last you saw of him?"

"Yes, it was."

Deepa's questioning was too gentle for my taste, and I didn't believe half of what Gabrielle said. She'd gone from being assertive and self-assured to being defensive, yet tough-talking. It all smelled like she was trying to create a false persona on the spot.

I broke in. "I think you're lying."

Gabrielle's mouth dropped open. "Excuse me?"

"Stuart Baker isn't the sort of man who apologises after an argument. He's an arrogant narcissist. He wouldn't take you flowers to make up. He'd expect you to apologise to him."

Gabrielle leaned back against her car, hushed and frowning. Deepa regarded me with a raised eyebrow.

I took Gabrielle's silence as evidence that I was on the right track. "So, what actually happened? What did you fight over? Something to kill him for?" Sometimes it was worth asking questions that shock. A suspect's lips might lie easily, but their eyes don't.

Gabrielle gasped. "I didn't kill him. It wasn't me! How dare you!"

"You said you argued. The next morning, he's dead. I'm asking what really happened."

"Listen, when I said we argued, it was only a trifle. I wanted to know about his antique shop business, complained about his long hours working there. That's all. It was nothing. Anyway, he got pissed off and didn't stay to eat the meal he'd ordered. I had mine, then went home and watched Netflix for hours, eating chocolate and drinking wine."

"On your own?"

"Yes. I was alone. That's not unusual, is it, watching TV alone?"

Deepa jumped in. "How long had you known Stuart?"

Gabrielle waggled her head. "He's been a customer at the bank I work at for years, but we've only been going out for a couple of weeks."

"And you have a key to his house? After only a couple of weeks?"

"No, I don't have a key? Why do you ask?"

I saw where Deepa was going with this. She was smart.

Deepa pressed the point. "So, you came to his house a few minutes ago with no key. How did you plan on getting in?"

"I… I thought maybe the police might have left it unlocked."

I shook my head. "I don't think they're quite that careless."

Deepa chuckled. "We didn't lock it when we left just now."

Damn. We'd have to go back. "All right. Let's all go back there now. Gabrielle, you may as well fetch the personal things you wanted, then we'll lock up. That okay with you?"

She regarded me with suspicion. "I guess so."

"And, before we go, let me have your phone number, in case I need to contact you again. I'm sure I will, and I don't want to have to go searching for you."

"Fine." She clipped the word in that way that meant it wasn't fine, but she gave me her number anyway.

Deepa was keen to drive again, but I insisted she give me the keys; the previous hair-raising journey still preyed on my mind. We got back into our cars and drove up the windy road to Baker's house.

Once there, Gabrielle searched through the house while we watched. She wasn't as thorough as Deepa and I had been, but she opened every cupboard and drawer downstairs and upstairs. Whatever she was looking for in those places, she didn't find it. Finally, she grabbed a few personal items from the bedroom and en-suite bathroom and said she was ready to leave.

In the hallway, I dialled the number she gave me. She pulled her phone out and answered. I heard her voice in my ear and thanked her. She peered back at me in consternation.

I smiled. "Just checking."

Chapter 31

Day 7 (Sunday, 20 August), evening

WE NEEDED TO EAT. I asked Deepa if she wanted to get some dinner somewhere. She declined. That was unusual. Guess I was still in her bad books, despite us working well together on the investigation.

"I'll drop you at home, then." I didn't try to conceal the disappointment in my voice.

We made our way to the car. I didn't get in. Instead, I stood outside, musing. Deepa's curiosity would soon reveal itself.

As I suspected, it only took a few moments. "What are you going to do next, Danny?"

"Well… if you aren't interested in having dinner, I'll carry on with the investigation. I have another lead." I pulled the 'Job for Brock' post-it note from my pocket and showed Deepa. "I'll see where this takes me."

Deepa couldn't resist asking. "What's that?"

"It's a note I found on the desk in Baker's living room. I want to find out who this 'Brock' is and what job he did for Baker. That might lead to another suspect or another crime."

"Or he could just be the gardener."

"A gardening job for ten grand?"

"Oh yep, I see what you mean." Deepa took a deep breath. "All right, I'll come with you. You'd just get into trouble again, if I left you to investigate on your own. I've always had your back, haven't I?"

144

"Yeah. Thanks. First, let's stop somewhere for dinner and talk things over." I finally got into the car.

Deepa got into the passenger seat. "What things?"

I sighed. "You know. Us. Our... personal bond."

"Our investigative partnership, you mean?"

"Sure. But I meant our friendship, and any misunderstandings we've had."

Deepa gave me an odd look. "We're friends. We work together on cases. What misunderstanding?"

I turned away, feeling out of my depth. "Deepa, don't be obtuse. I'm sure you know what I'm referring to."

"Why don't you spell it out for me?"

"You know, I'm not good at this sort of thing..."

"Talking shit, you mean?"

I frowned. "That I'm good at. I mean I'm not good at talking about friendships and emotions and stuff."

"Okay, I certainly won't disagree with you on that."

"It's just that... I thought that... we get on well together, we spend a lot of time together, we've worked together investigating cases and earning a living, we've even slept in the same place together—"

Deepa shook her head vigorously. "Oh no, Danny, we haven't slept together. I'm sure I'd remember that."

"No, I meant we've slept separately in the same place, in the same hotel room or in my apartment."

"Out of convenience or when a serial killer was on the loose and I was a target."

"Yes, that's true; even so, it strengthened our bond." I groaned inwardly. I knew I was making a hash of this, but there was no stopping now. I'd gone too far.

Deepa stared at me wordlessly, waiting for me to continue.

Heat rose in my face. My palms were sweating. I was as nervous as a junior pickpocket before his first theft. "I really thought we might have a more personal connection, you know, in time, become more than friends."

Deepa stayed quiet for a few moments. She didn't smile. Her eyes were hard. "You know, Danny, I thought the same until a few days ago. I'd asked you into my apartment, and you dashed off and banged that sex worker instead."

"She's not a sex worker. She's a stripper."

Deepa threw up her hands. "Oh! Sorry. That must be all right, then."

"I don't even remember the sex. I'd been hurt in a fight. She's my neighbour. She looked after me."

"She looked after you, all right."

"It really was not my fault."

Deepa raised her eyebrows.

"Okay, it was at least half my fault, but I had little control over the situation. Perhaps I'd had too much to drink. I don't remember. I don't even know how it happened."

"But it did happen."

I sighed and ran a hand through my hair. "I'm sorry. I was embarrassed about it, even before you walked in. When I saw you, I regretted what I'd done. Can we let it go? It's not as if we are a couple."

"I'll think about it. Now, you mentioned dinner. You're buying. And it had better not be burgers."

Chapter 32

Day 7 (Sunday, 20 August), evening

DEEPA CHOSE AN expensive Indian restaurant in Wigcrumb for dinner. She ordered for us both, too. Spicy, not mild. She knew I'm not used to spicy food. She could be mean like that sometimes—though only when I deserved it—but she'd deny it if I'd said anything. I drank a jug of water to douse the meal's fire. It meant two trips to the toilet before we left the place, but at least she seemed in a better mood when we departed.

It was eight o'clock. I thought it was time to phone Brock, whoever he was, and lure him into a meeting.

He answered hesitantly, maybe because he didn't recognise my number. "Hello? Who's this?"

"I'm Danny, and I assume you're Brock."

"Yeah, that's me."

"I got your name from an acquaintance, Stuart Baker. He told me you're the guy to call for jobs of my kind."

"Yeah. He can vouch for me. Shit, I mean, he could vouch for me if he hadn't died. May his soul rest in peace."

"May his soul rest in peace." I was damned sure it wouldn't. "I assume that you'd be interested in replacing that lost income stream, wouldn't you, Brock?"

"Of course I am. Let's not take this any further over the phone. We'll meet up, okay?"

I grinned. "Name the place and time."

"How 'bout in an hour at the Got Inn?"

"I'll see you there. How will I recognise you?"

"Ask Harry at the bar to point me out." He hung up.

I turned to Deepa. "I'm meeting him at the Got Inn. It's in Sintown, and it's a nasty place. Would you rather sit this one out?"

"Not a chance. I'll give you a minute, then follow you in and sit as close as I can so I can listen in without drawing too much attention."

I knew I couldn't talk Deepa out of going with me, no matter what the situation. In fact, she'd pulled me to safety more than once.

"All right, let's get a coffee on the way."

That proved to be more difficult than I thought. We drove around Wigcrumb, trying to spot cafés. The only one we found had been boarded up due to fire damage.

Deepa drummed her fingers on the car seat to some beat I didn't recognise, maybe impatience.

I'd gone through impatience to outright annoyance. "What kind of suburb is this? It's Friday night, and we can't get a coffee anywhere? It's like we're in the Dark Ages here."

Deepa noticed some youths tagging the steel roller door of a loan shark's office. "Perhaps we are."

We drove to the pub early and parked around the corner. As we'd agreed, I went on ahead. Locally, the Got Inn was known as the Grot Inn, and I soon understood why. The paint on the wooden facade was peeling. One of the 'n's on the name hung upside-down. The double doors had indentations from steel-capped boots.

Inside, it wasn't any better. The pub wasn't well lit or ventilated; instead, it was murky and stuffy. Muddy boot prints marked the floor. The place was half-full, and the patrons were well on their way to being totally smashed. Their inebriated conversation comprised the only ambiance in the room, such as it was. If I didn't have someone to meet, I would have turned around and stalked out immediately. Part of my job is to be inconspicuous, to fit in anywhere, but here even I stood out as an outsider.

Three patched members of the Gruesome Crew gang leaned against the bar, beer bottles in hand, laughing in that carefree way of the intoxicated. At a table, three minor criminals chatted to a greasy man in a suit. In one booth, a party of four had been reduced to only three who were conscious. In all cases, tattoos and shaved heads were more evident than unblemished skin and hair. Footwear was generally of the stamping and kicking variety.

I ordered a sparkling grape juice at the bar so I could keep my wits about me. The barmaid gave me an odd look, as if I'd asked for a bottle of warm milk, but she filled a glass for me and handed it over.

"Is Harry here?" I asked because both the people working at the bar were women.

"I'm Harry. It's short for Harriet."

I nodded. "I'm supposed to meet a guy called Brock. He said you'd point him out to me."

She glanced around. "I can't see him. Sit down, and I'll let him know where you are when he gets here."

"Thanks." I found an empty booth and slid in on a cushioned seat. The table hadn't been cleared of the previous customers' glasses. I pushed them aside.

Deepa came in. Heads turned, and I silently fumed as a couple of patrons ogled her up and down and exchanged lewd comments, judging by their expressions. She ignored them and made her way to the bar, ordered a Pimms, and surveyed the room. Our gaze met and held for a few moments before she turned back to collect her drink. She sat at a small table near my booth.

We waited at least ten minutes. I kept a close eye on everyone the barmaid, Harry, spoke to, so I could scope out who I was meeting. Soon, my drink was almost gone.

A man approached the bar. I couldn't see his face until Harry pointed at me and he turned in my direction.

I recognised Brock immediately. So did Deepa—I heard her sharp intake of breath. Brock was the guy who'd attacked me in my car. The car that he said had been stolen from him.

149

Chapter 33

BROCK DID A DOUBLE-TAKE when he saw me. For a few seconds, I thought he might drop his drink and bolt. He checked behind himself, maybe to see if the police were coming for him, then relaxed and sauntered over. If he'd noticed Deepa at the nearby table, he gave no indication of it.

He plonked his pint of beer on the table. "You again. Did you really get my number from Stuart—may his soul rest in peace—or was that a ploy to get me to meet you? What do you really want?"

I took my P.I. licence from my pocket and showed it to him. "I've got a few questions for you, if you don't mind." I fished out one of my business cards and gave it to him. He pocketed it.

"Yeah? Well, I do mind. Why should I talk to you about anything? Unless it's about you returning my car."

"The car you stole from someone yourself, you mean. No, it's nothing to do with that. It's to do with Stuart Baker."

Brock stopped scowling. He took a long swig of his beer before answering. "What about Stuart? May his soul rest in peace."

"May his soul rest in peace." I'd echoed the words before I'd even realised. "A man like him must have accrued a few enemies in his time."

"And friends." Brock gave a glimmer of a smile. It faded quickly.

"More enemies than friends, I'd guess. Any who might have wanted to kill him? For revenge, maybe?" A tinge of bitterness flavoured my voice.

Brock shook his head. "I wouldn't know about that. I only did occasional jobs for him. That's all."

"You did a job for him recently, I believe?"

"How do you know that?"

"I learned that from him." Or, rather, I learned it from a note I found when searching his house.

Brock seemed to accept this. Maybe he believed I was on the level. "You investigating Stuart's death? May his soul rest in peace."

"May his—" I interrupted myself. I wanted his soul to rot in hell. "Yes, I'm investigating. That's why I want to know about any enemies he had."

"As I said, I don't know anything about any enemies."

I glanced sideways at Deepa. She was discreetly paying attention, her phone in her hand, possibly recording our conversation amid the hubbub from the other patrons.

I tilted my head. "Mind telling me what job you did for Stuart?"

Brock's eyes flashed anger. "Why should I tell you that?"

"Maybe it has something to do with his death."

"I doubt it."

I leaned forward. "I won't inform the police about it. I don't care what dodgy thing you did on his behalf, but if you tell me what it involved, I can investigate whether it came back on your friend Stuart. The police won't be able to do that, but I will." I shrugged. "Of course, I can't force you to tell me, but if you want to ensure all avenues of investigation into his death are covered, you'd help me out here."

Brock seemed to consider this. His mouth turned down. His eyebrows scrunched together. Clearly, it was a tricky decision for him.

"I can give you a name, but I want something in return."

Here we go. How much palm grease was he going to ask for? "Yeah, what?"

"I want my fucking car back."

I shook my head in what I hoped was an apologetic manner. "I can't do that. I've already sold it on. There was a problem with it." The lie slipped out so easily I almost believed it myself.

"What problem? I never had a problem with the car. You're lying."

151

"No, the owner before you spotted it and accosted me. He said he'd go to the police. I had to get rid of it quickly."

Brock stared at me, trying to figure out if I was telling the truth. I held his gaze without blinking. Finally, he glanced away. "Damn. I loved that car."

"Yeah. Sorry about that. Anything else you want, or is justice for your friend enough?" I felt like a criminal. Lying outright, making promises I didn't know if I could keep.

"Okay. If you find his killer, that's good enough for me. The guy you should check out is Jaxon Coles. He runs a software company called SuperGames Apps."

I nodded. "Jaxon Coles, SuperGames Apps. Did he have any idea that Baker was behind whatever it was you did?"

"Maybe. I wasn't involved in that part of the plan."

"All right. One last question. Where were you at around eight o'clock on Friday night?"

Brock's nostrils flared. His face reddened. "Are you suggesting what I think you're suggesting? That I killed him?"

"I'm just asking. It's routine questioning. I'd appreciate an answer."

"Fuck you. You stole my car, then called me asking for help to do your job. I've been cooperative, I've helped you out with nothing in return, and you insult me like that. I should punch you in the mouth."

Silence descended on the pub. Somehow, amidst all the rowdiness of several groups talking, Brock's raised voice had caught the attention of several patrons. Heads turned in our direction.

"Fight! Fight!"

One of the Gruesome Crew gang members banged his pint glass on the bar counter, as if to egg us into a brawl. The suited guy and his likely henchmen joined in, thumping their table with their fists. The barmaids both ducked behind the bar. Deepa thrust her phone into a pocket and stood.

I tried to diffuse the situation. "Look, Brock, I'm not accusing you of anything. I have to—"

He leaned across the table and punched me so hard my head spun ninety degrees. I flopped sideways onto the padded seat.

"Fight! Fight!"

Most of the patrons were watching now. I scooted out from behind the table at the same time as Brock. "Let's not fight. I simply want to eliminate you from the investigation."

Brock swung at me again. This time I blocked it and punched him in the stomach, not too hard, but enough to make him pause.

He didn't pause. His next swing sent me to the floor, seeing stars.

The pub was in an uproar. Shouts of encouragement filled the air. Unfortunately, none of them were for me.

I stumbled to my feet, blood dripping from the side of my mouth down my chin.

Brock raised his fists once again.

Deepa moved in like a flash, gripping something in one hand. It was silvery metallic, but it flexed like a whip. She struck Brock across the arms with it. He gave a brief cry of pain and staggered back.

I reached for her outstretched hand. She seized my wrist and half pulled, half dragged me through the pub. Someone stepped forward, snarling, and Deepa slashed with her metallic whip, hitting him across the hip. He retreated with a groan. His companion started forward to block us, but I shoved him back.

The noise in the pub increased. Behind us, chairs crashed to the floor, people shouted, glass smashed and scuffles broke out. I glanced back. The Gruesome Crew trio had attacked the three guys sitting with the suited man, who was trying to keep out of their way. They traded punches and headbutts. Brock was scanning around for us.

Harry rose from behind the bar, wielding a shotgun, shouting for order.

We made it outside. The chilly night air cleared my head and sharpened my senses. Now I pulled Deepa forward. "To the car. Quickly!"

We hurried around the corner. A hooded stranger stood by the car, suspiciously staring through the passenger window. At the sound of us running, he glanced up, saw the weapon Deepa still carried, and scarpered.

Deepa thrust out her hand. "Keys!"

I dug them out of my pocket and handed them over. She was right; I was dazed and not in any condition to drive.

We got into the car. She started it up and screeched a U-turn, heading away from the Got Inn.

Chapter 34

I WOKE THE NEXT morning in my apartment. Chelsea hadn't been home when I'd returned the previous night, so I had no choice but to hope the police didn't come knocking on my door.

A shower revitalised me. Though I'd showered after getting home the previous night, I still imagined the murk and grime of the Got Inn infesting the pores of my body. I had a minor headache and slugged back some paracetamol and coffee.

I googled the contact details for that guy Brock had mentioned—Jaxon Coles, SuperGames Apps. The company was part of an office block in Baddington. Jaxon's mobile number was listed on their website. I noted it down.

A news article in the search results caught my eye. SuperGames Apps had suffered a break-in a few days ago. No equipment had been taken, but the intruder had wiped the main server's content. Brock's work, maybe?

I put on my coat and hat and left home. It was already ten thirty. For once, it was warming up a little. Spring was not far away, bringing new life to Quake City. Not for Baker, though. He'd stay as lifeless as stale bread.

After a second coffee and some toast, I fed Torquemada. As he sat purring contentedly on my lap, I phoned Deepa, but she didn't answer. I'd dropped her at home after we left the pub. I was sure no one had followed us. What if I was wrong, and they'd attacked Deepa in her apartment? I shuddered.

The cat noticed and peered up at me.

"I'll phone once more, Torquemada. If she doesn't answer, I'd better drive over to check on her. Make sure she's all right."

Ten minutes later, I reached Deepa's apartment in Splitstown. I rang the buzzer outside, but there was no answer to that either. My worry increased. What had happened to her?

My phone rang. I breathed a sigh of relief when I saw it was Deepa. "Hey, what's up? I've been phoning you."

"I'm at the *Richter Mail* offices. My editor wants to talk to me about the article I wrote. Said he might want me to do a series, 'the conman's crimes'. He's late, though. I'm still waiting for him to get here. I'll call you when I'm free, okay?"

"All right. I'm glad you're okay."

"Why wouldn't I be?"

"I don't know. This case—"

"Thanks for thinking about me. That's sweet. Talk later." She hung up.

I stared through the glassed door of her apartment building, feeling a little like a fool. She'd probably not heard the phone when I'd called earlier, and I'd rushed over without due cause. What would she think if she knew?

Time to contact Jaxon Coles. I dialled his number. A gruff voice answered. "Coles here. Who's this?"

"Mr Coles. I'm Danny Ashford, private investigator."

"What do you want? I don't need the services of a private dick." His voice was familiar, but I couldn't place it.

"I'm not offering you my services. I only have a few questions I'd like to run past you. Do you mind if we meet somewhere for a coffee? I'll pay." My expenses account could probably just handle that.

"No, I don't have time or inclination for that. I'm trying to recover my business after a break-in. Say what you want over the phone."

I'd rather interview him in person, but he hadn't left me any choice. "I'm investigating the recent crimes of a local conman by the name of Baker."

"I don't know anything about a conman. I really can't help you."

"It's possible he had something to do with the break-in to your offices.

156

Was anything taken? Any unusual communications afterwards?"

"Such as?"

"Demands for money, threats to expose secrets, blackmail, anything of that nature."

"Of course not. Even if there were, I wouldn't tell you. It'd affect the reputation of my company and me personally."

"I understand." Though I didn't, really. Jaxon's answers brushed off my questions too quickly, as if he'd prepared for questions like these. Perhaps he'd already answered the same questions from reporters. "The guy I'm investigating sometimes used false names. Does the name Jonathan Goodfellow mean anything to you?"

There was a pause before his answer. "Not in the slightest."

"All right. Now, this might sound like a strange question, but I'm asking it to everyone. Where were you on Friday night at around eight o'clock?"

"I was in the office. A few of us had a late work meeting."

"That is late."

"We watched a live webinar on some relevant code design features we're interested in."

"Fascinating." My voice was as dry as a parched desert.

"Yes, truly inspiring."

"Thanks for your time, Jaxon. Good luck with your games app. What is it about, do you mind me asking?"

"Not at all. Maybe you'll be a future customer. It's a kickboxing game. Something I designed myself. I've had years of training, so designing a virtual game seemed like the obvious next step to monetise that knowledge."

"Right. Of course." I had no idea what nonsense this was. Or why his gruff voice sounded familiar. Meanwhile, I was thinking of how to check his alibi. Ask his employees? They'd back him up, of course; they'd have to.

Jaxon cut into my thoughts. "So, just out of interest... what's the story with this conman you were asking about?"

"Oh, not a lot. He was found dead two days ago. The police are looking into it, and I'm running a parallel investigation."

"Any idea what he was up to, this conman, Stuart Baker?"

"All kinds of misdeeds. Please tell me, Jaxon, how did you know his first name was Stuart?"

"You mentioned it before."

"No, I only referred to him by his last name."

"Oh, well, I must have read about him in the newspaper."

Jaxon's comments didn't add up. "But you told me you'd never heard of a conman called Baker."

"It slipped my mind. I've got to go now. Good luck with your investigation." He finished the call.

Chapter 35

Day 8 (Monday, 21 August), morning

I RETURNED HOME, frustrated, and sat on the sofa with Torquemada and a strong coffee to clear my head.

My talk with Jaxon Coles had revealed little except that he was an arrogant, rude liar. I was sure he knew of Baker, even if he knew him under a different name, but he'd flat out denied that. And he claimed he had an alibi. I might have to check that out later.

Similarly, I'm sure Gabrielle Hocking hadn't told us everything. In fact, she'd barely told us anything. What was that lengthy search through the house for, when all she ended up taking was a few personal bathroom items? No, there was a lot more going on with her than she'd revealed.

Then there was Brock. I didn't even know his last name. He readily admitted to working for Baker. He'd probably been the guy responsible for wiping the server at Coles' software company. Industrial espionage? Or was there such a thing as software kidnapping? I didn't know. He'd refused to tell me where he was on the evening Baker was killed too.

I had to dig further into all this. And what about Sarah, the ex? I should question her further. And Mary Sanchez.

There was a knock at the door. I froze. Was that Nadia, the landlady? Sweat broke out on my brow. Would I have to leave via the window to get away?

"Danny? Answer the door. I know you're in there." The voice was soft, not the harsh, grasping voice of Nadia. It was Chelsea.

I opened the door, and she came in without waiting to be invited. She wore a long t-shirt bearing the slogan 'Muddle Earth' with a huge green question mark, some kind of comment on how we humans were screwing up the planet and did not know how to reverse it. That was my interpretation, anyway.

Chelsea stuffed her hands into the back pockets of her jeans. "I got called into work last night. You weren't around, so I couldn't let you in to my place. Sorry if that didn't work out for you."

"That's okay. No one came looking for me. Thanks, anyway."

"Don't get too relaxed. The cops came here a little while ago, but you were out. No, wait. They wanted to speak to me first. After that, they decided they needed to talk to you again. I said you were out, and they left."

I frowned. "Did they say why they wanted to talk to me again?"

"No."

"Or when they'll be back?"

"No. I think they weren't going far, just to get coffees or doughnuts or something like that. They eat a lot of fast food on TV, don't they?"

"Yeah. You've got to eat and drink whenever you get the chance when you're investigating."

"What's going on, Danny?"

I shrugged. "They might want to tell me in person they've eliminated me from the investigation, that's all. And apologise, of course. That'd be thoughtful of them." I doubted it, though. More likely they had more irritating questions.

"I guess. They could have apologised to me. They woke me up. It was only eleven."

"How inconsiderate of them. Was it that inspector with the ginger moustache? O'Toole?"

"Yeah, and a female officer with him."

I nodded. That would probably have been Debbie, the new sergeant.

"Nadia came around too. When you didn't answer, she asked me if I knew where you were. I said you'd told me you would be out all day."

"Great, thanks." That gave me another day to find the money to pay my outstanding rent.

Chelsea closed the distance between us. "Is there anything I can do to help?"

"Actually, there is. Can I sleep at your place tonight?"

Chelsea quirked an eyebrow in response. "Are you expecting sex?"

"No. I didn't mean like that. I need to hide from the landlady."

"And the police, too, I suppose."

"That would give me more time to prove my innocence and raise the money to pay Nadia. And pay for my car. If I'm stuck in jail, I won't have a chance."

"I see. Fine, then. Remember I sleep late, so don't be noisy in the morning."

"I can stay, then?"

"Sure. For one night to give you time to sort out your shit."

"Thanks, Chelsea."

"No problem. We need to watch out for each other. I'll get going. I need to pick up something from a repair shop. See you later."

After Chelsea left, I headed downstairs. It was lunchtime. I'd have to go to a nearby bakery because I had nothing suitable to eat in the apartment.

I'd no sooner stepped out the door when a hand clasped my shoulder.

I froze.

Chapter 36

Day 8 (Monday, 21 August), morning

"GOING SOMEWHERE?" Sergeant Debbie Hilton stepped out from behind me. Handcuffs jangled on her belt. She didn't let go of my shoulder.

"Out to get lunch." I tried to sound nonchalant and sophisticated, but I probably sounded like someone who doesn't have the time or skills to prepare their own food.

"Never mind that. I'll give you a sandwich down at the station."

I groaned. Not again.

Debbie escorted me to a police car parked nearby. Inspector O'Toole sat in the driver's seat, fiddling with his phone. He tucked it away as I was gently encouraged into the back seat.

O'Toole turned to face me. "Nice of you to join us."

"What do you want from me? I answered all your questions on Saturday night."

"Ah, but now we have more questions."

I fumed. This wasn't helping me—it was wasting my time. Not only that, they might not let me leave. Then my investigation would grind to a halt, and I'd have no way of proving my innocence and recovering the stolen money. "What do you want to know?"

"We'll talk about it at the station." He turned back and started the car now that Debbie had got into the passenger seat.

Two minutes later, we pulled up in the Crumbledon police station car park.

"We could have walked, you know, Inspector. It's not far."

O'Toole chuckled. "I don't walk anywhere if I can drive."

In the same bleak, impersonal interview room I'd been in last time, I sat across the table from them both. Debbie gave me a strong, bitter coffee. She'd forgotten the sandwich. I didn't bother asking for it.

O'Toole leaned forward, the chair creaking beneath him. He turned the digital recording on and declared the preliminaries of the time and people present. "Let's get straight to it. The reason I wanted to have this conversation here rather than at your apartment is—"

"Don't say it's because of the quality of the coffee."

"Ha. No. This is a more formal interview in which we want to double-check your whereabouts on last Friday evening. We're particularly interested in where you were at eight o'clock. Mind telling us again?"

"Sure. As I've already told you, I got home at eight o'clock and spent some time with my neighbour, Chelsea Whitlam. She can confirm that if you ask her. Apparently, you spoke to her this morning, so what's the problem?"

"She says she doesn't think she saw you before half-past eight."

"No, it was definitely eight o'clock."

O'Toole shook his head. "That's not what she says."

I fumed quietly. "Tell me exactly what she said, then."

Debbie spoke up. "If I may, Inspector. Ms Whitlam said she left for work at exactly nine thirty. She said that she spent about an hour with you. Working backwards, that means she said you arrived home at around eight thirty, not eight o'clock."

"Wait a minute. She said she spent 'about an hour' with me. 'About' is not an accurate description—it's an approximation. She's not sure when I arrived home, that's all you can infer from that."

Debbie nodded. "You're right. The important thing is that she isn't sure of the time. Therefore, we can't be sure whether you were at home at the time of Stuart Baker's murder."

"I don't believe this. I was home at eight on the dot. I told you that."

O'Toole shrugged. "I'd like to believe you, Danny, but..."

"But what?"

"You're not beyond telling the occasional falsehood if it suits you, are you?"

I reddened. Partly from embarrassment, but mostly from anger. "How dare you?"

The inspector remained impassive. "I'm simply saying it as it is."

I turned to Debbie. "Turn the recording off, please. May I talk to the inspector alone for a few minutes?"

She turned to O'Toole, and he nodded. With a glare at me, she switched it off, got up and left the room, shutting the door behind her.

I said nothing. After a few moments, O'Toole filled the void. "I know what you're going to say. You're going to remind me I owe you a few favours for all the help you've given me over the years. Aren't you?"

"Of course I am. It's the truth. You wouldn't be an inspector if I hadn't helped you solve some tricky cases… and helped cover up a few irregularities. Do you want the superintendent to hear about your past questionable investigative techniques?"

"No, I do not. See here, Danny, this is the situation. It doesn't look good for you. Now, I don't know if you confronted that conman and things got out of hand—"

"I didn't even see the guy. I certainly didn't kill him."

"Yes, we have your word for that, and a whole lot of evidence that says you were at his house that evening, and the timing of when you got home is a little uncertain. Surely, you can see why we have to follow due process here?"

"Come on, Inspector. You can't possibly think I killed that bastard. What would be the motive?"

"Revenge. He stole from you and your client. But maybe it was an accident. You fought, and he fell over the balcony. If that's the case, now's the time to tell us."

"That didn't happen."

"I see."

"So, I demand you let me go. If you don't, I'll phone my lawyer again. She'll complain to the superintendent about your harassment of me."

"There's no need to go that far. I'm being lenient on you. I could charge you, put you in the cells for forty-eight hours, but I haven't done that. I'll let you go out of professional courtesy. For now."

That caught me by surprise. Perhaps my unsubtle threat had eventually sunk in. Or maybe O'Toole really did respect and believe me. Miracles occur sometimes, after all.

"I appreciate that, Inspector. One more thing—if you're not already investigating Baker's bank accounts, you should. His personal accounts and those of his businesses. Some, if not most, of that money will be from the proceeds of his crimes."

"Thanks, Danny. I'll pass that on to the Financial Crimes team."

I stood to go. The inspector grabbed my arm.

"Danny, don't leave town. And be careful."

"Be careful of what?"

"Come on, I know you. You're going to get yourself into trouble no matter what I say. You're going to go out there and try to prove your innocence and solve this case using whatever means necessary. Just make sure that you don't break the law, otherwise you'll be back here and slammed into a cell in no time. Then you'll be screwed. The superintendent is demanding results from me, and as soon as I tell her the evidence we've got that points to you, she's going to want you locked up for sure."

I stared at him.

O'Toole continued. "Obviously, my team and I are hard at work trying to determine what actually happened, and we'll get to the bottom of it as we usually do."

Yeah, right. Occasionally, if you get a lucky break, you solve a crime. "If I'm stuck in the cells, I can't help you solve this."

"I know." The inspector leaned closer. "So, I repeat... be careful. Don't get into trouble. And, whatever you do, be damned quick about it."

I left the police station with his words ringing in my ears. Though O'Toole often talked a lot of rubbish, this time I'd listened intently. I had limited time before the superintendent would want to close the case, and then I'd be facing months in Quake City's jail on remand until trial. And I was damned sure I wouldn't survive that long, because some tough perps in there weren't grateful for my part in having them arrested and jailed.

No, I had to solve this case if I didn't want to end up murdered in the cells with a sharpened toothbrush.

It was a few minutes' walk home. The day was cool, overcast now, threatening rain, maybe thunder. It matched my mood perfectly. I phoned Julie Nicholls, my lawyer.

She answered almost immediately. "Danny, what's going on? Have you found my money yet?"

She caught me by surprise with that. I was about to tell her about being questioned by the police again. With all that was going on, I'd almost forgotten that she hired me to find the forty grand Baker had scammed out of her.

"Not yet, but I'm on it." That was stretching the truth a little. Although, I'd start on it as soon as I could.

"It should be easier to recover the money now, right? Baker's dead. He can't move or hide the money any more. So, what's the problem? Why haven't you found it?"

"It's complicated, Julie. As you know, I spent most of Saturday in the police station. Give me a chance. I'll get right on it."

"You just said you were already on it. Which is it?"

I could have slapped my forehead. "I am, I promise."

"Danny, I need that money back urgently. And, speaking of that, I'll send you an invoice for the work I've done for you so far. Would you mind paying that by tomorrow?"

"Julie, I'm not sure if I mentioned it, but I'm having a few cash flow issues at the moment. I thought that maybe we could offset your invoice against my own later on."

"That's not going to work for me." Julie's voice sounded strained. She'd spoken a little faster, higher pitched.

"Why don't you tell me what's going on?"

"I need that money back. Never mind why. That guy was a conman. Surely, the police know all about him by now. Make a claim on the funds or whatever you have to do. Or… or… You know a hacker or someone, don't you? Get that bloody money back for me. How difficult can it be?"

I was about to answer when she disconnected. I shook my head. Something was going on that she hadn't told me about. When she'd hired me, she'd been angry about the money, but now she sounded desperate. What had changed?

She hadn't even given me a chance to tell her that I'd been pulled in for questioning again.

Chapter 37

Day 8 (Monday, 21 August), afternoon

I WAS STARVING, so I stopped at Quake Burgers for a late lunch. There was barely any money left of what Julie had given me. Being pulled into the police station for questioning again had been irksome, but it showed me the police had got nowhere with the investigation. The only suspect they had was me.

Who else could I talk to? A list of victims, past and present, would really help me out here. But if he'd had one, Baker had either hidden it so well that no one had found it, or the police had it and couldn't or wouldn't access the information.

That reminded me of something. Gabrielle, his supposed girlfriend, combing the house. She'd said she only wanted to retrieve personal items, but I didn't believe that for a second. She'd dug into every drawer and cupboard there and even peered under furniture. No, she'd been searching for something that might have been concealed. What, though?

Was it a list of Baker's victims? That would imply she knew about his scams and cons. Or maybe she was looking for anything that incriminated her. Either way, she'd found nothing of the sort. The police may have got there first.

I needed to talk to her again.

Who else? Mary Sanchez, who took over the 88 Club immediately after Baker's death. Surely, that was too much of a coincidence. Had they signed a deal whereby she'd bought the club or was to manage it? Or was there foul play at work?

I left Quake Burgers. My confidence was returning now that I wasn't trapped in a police interview room. It was up to me to solve the case and prove my innocence before I got arrested.

The 88 Club wouldn't be open for business in the middle of the afternoon, but I drove there to see if the new owner or manager was there. A solitary heavy-set bouncer guarded the main entrance. I approached him.

"Is Mary Sanchez here?"

"Maybe." He flicked his chin up at me. "Who are you, and what do you want with the boss?"

"That's between me and her. Is she in or not?"

He eyed me suspiciously. "Yeah, she is. You didn't say who you are."

"I'll introduce myself, thanks." I made a move to go past the bouncer.

He blocked the entranceway. "We're closed."

I'd lost patience by now. My freedom, my life, was on the line. I needed to work fast to solve this case. I stepped forward again. When he blocked me this time, I shouldered him into the door jamb, then struck him on the neck. He dropped like a stone to the steps.

The bar area was empty. I advanced upstairs. Would there be more bodyguards? Baker seemed to have them everywhere, though that was when the club was open. At the top of the stairs, I turned left. Still no one. I knew the way to Baker's old office. The door was open. Inside, a middle-aged woman with red hair and horned glasses sat examining receipts and accounts.

My appearance startled her, and she jumped to her feet, reaching for her handbag hanging on the back of the chair.

"Relax. I'm just here to talk. Are you Mary Sanchez, the new owner?"

"Yes, I am. Who are you, and what do you want?" She clutched her lumpy handbag to her side. Was the lump a concealed gun? Probably.

I spread out my hands where she could see them and stayed in the doorway. "My name's Danny Ashford. I'm a private investigator. I've got some unfinished business with Stuart Baker."

169

"Is that so?" Her voice was strident, yet dismissive. "Then you're screwed. He's dead. I bought this place from him that same day."

"What a coincidence." I gave her my best deadpan expression.

"I don't appreciate sarcasm, and I don't like P.I.s. The two combined are intolerable. Get out."

I ignored her command, but kept a close eye on her handbag in case she scrambled for her gun. Surreptitiously, I brushed the pocket of my coat where I kept my Glock. It rested comfortingly inside.

She glared at me over the top of her glasses. "I told you to leave."

I decided to play it cool and try to calm the situation. "I apologise for my rudeness. I'm trying to figure out Baker's last movements. You have a reputation as a smart businesswoman around town. That's why I think you'd know of any personal enemies he might have had." I was totally guessing at that. I didn't know anything much about Mary Sanchez at all.

She mellowed. "Yes, I'm successful and respected. I have to say I didn't know Stuart Baker well, but he came across as the kind of man who would make a lot of enemies. Not me, though. Our interactions were purely business. He'd decided to get out of the club business and consider other opportunities. As I was already the owner and manager of a local club, I was the obvious person to approach to buy his business. It was purely good timing and luck on my part that we completed the paperwork for the deal just before his untimely demise."

Some of what she'd said might be true, but it sounded rehearsed. How much was lies? Had she forced her own luck? "Any idea who might have wanted him dead?"

"His staff told me he harassed them constantly, but I can't imagine any of them would have killed him for that. They could simply quit, couldn't they? By the way, that's changing under my management. I'll treat the exotic dancers and hostesses with respect."

"I'm sure they'd appreciate that. It'd be a welcome change for them. One other thing… where were you on Friday night around eight o'clock?"

Mary scowled. "You think I might have killed him? Of course not. I was at various places in Sintown all evening from seven o'clock onwards. Several people can verify that."

"You mean customers and drunks."

"I'm not passing judgement on them. They can do what they want, and some of them saw me around. And exactly what do you think you're insinuating? Fuck off. I don't want to help you any further." She turned her back on me.

"Just one thing more, please... do you mind telling me what lawyer arranged the sale on Baker's behalf? I'd like to talk to them in case they can help me."

Mary paused so long, I thought she wouldn't answer, but she relented and faced me. "Oh, lawyers weren't involved. It was a private deal we carried out. We signed the papers over coffee in a nearby café. It took only a few minutes and saved us both thousands in legal fees." She smiled.

Something wasn't right. Had she really been that lucky, buying the business hours before Baker's death? Or was she smiling because she was lying and didn't care if I believed her?

"What café was that? I'll get a coffee when I leave here. I don't know the area well, so I'd appreciate your recommendation."

She regarded me suspiciously. I tried to appear innocent and unsuspecting, a demeanour I've endeavoured to develop over time. It didn't come naturally.

"St Mark's Square café, other side of the street, down half a block. They serve great coffee and lamingtons."

"Great. Thanks for that, and for being so forthcoming with information."

"No problem. Danny, isn't it? I hope I'll see you back here as a customer sometimes."

"Sure. Thanks again."

The bouncer in the doorway was stirring awake. I stepped over him on my way out.

I made my way to the café. It was a small, untidy place crammed between a locksmith's and an op shop. Its outlook was onto a run-down part of Crumblo Street. There wasn't a square or piazza in sight; the main square in Quake City was cordoned off in the Red Zone about a kilometre away. I doubted this was the sort of establishment St Mark would frequent if he'd been visiting.

A couple of customers sat at a corner table, chatting quietly. I found a spot in the window and ordered a coffee and a lamington. The waitress scribbled my order on her notepad. While I waited, I kept an eye on the 88 Club. The bouncer was finally on his feet. He stumbled inside, presumably to speak to his boss, then resumed his position at the door. I wondered if Mary had sat here, at this very table, watching the comings and goings at the 88 Club before she acquired it for herself.

The waitress plonked the drink and cake on my table and presented me with a bill that made my eyes bulge. Ten bucks for the coffee, fifteen for the cake. Now I understood why the café named itself after St Mark's Square. It had nothing to do with the views, and everything to do with the exorbitant prices. So why did they have any customers?

I held up the bill. "This is damned expensive."

The waitress turned back. "Our customers pay for discretion. We have a lot of regulars."

"Okay, I get that. Maybe you can help me out. Do you know Stuart Baker and Mary Sanchez?"

"What did I just say about discretion?"

I didn't answer. I took out my wallet and withdrew a fifty-dollar note, putting it on the bill. "Keep the change. Were they customers here?"

"Yeah."

I waited, but the waitress didn't expand on that, so I asked another question. "Ever see them in here together? Especially this week? From what I understood, they weren't friends." I was testing here. I simply assumed they weren't friends because they were competitors.

The waitress glanced from me to the fifty-dollar note. Her meaning was clear.

I took out another fifty and added it to the first one. This was turning out to be an expensive afternoon tea. It had better be a damn good coffee and cake. With a side helping of getting my ass out of trouble.

"I've been working all week, and I've never seen them together. They were here at the same time once, a few weeks ago, but not together." She snatched the money and the bill and dashed away.

I knew that I wouldn't get any more out of her, but that was enough. Mary Sanchez had been lying about doing the deal with Baker in here. It hadn't happened.

I drank the coffee and ate the cake. Both were delicious.

Chapter 38

Day 8 (Monday, 21 August), evening

I RETURNED HOME, keeping a wary eye out for my landlady. I didn't see her, so I went upstairs and into my apartment, where I hung up my hat and coat. Torquemada smooched up to my leg, demanding attention and food and water. I complained to him about the case and how stuck I was with it. I needed a break, some angle, some new piece of evidence that pointed to anyone but me. I suspected everyone. Talking to the cat sometimes helped, but this time I was left as confused as when I'd started.

My phone rang. It was Deepa. I picked it up immediately and answered. "Hey, how are you doing?"

"Great. I'm finished with my work, and I wanted to see where you were at."

I filled her in on my latest trip to the police station and O'Toole's suggestion that I hurry up my own investigation before the superintendent decided she wanted me arrested.

"You're at home, aren't you? I'll come over. We'll talk about the next steps." Deepa disconnected.

She'd be only a few minutes. I could put the kettle on and make us drinks. But before I could do that, Torquemada caught my eye. On the windowsill, he was peering outside and swiping at the window.

I scurried over to check. My landlady, Nadia, had parked her Mercedes across the street. No doubt she was on her way to demand the rent I owed her. The trouble was, I still didn't have it.

She got out of the car and glanced left and right. Hell's teeth, I was right. She was about to cross the street. I drew back from the window in case she glanced up and saw me.

"Thanks, Torquemada."

I hurried out of my apartment, locked the door behind me, and scurried along the hall to Chelsea's door. I tapped on it lightly.

No answer.

I put my ear to the door and heard music. Maybe she hadn't heard me.

The front door downstairs opened. That would be Nadia. I had no time to lose. In seconds, she'd come upstairs and see me.

The handle of Chelsea's door turned freely, and the door swung open. I stepped inside, closing the door quietly behind me.

Chelsea was lying on the floor in a singlet and shorts, arms and legs wheeling in mid-air, keeping time with the music. She glanced at me, stopped her exercise, and rolled forward onto her feet. "Danny. Why didn't you knock before coming in?"

"I did." I kept my voice quiet, then raised one finger to my lips and pointed to the door. Shoes clunked loudly on the stairs outside.

"The landlady?" Chelsea mouthed it slowly, exaggerating the consonants.

I nodded fervently and made a charade of pointing a gun at my head and firing it.

Chelsea grabbed my hand and drew me away from the door. She pulled me through the living room into her bedroom. "Wait here. If she asks, I'll say I haven't seen you."

I breathed a sigh of relief.

The heavy footsteps reached the landing and continued past Chelsea's door and stopped. A knock sounded, but it wasn't on Chelsea's door. It was on mine.

I held my breath. It was impossible for Nadia to hear or sense me in Chelsea's apartment, but in my mind, I'd given her superpowers to root out renters behind in their payments like me.

The apartment building vibrated as she bashed on my door a second time.

"Danny Ashford! You bloody scallywag. You owe me two weeks' rent now. I know you're in there. Come out and pay up."

I stood still in Chelsea's bathroom, irrationally afraid that the least movement or sound might alert her to my presence. In the living room, Chelsea's music switched to a song with a faster beat. She was exercising again.

More thunderous bangs sounded from down the hall. Would Nadia smash the door's frosted glass with her thumps? Wouldn't she give up?

"You fucking worthless asshole. Don't hide from me. I demand you pay up now. If I bloody have to come back, I'll evict you. I'll blacklist you so you won't get a room anywhere in Quake City. I'll ruin you, you fucking wastrel."

I clenched my teeth, glad I wasn't at home. Nadia's temper had really let loose. A few seconds of silence from the hallway followed. Perspiration beaded on my forehead. What was she up to?

A door opened and closed. My door. I fumed. She'd gone inside to check if I was there after all. That was an infringement of my rights as a tenant. Not that she cared.

The door slammed shut a minute later. The heavy footsteps resumed. Then a knock came at Chelsea's door.

I swallowed involuntarily.

Chelsea answered it. "Yes, Ms Hart?"

"Oh, hi, dearie. Please call me Nadia. I hope you don't mind me troubling you for a minute. I was in the neighbourhood and called by, hoping to speak to your neighbour, Danny."

"I haven't seen him, Nadia. Is it important?"

"Oh, no, not really. We have a few things to discuss, that's all."

"You know, I think he's working really hard at the moment. He's hardly ever home. Not that I'm keeping an eye on him or anything, you understand."

"All right, dearie. Thank you. I hope you're settling in nicely."

"Yes, I am, thanks."

"Bye for now."

The door closed. I remained still while the boots clomped downstairs in case the slightest movement might cause a noise that brought Nadia running back. Chelsea crossed into my field of vision to the living room window, where she stood watching the street.

Finally, she turned away and beckoned me. "She's gone."

I exhaled a breath I hadn't realised I'd been holding. "Great. Thanks, Chelsea."

"I can't keep doing this for you, you know."

"I appreciate it. I'm in a bad spot at the moment. Once I solve this case, clear my name, and find the missing money, everything can go back to normal." I made it sound so easy.

She gave me a strange look. "I'll get back to my exercise routine. Hang around if you want. You're going to stay here tonight, aren't you?"

"Yeah, if it's not a problem. Nadia might come back."

"It's fine." Chelsea got into position on her exercise mat.

The stairs creaked. Someone else was coming upstairs. It couldn't be the landlady this time unless she'd removed her boots.

Chelsea got to her feet and cracked the door open to see who it was, then threw it open. "It's your girlfriend." She returned to her exercise mat.

Deepa strode along the landing and stopped outside Chelsea's door when she saw me. "Danny." Consternation swept over her face. "What's going on?"

"I had to evade the landlady. She was just here to speak to me. Come on in."

Deepa came inside, and I shut the door behind her. She glanced at Chelsea, who was lying on her back on the floor, panting, pumping her hips up and down. "Am I interrupting something?"

Chelsea answered before I could speak. "Never mind me. Just do your own thing. Danny's staying here to avoid the landlady until he can pay his rent."

I caught Deepa's eye. "It's not what you think. I'm going to sleep on the sofa."

Deepa rolled her eyes. Her expression darkened for a moment. "Sure you are. Fine. How's the investigation?"

I glanced at Chelsea. It probably wouldn't hurt to discuss the case in front of her, but it'd be unprofessional. Better to go out. I didn't want to risk returning to my own apartment in case Nadia came back.

"Let's take a walk. We can discuss it on the way."

Chapter 39

I GRABBED MY HAT and coat from my apartment, and we set off towards the river, a few minutes' walk away. Weeping willows hugged together along the riverbank, tendrils of leaves trailing in the water. A few people walked dogs. It was peaceful there. A sharp contrast to the turbulence in my mind.

I paused and peered out over the river. "I'm worried I'll run out of time trying to find the killer before the police come to arrest me."

Deepa stopped in the shade of a tree. "Where have you got to?"

"Baker had his sticky fingers in a lot of different crime pies. He hired someone called Brock to do a job for him. He's the guy I spoke to in the Got Inn. Would you believe, he's the dude who claimed my car is his."

"Small world."

"Yeah, I guess so. Anyway, he wouldn't tell me where he was when Baker was killed. He took a lot of offence at that question. But he did give me a name—the owner of the software company he'd robbed for Baker."

"Did you check him out too?" Deepa shivered and moved out of the shade. She started walking again.

I hurried to catch up. On the river, a pair of ducks glided in to land with a splash. "I phoned him. He was cagey, wouldn't confirm anything, even the theft, though it's in the newspapers. I didn't like him at all."

"You mean, you think he could be a suspect, or you didn't like him as a person?"

179

"Both."

"Anyone else?"

"Well, there's Gabrielle too. I don't trust her either."

Deepa gave me a sharp look. "Have you told O'Toole about any of these people?"

I shook my head. "No. There's no evidence that any of them have done anything. Hey, when was it you talked to Baker's ex-wife?"

"Friday night at about eight o'clock. I was with her for quite a while."

"That was the time of the murder, according to O'Toole, so that rules her out."

"And me." Deepa chuckled.

"That's not funny. You know I'm still the only suspect the police have."

"Yep, I know, but you'll crack this case, eventually."

"If I don't solve it soon, I'll have to do it from behind bars. Or you'll have to do it for me." I gulped down the anxiety rising from my stomach. Time was running out.

Deepa frowned. "You'd better get a move on, then."

"I'm trying to."

We strolled without talking for a bit. A slow rumble of a mild aftershock rattled under our feet, nothing to be concerned about, but nearby animals reacted. Dogs barked. Ducks quacked. Geese honked. Their cacophony made it hard to think.

My phone rang. It was O'Toole.

"Inspector? How can I help you?"

"Do you want to confess?"

I almost choked on my response. "Of course not. I haven't done anything."

O'Toole laughed. "Relax, Danny, this is just a friendly call. I'd like you to come back to the station. There's something we need to clear up."

I froze. The only way I was going back to the police station at the moment was if the police came to get me and I couldn't evade them. If I turned up willingly, they might not let me leave. My heart rate soared. I stared out over the slow-running river to calm myself. "I'm having a hectic day investigating this case, Inspector. Can't you ask me what you need over the phone?"

O'Toole hesitated before speaking. "I suppose I can. It's about Friday, the night that Baker was murdered. I need to confirm your movements between seven and eleven. That's the time range the coroner gave for Baker's death."

"Wait a minute. You told me earlier that a broken watch pinpointed his death at eight o'clock."

"Yeah, well, it turns out that's not reliable. Our forensics department, Jenny, found slivers of the watch face on the balcony. The second hand was there too. It must have been torn off the watch."

"So, Baker broke it on the balcony railing, not when he landed on the rocks. What difference does that make to anything?"

"It's where the glass and the second hand were found. They were against the wall by the French doors leading from the bedroom. See where I'm going with this?"

Hell's teeth. I did. "You're saying Baker wasn't wearing his watch when the murderer pushed him over the balcony. He'd come out of the shower wearing just a towel, so that's a reasonable assumption. The murderer then found his watch, smashed it, and threw it down to the rocks."

My mind raced ahead. The only point in doing that would be to mislead investigators as to the time of death. The murderer probably adjusted the time to eight o'clock because they could ensure they had an alibi for that time.

"You got it. Except for one thing. It wasn't even his watch. It was one just like it."

I frowned. "How do you know it wasn't his watch?"

"We talked to his ex-partner. His watch had an engraving on the back. This one didn't."

"I see."

O'Toole cleared his throat before continuing. "So, I want to re-check your movements. You said you were at Baker's house before eight—"

"Yes, but I didn't see him, and someone accosted me!"

"So you said."

"I said it because it's true."

"And—remind me—after that?"

"I was at home from about eight o'clock. My neighbour Chelsea was with me until she left for work at about nine thirty."

"That's right, I remember now. Though she said she was with you for an hour before she left for work."

"*About* an hour."

"And after that?"

"I slept on the sofa with an icepack on my head."

"On your own."

"Apart from my cat. Look, Inspector, I was in no condition to go out again. I'm sure my neighbour would confirm that."

"She's not a medical professional, though, is she?"

I fumed. "No."

"So, her opinion on your condition doesn't really count, does it?"

"Inspector, I've answered your questions. If there's nothing else, I need to get back to work."

"That's all for now. Thanks for clarifying that, Danny. I'll pass that on to my superintendent."

My stomach turned to ice. "When?"

"Tomorrow morning. That's the latest I can leave it. She's demanding answers. Don't be surprised if you're picked up for more questioning at the station. Or even arrested."

"Thanks for the heads-up."

"One more thing. The Financial Crimes team got back to me a little earlier about Baker's accounts."

"Already? They've investigated it all today?"

"Not exactly. They said they'll treat his funds as proceeds of crime unless something contrary to that comes to light. After the murder investigation is concluded, they'll confiscate the funds. They won't investigate where the funds came from."

"So, the victims of his cons won't get anything?" I was incredulous.

"Unfortunately, no. The Financial Crimes unit works to its own rules." The inspector lowered his voice. "I expect they skim some of the money they confiscate."

I thought so too. "Thanks for letting me know." Bad luck for my client and I, then. We wouldn't see our money again unless I came up with a creative plan to recover it some other way.

I finished the call. "Shit." I could have thrown my phone into the river.

Deepa seized my arm. "I think I got the gist of that. They're uncertain about the time of death now."

"Yeah, and I'm still a suspect, dammit."

Deepa set her jaw. "We'd better work fast, then."

Chapter 40

I TOLD DEEPA the police would probably confiscate Baker's money and that victims, including my client and I, would get nothing.

She nodded sadly.

We retraced our steps towards my apartment. I needed a damn good game plan.

"What's the next step?" Deepa's words didn't have their usual enthusiasm. Maybe she thought the situation was hopeless. Perhaps she was thinking about me spending the night in Chelsea's apartment. But where else could I go? I couldn't stay with her because the police might think to look there.

I shook my head in frustration. "I don't see how we'll have time to conduct follow-up interviews with everyone connected with the case."

"Then we won't try. Who's had the strongest motive to kill Baker?"

"That's easy. His ex had the most to gain, through her children."

We took the Audi and drove to Sarah Bailey's house in Leanwood. From what Deepa had said, she hated Baker, her ex, for failing to support her and their children, all the while enriching himself.

It was about eight o'clock, and we expected Sarah would be home with the young children settled in bed. I turned to face Deepa. "What time did you leave there on Friday night?"

"I was there between eight and eight thirty, then I caught a cab home."

"So, she could have gone out after that. She had plenty of time to kill Baker

184

before eleven o'clock."

"Yep."

"Her and everyone else." This made me rethink. Was Baker's ex really the most important person to interview now? What about Mary, Gabrielle, Brock or Jaxon?

"Let's see what she's got to say."

We parked outside her house and got out. Lights were on in several rooms. A pale streetlight showed a cracked and potholed driveway, peeling paint on the house, and an overgrown garden.

Deepa knocked on the front door. A security light came on and a woman's voice called out. "Who is it?"

"Sarah, it's Deepa Banwait. I've brought a colleague. Can we talk to you for a few minutes, please?"

The door swung open. Sarah stood there, knife in hand. I pulled Deepa back and stepped in front of her.

Sarah put the knife on a side table. "Sorry, it's for protection. Bad neighbourhood, single mother, vulnerable kids. I can't be too careful."

Deepa pushed past me. "It's okay, Danny. Sarah, I understand. You don't need to explain. Can we come in?"

Sarah opened the door wider and stepped to the side. "Sure."

She showed us into the living room. Once we were settled on the sofa, Sarah sat back and crossed her arms. "What do you want to know?"

Deepa spoke first. "Our condolences on your loss."

"Loss? You mean Stuart?" She guffawed.

I watched her intensely. That wasn't the reaction I'd expected.

Sarah continued. "It's the best thing that's happened to me and my kids for ages. Stuart had no other family. My kids inherit everything in a trust that I'm able to manage for their benefit until they're adults. Stuart had a lot of money hidden away in various places, I'm sure. The twins will get the whole lot." She swept her arm around the room. "We'll be able to move out of his shithole neighbourhood and crappy house into a proper modern home in a much better area. Or maybe out of Quake City altogether. Their lives are going to be so much better."

That was a powerful motive for killing her ex. "Sarah, if his money was earned illegally, it'll be seized by the police, and your kids won't get any of it."

"Come on. It can't all be stolen money. He had an antique business, a fancy car—"

"Which might have been bought with stolen money."

Sarah stared at me, eyes like fiery needles.

Deepa interrupted. "That's not certain at the moment. It's not what we're here about."

"Then what do you want?"

That was my cue. "After you talked to Deepa last Friday night, did you go out anywhere?"

Sarah stared at me as if I was suggesting the impossible. "No, I didn't. The kids were in bed. I couldn't go out."

"Can anyone confirm that?"

"I talked to my mother on the phone for an hour, but I don't remember exactly what time it was. The rest of the time I was reading. Does it matter?" Her eyebrows quirked. "You're not suggesting that I—that I killed Stuart?"

"I'm not suggesting anything, only asking. But you did have a powerful motive. His death could benefit your children directly, and you indirectly." It wouldn't if the police confiscated the money, but Sarah clearly hadn't thought of that.

Sarah's cheeks flushed. "Get out. Get out of my house this instant."

Deepa stood. "I apologise for my colleague. Sometimes he's a bit blunt. I'm sure he didn't mean to offend you."

"Just get out, both of you. Out!" She shouted the last word as she shooed us towards the door.

A child's cry came from upstairs.

"Now see what you've done! You've woken the kids!"

I followed Deepa into the hall and to the front door as quickly as possible. I hadn't expected such a vitriolic reaction from her, but I couldn't have guessed how she would react because I hadn't met her before.

We hurried through the front door and onto the cracked driveway. The security light blinked off, and the door slammed behind us.

"Great work, Danny." Sarcasm dripped from Deepa's voice like butter from hot toast. "Now we won't get anything more out of her." She headed for the car.

I followed, pondering exactly what was behind Sarah's angry reaction. Was it because I'd suggested she could have murdered Baker? Or was it because I'd said the police would confiscate his money and she wouldn't get any of it?

Chapter 41

Day 8 (Monday, 21 August), evening

STUART BAKER WAS DEAD. Brock had never had a chance to challenge him over the issue of the stolen car.

On reflection, though, he doubted Stuart had anything to do with it. He'd always been into bigger schemes, not minor things like stealing cars.

It was eight o'clock. Brock sat by a window in his apartment, turning the memory key over and over in his hands. What should he do with it? It was a copy of the information he'd given to Stuart. See what had happened to him.

The material on the memory key was worth a lot of money. Especially because Brock had wiped the main server of SuperGames Apps after downloading it. Stuart had paid him ten grand for stealing it. Now that Stuart was out of the picture, Brock had the chance to capitalise on the stolen info himself.

Just as well Brock had kept his own copy. He'd written down the contact details for the CEO of SuperGames Apps, too, just in case. Jaxon Coles, he was called. Brock had researched Jaxon. He was a business guy with a background in martial arts trying to make his fortune with video games.

He read in the *Richter Mail* how the company had been robbed and lost all their intellectual property and source code. They were on the verge of epic failure.

Brock didn't know if Stuart had contacted Jaxon before his untimely death or not. If so, how much money would he have demanded for the return of the precious material? Blackmail was dangerous—but lucrative.

He twirled the memory key in his hands, considering the options. The easiest and safest choice was to throw the memory key away and forget about the whole thing. But the alternative could make him a fortune—enough for a year or two, maybe more. How desperate would Jaxon be to get that information back?

He had little to lose by contacting Jaxon, and everything to gain.

Brock put the memory key on the window sill and picked up his phone. He dialled Jaxon's mobile number.

§

Jaxon put down his phone. Interesting. A second person had contacted him to sell his own company's proprietary software back to him. The price: fifty thousand dollars. Somewhat cheaper than the caller three days earlier.

He'd had little choice but to agree to the meeting at nine p.m. Otherwise, SuperGames Apps had no product. They'd go bust before they could redevelop the app. He'd have no alternative but to close the company down.

This was his way out.

He got ready and set off for the Got Inn.

§

Inspector O'Toole was in a foul mood. Overcast cloud and patchy rain made it a dark night, and eleven o'clock was a terrible time to be at a potential murder scene. He'd rather be home tucked up in his warm bed.

He and Sergeant Debbie Hilton stood at the side of a messy alley running behind buildings along Crumblo Street. They watched as Mikey, the coroner, examined the twisted body of a man. Debbie held a torch illuminating the scene. Without that, only the faint glow from a distant streetlight cast any light on the scene.

At the end of the alley by the main street, a constable took a statement from a man who'd spotted someone lying in the alley and called the police. Debbie had spoken to him already. He'd stopped to take a leak on his way home and seen the prone form in the shadows of some rubbish bins at the rear of the Got Inn.

O'Toole pulled his sports jacket around him more closely. He shivered. It was chilly. "Hurry, Mikey. We're freezing our butts off here. And it's late at night, for god's sake. We should all be in bed."

Mikey stepped around the body and regarded the inspector, his expression hard to read at the fringe of the torch's light. "People don't get killed only between nine and five, Inspector. Murderers work at inconvenient times."

O'Toole harrumphed. "So, you're saying it is murder, then?"

"Provisionally, yes. I'll examine the body more thoroughly tomorrow, but I can categorically say this unfortunate man was attacked. He's been hit on the face and his neck is broken. I can't say for sure, but it looks like his head was twisted laterally."

The inspector frowned. "What are you saying?"

Debbie interrupted. "Could he have broken his neck in a fall? Or do you mean that someone broke it for him in a fight?"

Mikey stood. "Neither. It's definitely not the result of a fall; the neck break seems too precise for that. And see his knuckles—there are no signs of grazing or impact damage that would suggest he was in a fight. No, he was attacked and couldn't or didn't fight back. It was probably over quickly. He never stood a chance."

O'Toole grumbled. "Sergeant, search the body. Mikey, how long ago was he killed?"

"About two hours ago, I'd say, based on the body temperature, give or take half an hour."

The inspector glanced at his watch. "You said he was hit on the face. What with? Any idea?"

"I don't know for sure, but my first guess is he was kicked, not punched or hit with something. Then, when he was stunned, the killer moved in and broke his neck with a swift movement."

"Someone who knew what he was doing, then."

"Definitely. There's nothing else I can do here, Inspector. I'll have the body removed to the morgue for examination tomorrow."

"Thanks, Mikey. Debbie, can you find any I.D. on this guy?"

Debbie rifled through the man's pockets. She stood. "I found this." She handed a wallet to O'Toole.

He flipped it open. "Brock Patterson. Never heard of him. Phone the station, will you? Find out what you can about him. See if he's got a record."

"Sure. But I found something else, Inspector."

He jerked his head up. "Yes?"

"He had this in one of his pockets." Debbie handed over a crumpled business card with 'Quake City Investigations' on it. "It's our friend Danny again."

Chapter 42

Day 8 (Monday, 21 August), evening

IT WAS GETTING LATE, and I didn't think Deepa and I could accomplish any more that night. We stopped for a late dinner. I tried to make a good impression, but that took a blow when I wasn't able to pay the bill. Deepa covered it.

I drove her to her apartment in Splitstown and made sure she got inside safely. At least that's what I told myself. Maybe I wanted to see if she would invite me inside, like she had a few days ago. But she didn't, so I went home.

It wasn't until I was climbing the stairs in my apartment building that I remembered I wasn't intending to stay in my own apartment. Chelsea had agreed to let me stay with her until I'd solved the case, so Nadia and the police wouldn't find me so easily. I didn't know whom I was most wary of, but I suspected it was my landlady. The police I could reason with to some extent.

Light seeped from under the door of Chelsea's apartment. Good. She hadn't gone to work yet, or she was having the night off. If she'd gone out, I'd have had no choice but to return to my apartment again or to sleep in my car.

Chelsea answered when I knocked and beckoned me inside. She was casually yet fashionably dressed in jeans with the knees torn and a black t-shirt with the slogan 'Bonsoir'. A pair of reading glasses sat astride her aquiline nose, and she peered over the top of them at me and smiled.

"Hi, Danny. You've been out investigating, I suppose?"

"Yes, I have, but I'm no closer to solving this case yet."

"Cheer up. It can't be that bad. You don't solve every investigation, do you?"

"I try." The one failure being finding the murderers of my parents when I was a child. For all I knew, the killers were still robbing banks and shooting innocent people who got in their way.

"So… how long do you want to stay here?"

This was the first sign Chelsea had given me that I might be imposing on her, but I'd expected that. We'd only just met. "Until the police aren't after me and I've paid my overdue rent, if that's okay. Are you working tonight?"

Chelsea smiled sweetly. "No, it's one of my nights off." She returned to the sofa, propped her glasses on her nose, and resumed reading her chic lit novel.

"Chelsea, I have a small favour to ask you."

She glanced up. "What's that?"

"Would you please pop next door and give Torquemada some food and water? Maybe spend a few minutes with him? He'll be lonely."

"Why don't I just bring him back here? Then you can spend time with him yourself."

"That sounds great, thanks." I hadn't thought of that solution. Hopefully, it wasn't too much of an issue. I handed over my keys. A few minutes later, Chelsea returned with the cat in one arm and the food and water in the other.

Torquemada scampered around her apartment excitedly, sniffing everywhere and exploring every corner. The rooms were the same layout as mine, and he seemed to enjoy discovering how Chelsea had arranged her furniture. Her apartment was stylish. Compared to hers, mine was a scrap heap with old furniture, a living room that served as an office, a messy bedroom, and a one-fingered salute to Feng Shui.

Chelsea took up her book and reclined on the sofa. "Make yourself at home, Danny. You're making me nervous, standing there."

I sat in an armchair and switched on a table lamp next to it. Light flooded my lap. This must be another of Chelsea's reading spots. I frowned; I should have asked her to bring me my laptop from my apartment. Instead, I took out my phone and dialled Julie Nicholls, my lawyer.

She answered after several rings, when I was about to give up. "Danny. How can I help you? Is it something urgent?" Music and chatter sounded in the background. She was obviously out somewhere. I needed to remember that most people have more active social lives than private investigators.

"Sorry for disturbing you. The police interviewed me again today. I'm running out of time before they arrest me on suspicion of Baker's murder."

"Why do you say that?"

"They haven't any other suspects."

"Okay, so you might spend a few days in the cells. Make sure you pay my invoice before that, okay?"

I thought I must have misheard that. "Sorry, what did you say, Julie? If it was about your invoice, which I hope it wasn't, remember I said my bank account was emptied by the same perp who scammed your money."

"Have you got cash?"

"Barely any. Can't it wait? I'm relying on you to keep me out of jail. I'll pay you once that's not likely any longer." And when I've got some money, I added to myself. I still owed Nadia and Jimmy Wang.

"I need it now, Danny. Tomorrow at the latest. And what about the money that conman scammed out of me? You're supposed to retrieve that for me. I need that tomorrow, too."

I couldn't see how that was going to happen. I had no money, and I needed Julie to pay me the remainder before I could pay her. Nor did I know where Baker had put the stolen money, and he certainly couldn't tell anyone now. I groaned. Maybe I could put these problems off for another day. "I'll see what I can do."

"Great. Thanks. I appreciate it. Remember, if you get arrested, call me."

"Of course I will." I disconnected.

She hadn't inspired me with confidence. Something was going on that I didn't know about. I thought lawyers were affluent; richer than private investigators, anyway. Why was she so desperate for money? Was she a secret gambler or had an overdue tax demand or something?

Chelsea glanced over. "More bills?"

"Unfortunately, yes. That was my lawyer."

"You're in deep shit, aren't you?"

I sighed. "Well and truly."

"I wish I could help you."

"You've done plenty, and I appreciate it. I just need to wait until the police move their attention to someone else."

"Do you think they'll do that?"

"No."

I'd planned to sleep on the sofa, but Chelsea was reading on it, so I lay back in the armchair and closed my eyes, thinking about the conversation I'd had with Julie. She'd barely listened to my concerns about being arrested. Her attention was on getting paid and getting her money back. But she'd sounded so desperate. Why was that?

A terrible thought entered my mind. Hadn't she said something about Baker being unable to move or hide the money now that he was dead? It sounded like she thought it would be easier to access with him gone. I'd told her the conman's identity just before he died. Had she killed him?

The idea swirled around and around in my mind until finally I fell into a fitful sleep in the armchair.

Chapter 43

Day 9 (Tuesday, 22 August), morning

THE STAIRS CREAKING disturbed my sleep. Several people, by the sounds of it.

"Open up. Police!"

I sat bolt upright in the chair. Torquemada sprang off my lap and raced behind the sofa. My back and neck twinged with the pain of sleeping in an armchair. What was going on?

The room was dim, but sunlight was streaming around the edges of the blind over the window facing the street. Morning.

A crash and splintering of wood came from along the hallway. I gasped involuntarily.

Chelsea tore from the bedroom, her t-shirt flapping, bleary-eyed. "What's happening?"

I lifted a finger to my lips. "Quiet. It's coming from next door. My apartment."

Shouts and the stomping of feet had followed the crash. The police raid team must have smashed through my front door with a battering ram. That was unnecessary, of course. They could have simply broken the frosted glass, reached in and opened the door, but they probably preferred to break down the door instead.

Fortunately, Torquemada was with us rather than in there. He'd have been petrified.

Now that they weren't shouting, I put my ear to the wall to hear what the police team were saying. About half of it was obscenities. I didn't recognise any of the voices; the group was one of their special teams of thugs, not the detectives I knew. They didn't sound pleased. They'd discovered my place was empty, and that had evidently pissed them off. There were three or four of them in my apartment, apparently going through my things from the sound of drawers and doors thumping. I knew from experience that it'd take me hours to tidy up the mess they could make in three minutes.

Chelsea grabbed my arm. She was shaking.

I tried to calm her. "Don't worry. They'll bang about for a few minutes, then depart. They'll take my laptop and any booze they can find. It's me they're after, and they'll soon leave to search somewhere else or go back to the station."

"Fuck, I hope so. They scared me half to death. What's the time?"

I glanced at my watch. "Six thirty. They like to strike early before their targets are up and about, and to claim the overtime."

Chelsea clung to me until the police team left a few minutes later. They clattered downstairs, not caring if they disturbed anyone. I'm sure I heard the clinking of bottles and a few chuckles.

"They're gone." I only stated the obvious because Chelsea still hadn't let go of my arm.

"Oh, Danny, this is too much. What if they'd broken in here too?"

"Try to relax. They're only after me. My time must have run out. The inspector warned me that the superintendent would want my ass back at the station. She must have decided not to ask me nicely to turn up at my convenience."

Chelsea giggled hysterically. "You're funny. Shit, I'd be terrified if I was you. What are you going to do?"

"Right now, try to catch a bit more sleep. After that, I'll keep doing what I've been doing until I solve this case. But I'll have to keep away from the police too." I smiled at her in what I hoped was a reassuring way. "Why don't you go back to bed too? It's early for you."

"My nerves are shattered. There's no way I could sleep now."

I frowned. What would help?

"I'm going back to bed. Come and sit with me, please, Danny."

"I don't think that's a good idea."

Chelsea's eyes were wide with anxiety.

Her worried expression swayed me. "All right. For a few minutes only, until you're settled."

She led the way into her bedroom. "That armchair must be awful to sleep on. Just lie down next to me. I'll feel much safer if you're here. The police raid team might come back."

"There's no danger. They're gone."

She lay on the bed and beckoned me. "Come to bed, Danny."

I was ready for this, but this time I wasn't giving in. I thought of Deepa. I'd betrayed her by sleeping with Chelsea that first time. She'd been hurt. I wasn't going to do that again.

"You'll be all right on your own." I smiled reassuringly and left the room.

§

I must have drifted off to sleep on the armchair again. The coffee machine in the kitchen woke me.

"Coffee's ready." Chelsea brought two steaming cups into the living room.

We sat in silence that became uncomfortable after a while before I broke it.

"Please understand, Chelsea, I don't want you to get the wrong impression. We slept together once. I think we should think of it as a one-off—"

"And that one time was great, wasn't it? There's a spark between us."

I couldn't deny that, but it wasn't the point. "I spend a lot of time with Deepa, my reporter friend, and I'd planned to—"

"I don't mind. Just go for it. I'm all fine with an open relationship."

"But it's not my style, Chelsea, and I don't think it's hers either."

She stared at me. "Then what the hell have you been doing? Leading me on? Teasing me? Asking to stay overnight? You even moved your cat in, for fuck's sake."

I explained yet again that I was dodging the landlady and the police, as she knew perfectly well. Then the stairs creaked. I froze. Someone was coming.

Maybe it was Nadia to claim the overdue rent or payment in kind.

A knock came on the door. I recognised the rat-a-tat-tat. It was Deepa.

Chelsea let her in and closed the door. Deepa glanced from her to me. What a contrast. Chelsea's expression was like a pending thunderstorm; I was calmer, but frustrated by Chelsea's attitude and expectations.

"Cosy night, was it?" Deepa's voice dripped icicles. "Just got up, did you, Danny?"

"It's been a rough night. And morning."

"I bet it has. I hope you're not too tired to do some investigating today."

"I slept in the armchair." I rolled my shoulders and rubbed my neck. "Did you see along the hall to my apartment? The police smashed their way in earlier this morning. If I'd been there, I would be locked up in the cells by now." Judging by Deepa and Chelsea's expressions, I might actually be safer there.

"I didn't observe closely, but I noticed that half of your door is lying on the floor outside your apartment."

Great. Nadia would probably charge me for the repairs too.

I put my coffee down and stood. I'd had enough feeling sorry for myself. I needed to move forward, solve the case, find the stolen money, get paid, and somehow repair the mess I'd got myself into with my neighbour and Deepa. That last goal was the most difficult of all.

The two women faced off against each other.

"If you'll excuse me, I'm going to nip back to my apartment for a shower and a change of clothes. If you hear anyone on the stairs, bang on the wall." It would give me some warning, at least.

By the time I'd returned, with some trepidation, both Chelsea and Deepa's moods had lightened considerably. Some womanly discussion had passed between them that I'd missed.

"What's going on?" It might have been wiser not to ask, but curiosity got the better of me.

Chelsea shook her head. "Nothing to worry about. I'll get us fresh coffees." She headed into the kitchen.

Deepa took a copy of the *Richter Mail* out of her backpack and laid it on the sofa. She pointed at a photo above the fold. "Recognise him?"

The front-page headline blazed 'Murder in Sintown'. My attention was drawn to the photo of the victim. It was Brock Patterson.

My mouth dried, and I gasped. I'd seen the guy less than two days before, and now he'd been killed. Whatever he'd done, he didn't deserve to be murdered for it.

"Coincidence?" Deepa quirked an eyebrow at me. She knew I didn't have much belief in coincidences.

I shook my head and pulled the paper to me to read the article. "Says here his neck was broken deliberately after being hit or kicked by his assailant." I closed my eyes for a moment until something clicked in the back of my mind. "I think I know who his killer is."

Chapter 44

THIS MIGHT BE my way out. If I was right about Brock's killer, I could turn him over to the police. Surely, he'd murdered Baker too. I'd prove my innocence and could move back into my apartment, free from police persecution.

"Let's move." I nodded to Deepa while I grabbed my hat and coat. "I'll fill you in on the way. We should hurry."

"Give me your keys, then. I'll drive."

I handed them over as we descended the stairs and hastened outside into the late winter morning. The weather was warmer than recent days, but the weather was always changeable in Quake City. I hesitated and checked my coat pocket for my Glock 17.

Deepa noticed me stop. "Something wrong?"

"No, just making sure I have my gun. I do."

"Okay." Deepa got into the driver's seat. "Where are we going?"

"A company called SuperGames Apps." I gave her the address in Baddington.

She started the car and screeched away from the curb. "That's the business Brock Patterson robbed, is it?"

"Yeah, but get this. They're building some kind of kickboxing game. According to their website, Jaxon Coles, the CEO, is a martial arts expert."

Deepa swerved around a corner. My stomach lurched sideways. "So, he has the ability to have killed Patterson, but is he the kind of man who would do that?"

"Yeah, he is. I'm almost certain he's the guy who attacked me outside Baker's house the night of his murder, too. I recognised his voice."

"Right. So, he's dangerous."

"He sure is. He had a motive, too. I learned from Brock that he'd stolen some information from SuperGames Apps. The next day, according to the *Richter Mail*, the company was struggling because their main computer server had been wiped clean. The CEO thought they might have to shut down the business."

"The motive was revenge, then. Or maybe Coles was trying to get the stolen information back."

The small brick office building housing SuperGames Apps came into view. Deepa parked nearby, and we headed to the entrance.

I didn't know what to expect. The building could be empty, abandoned by the staff, the business already closed down. Or maybe a handful of dedicated employees would be working hard, trying to recover whatever lost work they could. All I hoped for was that Jaxon Coles was there.

A young male receptionist asked us how he could help. For someone whose job could be under threat or gone any minute, he seemed upbeat.

"We're here to see Jaxon Coles. We don't have an appointment, but it's urgent."

"Your names, please?"

I gave them.

The receptionist made a call, then looked up in surprise. I turned and saw Deepa disappearing through the door into the inner offices. Someone had come out of there, and she had seized the chance to go through before the security door closed and barred the way.

Startled, the receptionist broke off his call before it had been answered. "She can't go in there. You both have to wait here."

I caught the door before it shut after her. "Forgive her, she's impulsive. I'll let her know." I slipped through the doorway after her.

Deepa strode along the edge of an open-plan office filled with people working at computers. She stopped outside a room at the end and examined a nameplate on the door. I caught up to her. It was Jaxon Coles' office.

Without a word, Deepa opened the door and marched inside. I followed on her heels.

A man with a slight beard and a bald head rose from behind a desk. "Who the hell are you two, and what are you doing in here?"

I stepped forward. "Mr Coles, I'm Danny Ashford, private investigator. We spoke on the phone yesterday. This is my colleague, Deepa Banwait."

"I don't know how you got in, but I've nothing more to say to you. I've already told you that."

The receptionist appeared at the door behind us. "Sorry, Mr Coles, they refused to wait."

"Forget it. Get back to the front desk. I'll sort this out."

The young man scurried off. If his job hadn't been under threat before, it probably was now.

Deepa spoke up. "Mr Coles, I'm a reporter. I understand that your company suffered a theft that meant the business couldn't continue. But, out there, everyone's working. May I write a story about how SuperGames Apps is up and running again? I assume your operation is back to normal."

Coles stared at her, and his expression softened. "Yes, please write that. It'll be free advertising for us. Our customers were disappointed when the press reported we were going under, so it'll be good news for them to read that we're back in business developing our kickboxing game."

Deepa nodded her thanks.

I tilted my head to catch Coles' attention. "What happened, then? Were you able to restore the wiped server? I thought you said it was impossible."

Coles glared. "Nevertheless, we have."

"If you couldn't recover the information from the server, you must have found it some other way."

Coles guffawed. "How could I have done that? I don't know who stole it."

"If the thief contacted you, maybe for money, you might have got it back from them directly."

"What are you insinuating?"

I spread my hands wide, trying to appear innocent. But my words conveyed a different message. "I'm not saying you know the thief's name, but he knows yours. Or I should say, he knew yours. Someone murdered him last night. Did you know that?"

"No, I didn't. Anyway, so what if a minor criminal is killed? In his line of work, it's an occupational hazard, isn't it?" Coles scowled. I sensed the only reason he hadn't demanded we leave was because he was curious about how much we knew or suspected.

Deepa interrupted. "Aren't you interested in what happened to the thief at all?"

"Of course not. Why should I be?"

Deepa and I exchanged glances. Her insightful question had set up a trap for Coles, and he'd fallen into it. She continued. "Yesterday morning your business lay in ruins. The thief had stolen your intellectual property and wiped it from your server. You must have wanted it back desperately, and they had a copy."

Coles' nostrils flared. His cheeks reddened.

Deepa carried on. "Naturally, you'd want to find out if he had a copy of your intellectual property on him or hidden at his home. You just told us you didn't know the thief is now dead. Surely, you'd phone the police straight away to see if you could get your stolen information back. But, this morning, your employees are all already working hard. Obviously, to be back in business, you've got it back already. Yet you told us you couldn't recover it from the wiped server."

I jabbed a finger at Coles, who switched his hateful glance from Deepa to me. "And the only person you could have got that information from was the thief, or the person who employed the thief. Both of them are dead. The thief was killed by someone with martial arts skills." I paused for effect. "Such as those you have."

Jaxon Coles became beet red. His scowl reformed as a snarl, and he stepped out from behind his desk towards us. Violence pooled in his eyes; I could see it in his expression. I knew, immediately, that I'd been right about Coles.

I pulled my Glock from my pocket, but Coles was too quick for me. I'd barely raised the gun when his boot kicked it out of my hand. It crashed into the wall. My fingers and wrist stung from the impact. He barged me with his shoulder, and I sprawled to the floor.

Coles toppled to the ground beside me, groaning. I looked up.

Deepa stood there brandishing a metallic baton in her hand. She grinned. "You're not the only one who carries a weapon." She collapsed it and put it back in her bag.

"Is that thing legal?"

"Not as far as I know."

I got to my knees, my hand still in a lot of pain, and fished in another pocket for a pair of handcuffs. I didn't have a key for them, but I didn't care. The police could unlock them later. I fastened one cuff around Coles' wrist and the other around a metal leg supporting his heavy desk.

The door opened. Some employees stood there, blocking the doorway, jabbering.

"What's going on?"

"What did you do to the boss?"

"We're calling the police."

Deepa took a photo of them, probably for the newspaper. "Call the police, then. That'll save us the trouble. Your boss is a murderer."

Coles stirred and snarled at me. "Let me out of here, you bastard. You'll regret this."

"No, it's you who will regret it, Jaxon. For life, I'd say."

Chapter 45

MOST OF THE CURIOUS employees moved away from the doorway. Some returned to their desks, muttering about Jaxon. A couple of them remained. They sounded unhappy and angry. After the few days of uncertainty that SuperGames Apps had put them through, seeing their CEO in handcuffs, accused of murder, was probably the final straw.

One of them, a young guy with a pointy beard, jutted his chin at us. "Who are you guys?"

Deepa flashed her reporter's I.D. I flashed my private investigator's I.D.

The guy's demeanour changed. He glanced at Jaxon. "Is it true? You're a murderer?"

Jaxon ignored him. Evidently, the young man and his co-worker took that as a tacit admission of guilt. Horror etched on their features, they wandered away.

Deepa grabbed my hand and thrust my car keys into it. "You need to get out of here before the police arrive. I'll fill them in on what Coles has done, but they're still searching for you. Unless he confesses to Baker's murder, you won't be in the clear yet."

A chill of anxiety swept through me. She was right. "Thanks, Deepa." I retrieved my gun and rushed from the building.

The sirens neared as I reached my car. I pulled away from the curb into a slow stream of traffic. Three police cars raced past on the other side of the road. I keep my face averted, just in case a constable glanced over. Most of them knew me, but I didn't think any of them would recognise my new car.

I may have solved the case. I didn't know. Even if I had, I wasn't finished with it. Coles had surely killed Brock Patterson, but I didn't know whether he had killed Stuart Baker. Little details about the crime scene pricked at my mind. Baker was struck on the head with a vase and pushed over the balcony next to his bedroom. If Coles was the killer, why would he hit him with a vase? He was a martial arts expert, a fighting machine who could kill with his hands or feet.

It wasn't safe to go home, so I drove to the Crumbledon library. It was one of the nicer, updated libraries until the earthquakes ruined it. Now it was a graveyard for books. Behind it was a carpark surrounded by trees that burst into pink blossom for two weeks a year. I sat there for a while and came up with a plan.

I phoned Julie Nicholls. She answered immediately.

"Danny, I hope you've got good news for me."

"Yes, I have. I think I know how to get your money back."

"That's great." The relief in her voice was palpable. "Thank you."

"I'll need your help, though."

"Tell me what you want me to do."

When I'd finished explaining, Julie told me to swing by her office in an hour to pick up the paperwork.

Good. I phoned Deepa.

She picked up the call. "I'm leaving the police station now. Coles has been arrested for Brock Patterson's murder. I asked Inspector O'Toole if that meant you were in the clear, and he said 'no'."

I groaned. "Did he say anything else?"

"Yep. He said that Coles has an alibi for eight o'clock onwards on the evening that Baker was killed. He was at work until nearly midnight, doing stuff with several colleagues."

"Stuff? What kind of stuff?"

"I don't know. Whatever stuff apps programmers get up to in their spare time, I suppose. Anyway, the inspector asked me to tell you to come to the station for questioning. He doesn't like having to use his resources looking for you."

"Then he can stop looking. I'm not going into the station before I've solved this case."

"I told him that's what you'd say."

"Want some lunch? I'll meet you at the Cupquake Café in a few minutes." It was only a few minutes' walk from where Deepa was.

"All right. See you there."

Over sandwiches, Deepa pressed me on what I planned to do next. I explained that I had another lead to try.

"I'll come with you."

I shook my head. "I've got to do this on my own. The person I'm going to see isn't very trusting. Why don't you write another article on the case for the *Richter Mail*? You've got a brilliant angle, the inside story of how we brought Coles to justice."

"But I want to come with you."

Why did I tell Deepa about the meeting? I should have kept quiet. Now, I wouldn't be able to shake her off.

After a while, I excused myself to use the bathroom. While she was working on her laptop, I slipped out the side door of the café. I knew I had a better chance of getting my lead's cooperation if I went alone.

§

I picked up the legal document from Julie, then drove to Sintown to speak to Mary Sanchez again. It was after noon now, and she might be in the club. If she wasn't, I'd have to go searching for her.

The entrance to the 88 Club was closed, as I'd expected. It was a nightclub, after all. There wasn't a bouncer at the door now. Maybe he'd been fired after I got the better of him last time. I pushed at the door and it swung open.

Dim illumination revealed no one in the main downstairs part of the club. Why had she left the front entrance unlocked? Thieves might raid the club to steal the booze. Unless, of course, criminals knew better than to mess with Mary Sanchez.

If so, what had she done to earn a fearsome reputation in a place like Sintown? Was it by killing Baker? Or was it simply by taking over the 88 Club in a bloodless coup?

I took the stairs to the second level. The thick carpet concealed my footsteps as I made my way to Mary's office, formerly Baker's office. As before, the door was open. I stepped inside and froze.

Mary Sanchez sat at the desk, a huge handgun pointed at my stomach. "I upgraded the security system. A silent alarm alerted me to your entry, and I watched you come up the stairs on these screens."

"All right. Do you mind putting the gun away? I only want to talk."

She motioned with the gun to a chair in the corner. "Sit there."

I did so. She hadn't put the gun down. Now it was level with my chest.

"What do you want this time, P.I.?"

This wasn't going the way I'd planned, but it was too late. "I think we can help each other out, Ms Sanchez."

"Is that right? And how do you propose to help me?" She smirked. "I'm not hiring dancers at the moment."

I smiled. "That's not my thing. No, the way I'm going to help you is by not turning you in to the police for fraud. As soon as you heard he was dead, you forged Baker's signature on the change of ownership papers for the 88 Club. That's how you bought this place for next to nothing, isn't it?"

"Are you implying I killed him too?" The angle of the gun changed slightly. Now I was staring right down the high-calibre barrel.

"No, I'm not. You have alibis. Dozens of people saw you." Sweat prickled on the back of my neck.

Mary stared at me for a few moments and came to a decision. She put her gun on the desk. I let out a breath that I hadn't realised I'd been holding.

She crossed her arms. "Do you have any proof of the fraud you're claiming I did?"

"Of course I do. Not only that, but I've left proof with a close associate. If you kill me, they'll go to the police." I hadn't told Deepa, or anyone else, but it's surprising how easily a lie slips out when your life is under threat.

Mary's gaze bored into me. She was clearly contemplating what I'd said, perhaps wondering if I was telling the truth. I returned her gaze steadily, not looking away, not swallowing nervously, breathing slowly and deeply to keep myself calm. My phone vibrated in my pocket—I ignored it.

"I'm not admitting anything, but let's say you're right, just for the sake of argument. What do you want in return? Money?"

I shook my head. "All I want you to do is forge Baker's signature again."

"That's all?"

"You'll have to go to his bank with me."

Her eyes twinkled with mischief. "And why do you want me to do that, private investigator? Are you going over to the dark side?"

I actually laughed. "No. My money, and a client's, disappeared to the dark side. Baker scammed us. I merely want to get it back, and I'll need you to forge his signature to transfer some money out of his accounts."

"You're sure we can do this without being recorded on security cameras?"

"Positive." I hoped I was right about that. If not, we were potentially screwed.

"And how do I know you won't turn me into the police anyway after that?"

"Mary, you sound like you don't trust me. I don't care about your forgery to get the 88 Club. I only care about the money Baker scammed from me and my client. If I can recover that, I'm happy."

"Fine. I agree. When are we doing this?"

"How about right now?"

Chapter 46

MARY INSISTED ON driving her car, a black SUV, rather than taking mine. It gave her some control over the situation. Her gun sat in the door pocket, easy to access in a moment. She could drive me anywhere she wanted and get rid of me. I tried to appear relaxed, despite the trickle of sweat sliding down my neck.

Baker's bank was in Ricketyton, a ten-minute drive. Mary found a park on the street a block away. She put her gun into her purse. We got out of the car and proceeded past several damaged and collapsed shops to the edge of the mall, which had survived the earthquakes. The bank was inside the mall.

She nudged me as we entered. "If I suspect that I'm being set up, or anything goes wrong, I'm out of here. And I'll come after you for revenge. Understand?"

"Yeah. Don't worry. We've got this."

The bank was spacious, with tellers spread out to give customers privacy. Lavish furnishings allowed somewhere for people to wait. They'd spared no expense. Banks always had plenty of money. Unless you wanted a loan from them.

I scouted around for Gabrielle. She wasn't in sight. Damn. My plan wouldn't work without her. I stopped in my tracks.

Mary collided with me from behind. Her forehead creased with concern. "What's happened? Is there something wrong?"

A door behind the tellers opened and Gabrielle came out. Perhaps she'd been on her lunch break. She took a position alongside the other tellers.

"No. Quite the opposite." I kept my gaze fixed on Gabrielle. She caught sight of me and stared back, aghast. I strode over, grinning, followed by Mary. "Gabrielle, nice to see you."

"What do you want?" Her voice was a hushed rasp. She glanced between me and Mary, who watched with a quirked eyebrow, probably wondering what was going on.

"Have you got an office where there's no security cameras and we can discuss a few things in private?"

She came around the counter without responding and led us to a small room with a desk and three chairs. It could have been any meeting room anywhere, apart from the bank's logo plastered across every surface.

Gabrielle sat behind the desk. "You'd better tell me why you're here. Who's this?" She gestured to Mary.

Mary nodded at me. "Show her the legal document."

"In a moment. There's something I want to say first. So, Gabrielle, I expect Baker came here frequently. A well-dressed man with dollops of cash. He caught your attention, didn't he?"

"What's wrong with that? We were both single."

"Nothing is wrong with that, per se. But you know what I think?" I paused and observed her. She frowned and her breathing quickened while she waited for me to carry on. "I think you figured out that Baker's money was the proceeds of crime, and you wanted a piece. That's why you got close to him. Then, when you searched his house for your 'personal items', you were actually looking for any evidence that might have linked you to him, weren't you? You were involved in his illegal schemes, weren't you, Gabrielle?"

Her gaze became needle-sharp. "What do you want? What proof do you have to back up these accusations? And who's this?" She gestured towards Mary again.

Mary introduced herself, saving me from answering Gabrielle's other questions, before glaring in my direction. "Hurry this up, Danny."

My phone vibrated. Once again, I ignored it. I leaned forward and clasped my hands together. "Listen, Gabrielle, if I investigate your involvement with Baker and find anything to suggest you were working with him, I could go to the police and you'd face a lengthy prison term. Even a quiet word to the bank would probably see you lose your job. You don't want either of those outcomes, do you?"

She shook her head, her lower lip trembling. "All right. You got me. But I did nothing wrong. I only wanted to get some money out of Stu for hiding his suspicious transactions. He's a criminal. Why should anyone care if I get a cut of his stolen money?"

"That doesn't matter. What matters is that you're potentially in trouble. Big trouble. Fraud, blackmail, concealing crimes are all on your resumé now. But I'm offering you a way out. If you do what I ask, you'll be fine. The police and the bank won't hear anything from me."

Gabrielle thought about it for a minute or two, her brow glowing with sweat in the artificial light. "Okay. I'll do it, as long as you go away and I don't see or hear from you again."

"It's a deal." I reached into a coat pocket for the legal document that Julie had prepared for me. Mary had already signed it, once as herself, and once forging Baker's signature. I slapped the single piece of paper on the desk. "This document declares that Stuart Baker's antique shop bank account contains money from the 88 Club, which Mary now owns, and that it should be transferred to her."

Gabrielle picked it up. "I didn't see this being signed. I can't give you access to his account with this." As soon as the words were out of her mouth, realisation hit that she didn't have a choice. "Oh. You bastards."

I grinned. "We're in this together, remember. We have to trust one another, or we all go down. Understood?"

Gabrielle nodded slowly.

"This is the story, then. Mary, you can confirm that Baker signed this document when you bought the 88 Club from you, can't you?"

She smiled mischievously. "Of course he did. There's his signature and the date right there."

"So, Gabrielle, please open a new account in Mary's name. You'll transfer the money to that account, and then she'll transfer it out again to a separate new account."

Mary turned to me. "Wait. What did you say?"

"The money's not for you, Mary. It's destined for other people. I only needed your help to access it. The police might investigate Baker's accounts, and if they do, they'll see this transfer was made according to this legal document. There would be no reason for them to follow the money any further."

"You tricked me."

"No, I never said you would get Baker's money. I only said you had to sign on his behalf." I couldn't bring myself to say 'forge' out loud, even though we all knew that's what had happened.

Mary lifted her chin in a huff. "I see. You're taking the money, are you?"

"No. I'm going to return what I can to the victims of his scams. The rest will go to charity. Look, you've done well out of this. I bet you made sure you got the 88 Club at a dirt-cheap price."

Mary pursed her lips.

Gabrielle interrupted our side conversation. "If you're ready, you two, I've created the new account in the name of Mary Sanchez and transferred the money from Stu's account into it. Now what?"

"Now, create a new account in the name of this entity." I pulled another legal document from my coat pocket and put it on the desk.

Mary placed her hand on it so Gabrielle couldn't pick it up. "Just how much money are we talking about here?"

Gabrielle took a deep breath. "A little over two million dollars."

Both Mary and I gasped.

Gabrielle retained a professional expression. "Stu was a workaholic. Always scamming or conning people. He barely rested."

Mary drew herself up in her chair and glared at me. "There's no way I'm letting two million dollars slip through my hands without taking at least a cut of it." Her hand drifted towards her bag and the gun.

Chapter 47

THREE SCENARIOS passed through my mind in rapid succession. I could pull out my own gun and risk a gunfight. Or I could tackle Mary and risk being shot anyway. The alternative was to negotiate, fast.

"All right. Take a cut. That's reasonable."

Mary relaxed. "Ten per cent."

I countered. "Two per cent. This money belongs to Baker's victims."

"You'll never find most of them. I'm taking an enormous risk here. Eight per cent."

We haggled like Mediterranean market traders while Gabrielle glanced between us. Finally, we settled on five per cent.

"Great." Gabrielle smiled at our agreement. "That's five per cent each, then."

"You learn fast." Mary smiled.

I shook my head. "No, that's—"

Gabrielle's smile didn't slip. "It's two against one. As you said, we're all in this together. I'm taking a risk here too. I'll take the same cut."

I fumed, but I couldn't see any way to convince them otherwise. "Fine. Do that, then. I will not take a cut. The rest of the money goes to the victims."

Both women nodded their agreement. Gabrielle carried out the transactions to redirect their cuts of the stolen money to their personal accounts.

Gabrielle picked up the document I'd put on the desk. "So, you want me to make a new account in the name of 'Victims of Stuart Baker' and transfer the remaining money into it. I'll do that now. I only need your signature on that, Mary."

She complied. "If you don't need me any longer, I'm off. Nice to do business with you, Danny." She stood, tapping the side of her bag, where her gun made a bulge, as a reminder. She left.

Gabrielle's confidence had picked up. Being a hundred thousand dollars richer for a few minutes' work did that. "What are you going to do with this money, Danny? Do you know who his victims are?"

"Yes. My client is one. He scammed her out of forty thousand. I'm another; he stole three thousand from me." I gave her a slip of paper with bank account details. "Please transfer the money."

Gabrielle swiftly did that. I breathed a sigh of relief. I'd let Julie know as soon as I could.

"Is that all for now?"

"No, there's one more transaction. I expect you can get the payee's details from Baker's account." I gave her the name and the amount. "And after that, I'll call you if I learn of any other victims to be refunded. I probably won't find many, though, but my partner and I will do our best. All right?"

She nodded. "Sure."

I waited until she'd finished with the last transaction, and then I left.

I caught a bus back to Sintown, where I'd left my car. I'd barely got there when Deepa called again. It was the fifth time she'd called since I'd left her in the café. I'd put my phone on silent, and I'd been ignoring the vibrations. She had also sent twelve texts, each more vehement than the one before.

"Where are you, Danny?" She sounded angry or upset. Maybe both.

"I had some dangerous business to attend to, remember?"

"I don't appreciate being dumped like that."

"Can I make it up to you?"

"How the hell do you think you can do that?"

I chuckled. "I've got a story idea for you."

§

I drove back to the Cupquake Café. I'd intended to go straight there anyway. I needed a coffee.

Deepa was at the same table as before, working on her laptop. I ordered lattes and pumpkin chocolate chip muffins for both of us and joined her. Hopefully, the muffin would sweeten her up a little.

Her expression was sharp enough to split a hair in two. "Did you get done what you needed to get done, whatever it was? What was so important and dangerous that you had to abandon me here? I've always had your back—and can handle myself better than you can, most of the time."

"I know. But I had to take the risk alone, and I can't tell you the details. If you'd joined me, I doubt my contact would have cooperated."

"But then I would have a story to write."

"I've got a better alternative for you."

Her face brightened. "So, now we're at the bit where you're going to explain how you make it up to me, right?"

"Yes." I fished in my pocket for my car keys and handed them to her. "You'll need these."

Our coffees and food arrived. I kept her on tenterhooks while we ate and drank.

After I'd finished telling Deepa what I'd done and why, her ire had disappeared as quickly as the muffin. She gave me a friendly smile that almost melted my insides. She'd always had that effect on me. She packed up her laptop and patted me on the shoulder when she left.

I pulled out my phone and called Julie Nicholls. She answered immediately. I'm sure she'd been waiting for my call.

"Julie, it's done. The documents you drew up were perfect. I got the money withdrawn to a new account, and I've transferred the forty thousand dollars that Baker scammed back to you."

"Brilliant! Thanks, Danny." In her excitement, her voice rose louder than its usual whisper. "I had gambling debts."

"Is that so? What kind of gambling debts?"

"The kind that were going to attract crippling interest if I didn't pay them off quickly. The way they emphasised the word 'crippling' concerned me."

"I understand. Julie, I still need your services as my lawyer. The police haven't closed the case of Baker's murder, and they want to interview me again."

"No problem. I'm on call for you when you need me."

"One more thing, Julie. I'll send you my invoice in the next few days." In reality, I wouldn't send it until I could safely return to my apartment without being arrested or accosted by the landlady. "But I'd appreciate it if you could send me another advance."

"Sure, I can do that now that you've got my money back. How much do you need?"

I told her the amount that would cover my rent in arrears and what I owed Jimmy Wang for the Audi. "One other thing, Julie. If you charge me your fees for representing me so far, I'll have to charge those back to you. Your legal fees are part of my investigation expenses. I'm sure you'll understand."

Julie was silent for a few moments. "All right. You should have been a lawyer, you know, thinking like that. Call me if the police take you in for interview again." She hung up.

I wasn't sure where to go, so I ordered another coffee. I'd concluded the case for Julie by getting her money back. I'd also recovered mine. Along the way, I'd uncovered a murderer: Jason Coles. He'd killed Brock Patterson, but he hadn't killed Stuart Baker.

I still didn't know who Baker's killer was.

Chapter 48

DEEPA ARRIVED IN Leanwood and parked Danny's car outside Sarah Bailey's house at around two o'clock. Sarah's boys would be at school.

She rapped on the door and stood back.

Sarah's face appeared at the narrow window by the door. She opened the door, scowling. "What do you want now?"

"Can I come in? There's something I need to tell you."

Sarah huffed. "Just as long as you don't accuse me of anything. And I don't have long. I have to leave to pick up the boys from school in forty minutes."

"It won't take long."

Sarah showed Deepa into the living room. A basket of washing sat on the sofa. She didn't move it. They stayed standing.

"What is it, then?"

"I know you must be concerned about your financial situation now that your ex-husband has passed away."

"Now that someone finally took revenge on him for whatever he's been doing, you mean. It won't make a hell of a lot of difference. He paid barely any child support as it is. The person who'll be shedding tears for him will be his accountant."

Deepa nodded. "Maybe that's true. But you may have thought your kids would inherit his money when he died."

Sarah's eyes narrowed. "If you're going to accuse me again of killing him,

219

you can leave now."

Deepa shook her head. "No, but I need to remind you that the police are likely to seize all his money—or all they can find—as proceeds of crime. There won't be an inheritance."

"Your partner told me the last time you were here. I'm not surprised, but I am disappointed."

"But here's the good news." Deepa smiled broadly. "A new organisation called 'Victims of Stuart Baker' has been formed. It doesn't expect to find all of his victims, so there will be money that can't be returned to its rightful owners. As a result, the organisation has deposited a sum of money into your account."

"They have? How much?"

"Enough to make your life a whole lot easier. Check your account, Sarah."

Sarah tapped at her phone for a minute. "The money's already there. I don't know what to say. How can I thank you?"

Deepa took out her phone. "There is a way. I'd like to write an article about you for the *Richter Mail*. It'll be about Stuart too. We—that is, the 'Victims' organisation—think it might encourage other victims to come forward. May I interview you when you get back from picking up your boys from school? Not in front of the kids, of course."

Sarah smiled for the first time. "Sure." She moved the laundry basket off the sofa.

Chapter 49

Day 9 (Tuesday, 22 August), evening

DEEPA PICKED ME UP after she'd seen Sarah. To my surprise, she agreed to go to Quake Burgers for dinner. We sat near the staff entrance in case any police constables came looking for me. Some of them knew the places I hung out.

By now, they probably had at least one stakeout car watching the entrance to my apartment building. I couldn't safely return without being spotted.

I couldn't think of anywhere else to lie low except Deepa's place. I wasn't sure how she'd react to me asking if I could sleep over. It was probably better not to even try. The money Gabrielle had transferred to me would pay for a hotel, but I wanted to save it for the rent I owed and to put towards what I owed Jimmy Wang for the Audi.

I took Deepa home. She didn't ask where I was going to stay, and she didn't invite me in. I wasn't going to press the issue.

After dropping her off at her apartment, I drove towards my apartment building and parked a block away. I pulled a powerful pair of mini binoculars from my coat pocket. For several minutes, I scanned every parked car, every doorway, every person on the street, searching for anyone who could be monitoring the entrance to my apartment.

I couldn't see anyone obvious.

That didn't mean there wasn't someone inside one of the other buildings keeping watch on mine. I started the car and drove around the corner, where

I parked and repeated the process. I spotted a car parked near the corner with a view of both streets and the entrance to my apartment. Two guys sat inside, chatting intermittently. They were probably there to watch for me. It was too chancy to risk it.

I drove further away and sneaked back, keeping to the shadows wherever possible. Fortunately, with the poor and unrepaired street lighting, shadows were plentiful. I took a detour and turned into a street that ran parallel to mine.

Google Maps showed me where I was in relation to my apartment building. When I was as close as I could get, I quietly entered the property that led towards the back of my building, cautiously, in case there were dogs. All was quiet. I sneaked to the fence bordering that property and my apartment building, and clambered over it.

For a minute, I stayed quiet, listening. No movement or sound anywhere. I hadn't been detected.

Now I needed a way in. Fortunately, I was in luck. A window in Chelsea's apartment was open. Wisps of steam emerged. I needed a way to reach it, though. But how?

I inspected the area. All I could see were the wheelie bins for the rubbish and recycling for the different apartments. Would they hold my weight? Maybe. I'd have to stack them up. If they collapsed under me, they'd make a hell of a racket. But what choice did I have?

Somewhere in my coat pockets was a small roll of duct tape. When I found it, I taped three of the wheelie bins together and fastened another on top. I manoeuvred them to below the open window.

I hauled myself up and stood on the top bin, holding onto the brickwork of the building. The window ledge was just within reach. I put my hands over it and jumped, thinking I could spring up and dive through the open window. Perhaps I might have achieved that if I'd done more exercise and eaten fewer burgers, or if gravity didn't exist. Unfortunately, it didn't happen.

The bins scraped noisily as my feet pushed them away from the wall. I got my arms into the bathroom, but no more. I hung there, hanging on from the upstairs window, my legs swinging with nothing but air below.

I called out. "Chelsea. Are you there? Chelsea?"

No answer. I felt myself slipping and pulled myself up with renewed effort, but only chest-high with the window ledge.

A toilet flushed. Great. She'd come into the bathroom in a few seconds, and she could help support me while I climbed in.

Again, she didn't respond.

I called again, louder this time. I didn't want to shout too loud in case the stakeout team heard me.

Once more, nothing.

I couldn't hold on much longer. Right now, the gym membership I'd decided not to sign up for sounded like it would have been a good idea. If I'd done that, maybe I could have dived through the window like James Bond or Jessica Jones.

I put in one ultimate effort, straining my arm muscles, until I heaved my stomach up onto the window ledge and tipped myself forward into the room. I landed on the tiled floor with a thump and lay there, eyes closed, panting.

"What the fuck are you doing, Danny?"

I opened my eyes.

Chelsea stood above me, a white towel wrapped around her body and another one tying up her hair. She stared at me with consternation. She waved a bare arm, clearly agitated. "Couldn't you simply knock?"

"No, there are guys watching the front entrance of the building. I couldn't risk coming in that way."

"Whatever." She tapped her foot a few times, obviously thinking about that, then reached down with a bare arm to help me get to my feet.

"Thanks." The floor had been wet in places. Dampness seeped through the back of my pants.

"Come on. I'll make us some coffee and get some snacks together. I'm sure you need it."

"Yeah. Thanks."

I followed her to the living room. She continued on to the kitchen. I glanced around. Where was Torquemada? Had he settled into his temporary home? Hopefully, he didn't like it here too much, otherwise he'd be reluctant to leave when it was time to go home.

Finally, I spotted him. Torquemada was curled up at the top of a bookcase, between a small glass vase and a cute ceramic pot. I reached up to him, and he scrambled to his feet and leaped into my arms. In doing so, he knocked the pot off the top of the bookcase.

I caught the cat but watched the ceramic pot fall. Before it could smash on the floorboards, I stuck my leg out to break its fall. It bounced off my leg near my foot and rolled onto its side.

A watch fell out. My eyes widened.

Chapter 50

I LET TORQUEMADA down gently by the coffee table and picked up the watch. A Seiko, the same model as Baker's. I turned it over. There was an engraving on the back: 'To Stuart, my fairy tale prince, love from Sarah.'

This *was* Baker's watch. Why did Chelsea have it? And why had it been hidden? Surely, there could only be one reason…

And then it all clicked into place.

Did the time fit? She'd left my apartment at nine thirty that night. She hadn't been due to start at the club until ten thirty. Yes, there was time for her to drive to Baker's house, kill him, and get to the club.

She'd told me that Baker had asked her to take his watch in for repairs because it had stopped working. Maybe that gave her the idea of fixing the time on the watch. But the repair hadn't been done in time, so she bought an identical watch.

She'd murdered Baker at about ten o'clock, yet tried to make it look like the time of death was two hours earlier. She'd deliberately created an alibi for herself by being on the phone with a friend from seven p.m. onwards until she saw me, then being with me until nine thirty.

Everything had been premeditated. A cold-blooded killing.

I pulled out my phone and took a photo of the engraving on the watch. Then I switched on the voice recorder and placed my phone on the floor below the coffee table. If I could get Chelsea to admit it, then give the recording to the police, they could follow up.

A wooden tray plonked onto the coffee table next to me. I turned. Chelsea had brought the coffee and some home baking. Both smelled divine.

Chelsea smiled as she sat on the sofa. "Playing with the cat?"

She hadn't seen what I was doing. I took the other end of the sofa and showed her the watch in the palm of my hand, not saying a word.

She paled momentarily, then recovered her composure. "I can explain everything."

I raised my chin, expressing disbelief. "I'd like to hear it."

Chelsea picked up a coffee and sipped at it.

I waited while she drank more. I leaned over, put the watch on the table, took the other cup. The flavour of the hot coffee was delicious, but it appeared cloudy and was a little gritty in my mouth.

"You remember what I told you about Stuart as a boss. He was a total arse, harassing us girls, making our nights' work hell. Well, one time when I was performing, he stole my ring and replaced it with a cheap copy. It wasn't even a good copy."

"Go on."

Chelsea crossed her arms. It tugged the top of her towel down slightly. "So, I repaid him by swapping his watch with another one. He hadn't noticed yet. I was going to tell him he had to return my ring if he wanted his actual watch back. It was a gift, apparently."

"I can see that."

"That's it. Unfortunately, he... passed away first."

I shook my head. "How do you know it was Baker who took your ring and not anyone else working at the club?"

"It was obviously him. Everyone else is cool. He's a dishonest creep." She leaned back on the sofa and slowly spread her knees apart.

I glanced involuntarily. She was trying to distract me. I returned my gaze to her face and drank my coffee.

What I hadn't yet worked out was the motive. Why had Chelsea killed Baker? Getting revenge for him stealing her ring seemed too extreme. Maybe it was about the sexual harassment.

Meanwhile, Chelsea kept up her denials. "Come on, Danny, you might think it's funny to accuse me of killing my boss, but honestly, that's the stuff of fiction. It's not a fucking joke."

I shook my head. "I'm serious. You've got his watch. Maybe it's a souvenir. Maybe you just haven't got rid of it yet. Either way, it's evidence."

"Give it up." Now she leaned forward, giving me more of a view of her cleavage.

My breathing quickened and my face flushed. Concentrate! All these sexually alluring tricks of hers made me more certain she was trying to deceive me. It was almost intoxicating, like I'd been drinking, even though I hadn't.

Chelsea's story about her early life swirled in the back of my mind. An absent father. Living in poverty as a child. Difficult teenage years. Her mother drinking herself to oblivion and then committing suicide. Chelsea having to fend for herself from sixteen years of age.

Was it even true? Or had she made it up, so I'd feel sorry for her?

Chelsea interrupted my thoughts. "Danny? That was an awful joke, but I'll forgive you. Why don't you take off your wet clothes, dry off and have your drink? Let's put this ridiculous prank of yours to bed."

I didn't miss the subtext of that, but I was still thinking about how she'd told me her family history. She had sounded genuine. I put my cup down. The coffee was making me nauseous.

And now it made sense. The cloudy, grainy coffee had been drugged. The nausea, intoxicating effect, and weariness. What had she drugged me with? Think! It would have been the new Rohypnol, manufactured to make it easier to detect. But I hadn't detected it because I'd been distracted by Chelsea sitting there, barely covered by a towel. Could I have been more stupid?

Actually, yes. She must have drugged my whiskey on the night we slept together. Alcohol enhances the effect of the drug. That was why I'd woken up feeling hung over and couldn't remember much about it. It was a Rohypnol blackout. Maybe we'd not even had sex.

My phone was on the floor recording everything. How much time did I have before I passed out? I had to get her to confess before it was too late.

But why had she killed Baker? Even as I asked myself the question, I realised the answer. The motive had been staring me right in the face. Literally.

Chelsea's aquiline nose was a perfect match for Baker's. Their hazel-green eyes matched too.

I held her gaze. "Stuart Baker was your father."

The self-assurance drained from Chelsea's face. "That's—"

"There's no point denying it. Even if it's not on the birth certificate, I'll find out by talking to your mother's friends and relatives. Anyway, I can see it. You have his features. Your mother told you before she died, didn't she?"

She didn't reply.

I continued. "You started work at his club so you could get close to him. You were angry that you and your mother lived in poverty while he was well off from his crime and business proceeds."

Once again, Chelsea didn't respond.

"You didn't tell him who you were. It must have made you sick, when he tried to get you to sleep with him."

"Yes, all right. I knew he was my father. But he didn't know I was his daughter."

"You were after revenge for the way he'd treated you and your mother. You blamed him for your mother's suicide. You hated him, didn't you?"

"Of course I fucking did. That doesn't mean I killed him, though, does it?"

"I know you did. You established an alibi for yourself for eight o'clock that evening. After you left me, you drove straight to his house, snuck inside and pushed him over the balcony. Then you set the time of the watch you bought to eight o'clock, smashed it, and threw it onto the rocks after him."

Chelsea held my gaze for a few seconds, but her resolve faltered. She realised I knew too much, and I'd figured out the rest.

Chapter 51

Day 9 (Tuesday, 22 August), evening

MY BODY WAS WEARY. This case had taken its toll on me, and now the Rohypnol was taking effect. Time was running out. If I passed out, what would Chelsea do? Escape? Kill me?

"Okay, Danny, I admit it. That bastard was my father, and I killed him for what he did to my mother. But tell me this: who would miss him? He was a narcissistic sociopath."

"That may be so, Chelsea, but you've committed murder." My voice was starting to slur. Only a mammoth effort enabled me to keep my eyes open and my head from drooping.

She stared at me for a few moments, then stood. "We can put that behind us. Forget him." She tugged at the knot in her towel, and it dropped to the floor around her feet. She stood naked before me, beckoning salaciously. "Come to bed, Danny."

My lip curled at the thought. She was still using sex as a weapon.

"Never. You're going to jail, Chelsea."

I'd done it; I'd got her confession, safely recorded on my phone. Now, all I had to do was call Inspector O'Toole.

But my body wouldn't cooperate. I tried to ease myself forward off the seat, but I didn't have the strength. My head swam. My limbs weren't in my control any more. Had she given me something else with the Rohypnol?

My Glock was in my coat pocket, hanging up on the door, impossible for me to reach.

I was completely at her mercy.

Chelsea smiled. It wasn't a friendly smile; it was the smug smile of someone who'd got what she wanted.

"I'm disappointed in you, Danny. I've rid the world of a wicked man, and you want me to go to prison. I've done Quake City a favour. You should let me go."

I couldn't speak—could barely think. I shook my head slightly.

"What a shame." Chelsea strolled, naked, to the bedroom. She returned moments later, wearing her dressing gown flowing loose around her body, and approached my coat hanging on the door. She patted the pockets, then withdrew my Glock 17 and put it in a pocket of her gown.

I winced and tried again to move, but I was paralysed. Maybe she'd given me ketamine with the Rohypnol. Whatever the concoction, it was playing havoc with my bodily functions.

Chelsea came over to me. She slowly tugged the robe's fastening cord free of the garment. I stared in horror, unable to move, the hairs rising on the back of my neck.

Wordlessly, she sat astride me, her thighs squeezing my legs. In my mind, I raised my arms to push her away, but in reality, they lay unmoving on the sofa.

Chelsea wrapped the dressing gown cord twice around my neck and pulled both ends. Searing pain erupted in my throat as the airflow and blood flow were restricted. I gasped breathlessly, helpless to do anything but gaze back with bulging, bloodshot eyes.

I would die here. Strangled.

She eased off the pressure for a few seconds and I gasped, my eyes streaming. Then she shoved something deep into my mouth—Baker's watch.

She resumed squeezing the life out of me. How would she explain this? A sex game gone wrong? Or would I be dumped into the harbour late at night? Either way, no one would ever know what she'd done.

I gasped, unable to breath. She was choking me. A red mist descended over my eyes.

The door flew open. Deepa burst in and gasped. "What the hell's going on?"

Chelsea glowered at her. "We're just having some fun."

Deepa glanced at me, distraught. Her gaze focused on mine, and then on the watch stuffed into my mouth. I couldn't breathe, and my lips may have been turning blue. Her eyes flashed understanding of the peril I was in. She moved fast, digging into her bag.

But Chelsea was faster. She dropped the cord and reached for her pocket. She pulled out my Glock 17.

Deepa froze, the handgun pointed at her face.

I gasped for air, my throat rasping and burning like sandpaper on fire. Somehow, from some frantic depths of willpower, I found the energy to swing part of one leg. I kicked Chelsea behind the knee.

She stumbled forward. The gun went off. A window pane tinkled as the bullet passed through it, out into the night.

Deepa seized the moment and pulled an object from her bag. It expanded into a flexible metal baton as she swung and crashed down onto Chelsea's arm. Chelsea screamed and toppled to the floor. The gun went flying.

Then the mist descended, and I passed out.

§

I woke in a hospital bed with a throbbing headache and feeling like crap. My throat burned like there was a fiery lump of coal lodged in my windpipe. At least I was alive. My first thought was wondering if being dead would be more comfortable. My second was that I wasn't in jail—yet.

"Good, you're awake." A registered nurse approached and took my pulse. "You've had a nasty mixture of drugs. We've had you under observation overnight. You won't feel like your normal self for a few days."

"What happened?"

"There was Rohypnol and ketamine in your bloodstream. You're lucky to be alive. It was almost a fatal dose."

"I don't remember much from last night."

"Memory blackouts are usual with Rohypnol. You might never fill in the blanks."

"My neighbour spiked my coffee. I remember that. Nothing afterwards."

"Someone's been waiting to see you. A woman. Are you up to having a visitor?"

"Sure." Was it Deepa? I hoped so. But would she even know I was in hospital? Maybe it was the police. Or… Horror swept through me. What if it was Chelsea, come to finish me off? But did she even know that I knew she was the murderer? I remembered figuring that out, but not what happened after.

Nadia wandered into my room. "Danny me boy. You've been in the wars. I came to see how you are."

I was speechless.

She plopped onto a seat by the bed. "You're not looking so good. You need to take care of yourself. Always getting yourself into trouble, you are. Now, I don't want you to worry about the rent, or paying for your busted front door." She patted me on the arm and smiled in a friendly way. "Not till you're out of here, anyway. Get better. Lovely talking to you."

Nadia got up and left. I hadn't even said a word.

I dozed off.

When I woke, Deepa was sitting where Nadia had been. She smiled at me, and I smiled back.

I tried to sit up and failed. "I know who the murderer is. It's my neighbour. She drugged me. I've got to tell the inspector."

Deepa placed her hand on my arm and left it there. "It's all right, Danny. The nurse told me you can't remember because that crazy bitch drugged you. I know all about how she killed Baker."

"Does the inspector know?"

She smiled again, her beautiful, gleaming smile that sent pleasant shivers down my spine. "He does. She's been arrested. You're in the clear." Her expression became serious. "When I arrived last night, she was strangling you. You were actually turning blue."

"You saved me?"

"We saved each other. You stopped her from shooting me with your gun."

"I did? I don't remember."

"I know." She yawned. "I've been up all night writing an article for the *Richter Mail*. I need to sleep. I'll come back later."

She leaned over and kissed me.

THE END

Reviews

If you liked this story, please consider leaving a review on Amazon to help other prospective readers decide if it's for them. Even a sentence or two will do.

Also, please consider following me on the sites below for details of my new releases:

Amazon

Bookbub

The Quake City Investigations series

Contemporary crime noir mysteries and thrillers set in the ruins of a post-earthquake-hit city.

The stories can all be read independently. However, this is the publishing order:

The Drowned Dockworker (prequel novelette)
   In Quake City, don't go down to the docks at night...

Shooting Messengers
   What if delivering the mail was a matter of life and death?

The Possum Fur Plot (novella)
   A million dollars of goods are stolen... but the insurance company doesn't want to pay out.

To Kill A Conman
   Everyone succumbs to the conman... until one of his victims fights back.

About the Author

You can connect with me on:

🌐 http://kevinberrybooks.com

🐦 https://twitter.com/KevinBerryBooks

🔗 https://books2read.com/ap/8prEjA/Kevin-Berry

🔗 https://www.amazon.com/Kevin-Berry/e/B00G23NDFI

🔗 https://www.bookbub.com/authors/kevin-berry

Subscribe to my newsletter:

✉ https://landing.mailerlite.com/webforms/landing/f5k0c7

Also by Kevin Berry

My books span a variety of genres and character voices. Every book I write includes humour because I think reading should be entertaining.

These include:

Contemporary Crime Noir
  The Quake City Investigations series:
  The Drowned Dockworker (prequel novelette)
  Shooting Messengers
  The Possum Fur Plot (novella)
  To Kill A Conman

Humorous Literary Fiction
  Stim
  Kaleidoscope

Interactive Fiction (ages 10-14)
  Stranded Starship
  Duel at Dawn
  Movie Mystery Madness
  Past Present Future
  Secret Project

Dystopian Cyberpunk Science Fiction
  Teleport

My work has so far produced:
  Winner: Sir Julius Vogel Award for Best New Talent (shared);
  Finalist: Sir Julius Vogel Award (5 times, various categories);
  Semifinalist: Kindle Book Review Awards (Literary Fiction, twice);

Awesome Indies Seal of Approval (twice);
Category Finalist: Eric Hoffer Award;
Finalist: Wishing Shelf Award;
Amazon (US) #1 Bestseller ranking in Australian & Oceanian Literature;
Amazon (CA) #1 Bestseller ranking in Noir Mysteries and Thrillers;
Amazon (CA) #1 Bestseller ranking in Hard-boiled Mysteries.

www.ingramcontent.com/pod-product-compliance
Lightning Source LLC
Chambersburg PA
CBHW060632260626
47161CB00008B/2874